With a shock, Phyllida realized that Gerard had no idea of all that had happened since their last meeting. Her world had been turned upside down, her heart had been broken, and Gerard knew nothing of it.

Gerard listened to her story in horrified silence.

"What you've been through, my poor, poor darling," he said at last. "If only I'd known. Then it would have been me that you married, instead of him. If only we'd been married . . . but then we would have still had to face the heartbreak of parting."

"You are sailing soon?" Phyllida did not even dare to think of the bliss that might have been hers.

Before Gerard could reply, he let her go and sprang back.

"What is it?" Phyllida whispered in alarm.

"There is someone watching us, there in the trees."

Phyllida

Irene Northan

A FAWCETT CREST BOOK

Fawcett Books, Greenwich, Connecticut

PHYLLIDA

THIS BOOK CONTAINS THE COMPLETE TEXT OF THE
ORIGINAL HARDCOVER EDITION.

Published by Fawcett Crest Books, CBS Publications, CBS Consumer Publishing, a Division of CBS Inc., by arrangement with Robert Hale & Company.

ISBN: 0-449-23459-2

Printed in the United States of America

10   9   8   7   6   5   4   3   2   1

One

Phyllida lay gazing up into the darkness of the bed canopy, trying to think what had woken her so abruptly. Something had disturbed her she was sure, yet the house was quiet enough now. Tense and still she strained her ears to catch some sound, but none came.

For a long time there was silence. Gradually she relaxed, and had all but drifted back into sleep when a dull thud came from below stairs. A thud, as though a door had blown shut.

Pulling back the bed hangings she got up and groped her way among the unfamiliar shapes of the furniture until she reached the window. No streaks of light brightened the sea; dawn was obviously a long way off, so no servants should be astir. It was unlikely that a door had been left unlocked—unlikely but not impossible.

"I suppose I must go and see," she decided, and quietly opened her bedroom door.

Once on the landing she began to have second thoughts. The darkness of the great staircase loomed before her in an almost sinister fashion, but after a moment she pushed her fears away and began to move downstairs. She fumbled her way down, her bare feet exploring each step. Furze House was still an unfamiliar place to her, and she found it difficult to judge exactly where she was.

"A candle would have been a help," she thought. "But it's too late for that now."

At last the coolness of marble under her toes told her that she had reached the hall. Standing still for a moment she tried to get her bearings. The only sound now was the whir of the long case clock. As her eyes grew accustomed to the gloom she looked about her. The hall was not quite in total darkness, the fanlight above the solid oak door showed up pale, and cast a lighter pattern upon the tiled floor.

What had been banging? The front door was shut, and as far as she could make out, so were the others that ranged round the hall. That left only the baize door into the servants' quarters.

As she looked a faint glimmer of light began to creep beneath the door, growing brighter and brighter as someone approached from the other side. A prickle of fear went down Phyllida's back, and she wished suddenly that she had not come alone to investigate. It was too late now to rouse the servants.

The door swung open and a sudden burst of candlelight blinded her for a moment. She flung up an arm to protect her eyes, still unable to make out who it was who had come out of the servants' hall so unexpectedly. Who ever it was, he was as startled as Phyllida, for there was a gasp, and for a second the candle wavered precariously.

"The Lord is my light and my salvation; whom shall I fear!" The voice that boomed out the quotation from the Scriptures was familiar, and the scream that had risen in Phyllida's throat died away.

"Hembury!" she exclaimed, blinking rapidly. "What are you doing downstairs at this time of night? Why, it's past two!"

The butler hesitated. "I was not sure that I'd locked the back entry door, madam," he said at last. "So I came down to make certain."

Phyllida felt at once that he was lying. For ever-careful Hembury to forget to lock a door, when she knew that he double-checked every night—no, that was not possible.

Hembury sensed her doubts, for he added, "I wanted to be extra sure, particularly as the master is away. 'There shall no evil befall you, for He shall give His angels charge over thee.'"

Phyllida stepped back a little, startled. She wondered if she would ever get used to Hembury's way of quoting from the Bible at every turn. She knew he was an avid

6

follower of John Wesley, what her grandfather would have called "a damned canting Methodist." Grandfather would not have tolerated him as a servant for one day, yet in this household no one seemed to consider it strange to hear the butler giving vent to his religious views.

Then she noticed something else about Hembury.

"You're fully dressed," she said accusingly.

He looked down at himself as if to consider the matter.

"I had not properly retired for the night, madam. I do not sleep well. Can I get you something? Some tea, perhaps?"

"Thank you, no."

There was something not quite right. Something that Phyllida just could not identify. But what?

"Some wine, then, madam? Or shall I call your maid?"

With a shock she realised that gently, imperceptibly, Hembury was edging her away from the baize door.

"No thank you. I want nothing." Her voice shook a little. Then she realised what was amiss. There was a smell of cooking. Although it was well past two in the morning a strong smell of fresh cooking had wafted in as Hembury came through from the servants' quarters. Hembury noticed her sniffing and gave a small cough.

"I took the liberty of warming a little broth for myself, madam. I hope that was in order."

Another lie! She could recognise fried bacon when she smelt it. But why should he even bother to lie? He was the butler, not the under kitchen maid, he could surely help himself to a slice of bacon without permission. It seemed such a pointless falsehood.

At that moment, from behind the baize door, there came a sound. It was faint but unmistakable, like the scrape of a chair or table leg. Hembury heard it too, she was certain, but he just stood there, his candle held aloft.

"May I be permitted to escort you to your room, madam. This staircase can be treacherous in the dark." Hembury's squat, crooked figure moved forward a fraction.

Phyllida opened her mouth to demand an explanation of the noise—then closed it again. The chill of fear was with her once more. Someone was in the servants' hall, of that she was certain, but Hembury did not want her to investigate.

If she protested, what then? Was there a servant in the whole house who would come to her aid? She doubted it very much. In the few days that she had lived at Furze House she could not help but notice how hostile the servants were towards her. No, hostile was too strong a word. Suspicious, perhaps, or watchful. It made no difference to her situation now, though. She knew full well that she did not have a friend in the whole house.

Hembury's hand tightened on her arm as he guided her upstairs.

"For Thou wilt light my candle; the Lord my God will enlighten my darkness." Hembury stopped outside her bedroom door. "If I may say so, madam, if anything disturbs you again it would be wiser to call Joseph or myself. These are wicked times we live in, and you do not want to come face to face with an intruder."

In her nervous state she wondered if his words were the friendly advice they seemed, or a veiled threat. His expression gave nothing away.

"Thank you, Hembury," she said, keeping her voice level. "I will remember that. Good night."

Inside her bedroom she leaned against her closed door, listening until Hembury's irregular footsteps had limped away, then she made a dash for the warmth and security of her bed.

Lying there in the darkness, hugging the feather bolster for comfort, it was loneliness that pushed away her fears. Furze House was now her home, but it was still so strange and friendless to her. She had never expected to feel homesick for her grandfather's house, after all it was less than a week since she had run away from there. She settled herself more comfortably among the pillows and began to think of Barton Hall. So much had happened since she had left there. How clearly she could remember the day that Sir Walter had summoned her to his room.

"The last of the Bartons!" Old Sir Walter Barton gazed at his grandaughter with derision. "Look what we've come to! If you were comely, wench, or had taking ways I might make something of you, but you're a maypole, just look at you! And black as a gypsy!"

Phyllida had come with her back straight and her chin raised high, determined not to let her grandfather's words hurt her, but as always his barbs got through her defences. She was all too well aware that she was tall and gawky, and that she had long since grown out of her gown.

Sir Walter frequently goaded her about her appearance. He never noticed that her height, her colouring and her strong features were all inherited from him. A more kindly eye would have noted that Phyllida, with her slender build and that proud tilt of her head, was a striking creature. She would never achieve the pink and white bergere type of prettiness so much in vogue then, at the latter end of the eighteenth century, but all she needed to become a most elegant figure was a little contact with polished society.

"Eighteen and not wed yet." Sir Walter gazed at her with dislike. "Most girls of your age have a husband and a flourishing nursery by now, so why not you, eh?"

"I have never been anywhere to meet any eligible gentlemen," Phyllida retorted. "And you must admit, sir, that there are few enough of them at Barton." She was determined to show that his jibes did not hurt her.

"I've told you before you're not worth dragging to London or Bath. If you had beauty I might have stirred myself, but it would be a waste of time. It's fortunate for you that you've a good inheritance due to you, since you've little enough besides to recommend you. Ten thousand a year clear, at least, that's what you'll have when I'm gone, as well as one of the best estates in the county. It vexes me that it'll all go to a female who'll no doubt hand it all over to some silver-tongued fortune hunter before I'm cold in my grave. If only you'd been a boy then I'd have been spared all this worry." His black eyes glittered malevolently out of his pale wizened face.

Phyllida looked at him, sitting bolt upright in his chair, the long amber-topped cane gripped between his bony fingers, and wondered why he had summoned her. This was all old ground that he was covering, complaints that she had heard a hundred times before. If she had done something specific that angered him—something apart from merely existing—then Sir Walter would have rated her soundly long before now.

Her grandfather rapped sharply on the floor with his cane to ensure her attention.

"As least while I'm alive I'll make sure that you don't fritter away any of my money. Any husband for you will be of my choosing."

"I would prefer to choose for myself, sir." It was foolish to argue with Sir Walter, but Phyllida could not help her exclamation.

She had very clear ideas about the man she would marry. Many of her solitary hours had been spent dreaming about her ideal. He would be handsome of course, and amusing (there was little enough humour at Barton Hall and she dearly loved to laugh). But most of all he would be desperately in love with her, someone who did not share her grandfather's views that she was plain and awkward. As for wealth, she did not even think of it. With such a man money would be a very trivial consideration, something of little importance.

"Oh, so you would prefer it, eh?" Sir Walter's harsh voice brought her back to reality. "Well I fancy you're a little late to start looking. I've received an offer for you. Moreover it's from a gentleman I consider suitable— or at least it's the best you're likely to get. So the Barton inheritance has already found you a husband."

Phyllida was dumbfounded. Dazed, she rocked back on her heels. This was the last thing she expected. Here was her grandfather arranging her whole future, and he was talking about it with the same emotion as he would the sale of a horse or a cow. Inside she was shaking, but she pressed her lips together and raised her chin.

Sir Walter interpreted her stance as a sign of dumb insolence.

"You're to be civil to him, mind. None of your damned surliness or he'll back down, and I doubt if you'll get another such offer. Not one that I'll approve of, anyway. Still, he's been married before so I expect he can handle obstinate females."

A sick feeling settled in the pit of Phyllida's stomach. She knew of no-one who could possibly be described as a suitor, and her grandfather's scant description seemed a long way from the husband she dreamed of. She longed to ask who he was, just to end her awful suspense, but she knew that her grandfather was withholding his name on purpose to torment her.

"Aren't you interested in the name of your future husband?" Sir Walter's face cracked into the semblance of a smile.

"I dare say you will tell me in your own time, sir." Phyllida refused to give him any satisfaction.

"You know him well enough, he's dined here often." Sir Walter's face darkened. "He's Mr. Richard Compton, the merchant from Tormouth."

That was the last name she expected to hear. Richard Compton! Why he was middle-aged, five and thirty at least, and he'd been a widower for about ten years. Phyllida closed her eyes for a moment, her romantic dreams crumbling into dust.

Sir Walter took no notice of her reactions, but went on talking, half to himself.

"I'll admit I'd have preferred a bit more breeding, though I believe his mother was of good birth, but he's sound. A steady individual who won't spend your money at the gaming tables or on some painted doxy. Besides, his own pockets are pretty well lined. Yes, a bill on Richard

Compton holds good the length and breadth of the country, though he obviously has some use for more money, otherwise why would he offer for you? All in all I think he'll do. Besides, as I have said, I hold few hopes of you getting a better proposal."

Phyllida had not been attending to her grandfather's observations upon Mr. Compton. The enormity of his announcement had taken her breath away, but gradually the full truth began to dawn on her. Married to Richard Compton! He was so much older than her. He was her grandfather's friend, or rather her grandfather's business associate, since both were trustees of a large local charity school. Mr. Compton came to Barton Hall about once a month, since Sir Walter was too old to attend the regular board meetings, and together they discussed any business connected with the school. He usually stayed to dinner, but even then he had never taken more notice of Phyllida than was decreed by good manners. His talk was always of politics or the war with the American Colonials. She could never remember him saying anything amusing, and now she was to spend the rest of her life with this humourless man whose only interest in her was her money.

"I can't do it!" she said out loud. "I can't do it!"

Sir Walter stiffened. "And pray, what is it that you can't do?"

"Marry Mr. Compton."

"Is there some reason for this decision of yours? Have you perhaps received an offer from a duke or a marquis of which I am unaware?"

"No sir."

"Then it must be Mr. Compton himself. Have you heard that he has at least two mistresses and a brood of natural children?" The sarcasm in his voice grew more biting.

"No, sir."

"Then why in thunder can't you marry him?"

"Because—because I don't love him."

There was a pause, then Sir Walter let out a crack of laughter that startled the sleeping spaniel at his feet, but

12

there was no amusement in the sound.

"What can you know of such things, miss? If that is the sum total of your objections I think we can dispense with them altogether."

"I won't marry him!" Phyllida spoke through clenched teeth.

"Oh, so it's won't now, is it?"

"I won't marry Richard Compton and you can't make me," cried Phyllida with an assurance she was far from feeling.

"We'll see." Sir Walter was confident of his own powers. "A few days locked in your room on a diet of bread and water will soon change your mind."

"Never! Never! Never!" was Phyllida's reply, but she was wrong. Four days on such a diet, kept within the confines of the same four walls were a terrible hardship to her. She knew also that her grandfather would never relent. If only there had been someone who would mediate on her behalf she might have stood a chance, but as there was not she knew it was hopeless. On the fifth day she gave in.

Richard Compton came next day to make his formal proposal, and their betrothal was made public at once.

It was then that fate played a cruel trick upon Phyllida. One week after accepting Mr. Compton she met Lieutenant Gerard Lacey, and knew at once that this was the man she could really love.

He should not have been in Barton Woods at all, of course, but there he was, sitting on a tree stump, pelting beech masts at a rock.

"You are trespassing, sir," she informed him with cold politeness. "This is private ground."

He sprang to his feet, towering above her and looking unbelievably handsome in his scarlet jacket.

"Your pardon, madam." He made a neat bow. "But I had no intention of doing so. I thought I knew a short cut to the camp, but the truth was that I didn't. I must confess that I am hopelessly lost."

"You are from the camp near Farmer Whiddon's land?" Curiosity got the better of her haughtiness. Few soldiers found their way to Barton. Usually they preferred the livelier attractions of the larger village of Moreton.

"Yes, madam, but just until our embarkation orders come, then it's down to the coast we'll march to take ship for America. May I introduce myself—Lieutenant Gerard Lacey at your service."

To her surprise his dark eyes were viewing her with bold approval, and to cover her confusion she said, "You are well out of your way for the path to Whiddon Farm. It is not on our land at all, but down there, beyond the stream."

"Your land? Then I must be addressing the charming Miss Barton."

I am Phyllida Barton, certainly." She was trying to keep her voice stern, but it was very difficult.

"Then I'm very glad I did trespass, or I would never have encountered such beauty."

Phyllida drew in her breath at such an outrageous compliment, but he removed all offence by adding in a chastened voice,

"There, you may call your keepers now and have me shot for such impertinence. But I warn you, I'll die happily at your feet like a spaniel."

Phyllida burst out laughing, unable to stay affronted for long. No one had ever paid her extravagant compliments before, and though she knew it was mere nonsense she had to admit that it was very pleasant.

"Just this once, instead of having you shot I'll show you the real path," she retorted.

"Beauty tempered with kindness. What more could I ask?"

He bowed low and offered her his arm as they went along the rutted track to the shortcut. All the way he kept up a flow of such nonsense and teasing that Phyllida was breathless with laughter by the time they reached the stile that marked the boundary of Barton Woods.

From its top step the lieutenant turned and smiled at her, his white teeth gleaming.

"I think I've a mind to trespass here again tomorrow. Shall we say at this stile at about eleven?"

Then off he went, jumping up now and again to wave to her over the tall Devon hedge.

"Saucy fellow, how dare he expect me to meet him again!" Phyllida pretended to be angry, but the next day found her at the stile in the woods, and the next, and the next.

Each meeting with Gerard was a time of wonder for Phyllida. She had never really expected to find anyone who matched up to her dream, and yet here he was. It was not just that Gerard was handsome, there was so much more to him than that. Part of his charm was the way he looked at her with his dark brown eyes, as though she were the most precious creature in the whole world.

When she was with Gerard she felt beautiful. She forgot that she was plain and gawky. But most of all she felt loved. This was a totally new experience for Phyllida, to be of such importance to someone, and it was wonderful.

Their moments together were brief, but to Phyllida they were the only real things in her life. Her grandfather, Mr. Compton, the plans for her wedding, all faded into a blur. She thought only of Gerard and of their love for each other. Every moment was wasted when it was not spent in his arms, listening to his deep voice telling her that he loved her. Even the many difficulties that beset them faded into insignificance because she was so certain that the strength of their love would solve them all. Her greatest worry, though, was that Gerard's regiment would receive orders to leave Barton.

"It's so unfair. Why should you be sent into danger just because some colonists and plantation owners rebel?" she complained.

Gerard laughed. "But danger is my trade, my sweet. Besides, but for this war I would never have met you.

Think what would have happened if I'd never come to Barton."

The enormity of being without Gerard shocked her into silence for a moment.

"So many obstacles are in our way," she said at last. "Why must we have all these difficulties?"

"Poor darling." Gerard put his arms about her. "If only we could go somewhere away from your grandfather and that dull stick he is forcing you to marry, how happy we could be together." He sighed. "I wish my own prospects were better, but I have only my army pay. That would not be enough for two."

"I wouldn't mind being poor," cried Phyllida, but Gerard only smiled and kissed her gently to change the subject.

Phyllida imagined that these precious meetings with Gerard were her own secret, but Barton was a small place, with little to occupy the inhabitants apart from observing their neighbours. It was not long before gossip that Miss Phyllida from the Hall was meeting a handsome soldier reached the ears of Sir Walter.

Phyllida had never seen him so angry. His face was purple with rage.

"This fine soldier of yours, I mark that he was not man enough to come to the house to meet me face to face," he snarled.

Phyllida said nothing. She knew that she was not expected to speak.

"And what was to come of this little escapade? Were you planning to part cheerfully or had you something else in mind? Such as joining the other camp followers that always trail behind such as him?"

Although she was smarting Phyllida still said nothing.

"You do well to keep silent. Shall I tell you what will happen? Nothing! This young buck of yours, he knows well enough that you are betrothed. He knows equally well that I would never countenance any connection between my granddaughter and a penniless red-coat. Shall I tell you what he's doing? Amusing himself! Passing the time before marching on! No doubt he does the same at every billet." The words spat out with a snarling violence.

"No!" Phyllida had to speak. "No, he loves me."

"Loves you, eh? That's a word you're very free with." Sir Walter was enjoying himself now. "You can tell him from me that if you continue to see him I'll cut you off without a penny. Then see how strong his love is."

"You're wrong. You don't know him." Phyllida was having to fight to hold back the tears.

Sir Walter's gloating smile changed. "No," he said sharply, "and I never shall. Do you know why? Because for one thing you're never to see or contact this mountebank again. And for another, I shall see to it that you are safely wed to Compton within the week. Oh don't worry. I shan't mention this disgusting episode. I don't want to frighten Compton off. I shall write to him saying that I an an old man and fear my days are numbered, so I'm eager to have my only granddaughter, (though heaven knows what I did to deserve one such as you,) settled before I die. That should do it."

His words were like a curse, and Phyllida knew all too well that he meant every one of them. Unable to face him any longer she turned and fled to her room, to find relief in a storm of weeping.

Tears will only last so long, and when at last all hers were spent Phyllida lay on her bed staring blankly at the ceiling, trying to think of a way out of her problems. She dreaded the thought of parting from Gerard and shuddered at the prospect of marrying Mr. Compton.

"I wish I could be miles away from here, in some safe place with Gerard. Without a grandfather to hound me, and no Mr. Compton to . . ."

She sat up suddenly. Her words were almost the same as those that Gerard had uttered. Some place miles from Barton Hall. Gerard's words had been mere dreams but the situation had changed critically since then. To run away together was not the only solution. Gerard wanted to be with her, had not he said so?

"We can be married somewhere at once, then he will have time to get back to his regiment before it moves."

Phyllida let her thoughts run on, calmer now she had some ray of hope.

"Yes, it's the only solution. Even my grandfather could not part us once we were man and wife." Man and wife! How beautiful that sounded. "Becky must take Gerard a letter, thank goodness she's such a loyal little maid, so there is no problem there. Now where can we meet? Exeter. Yes, Exeter should be large enough to hide us for a day or so until we can be married."

Exeter was also the total extent of Phyllida's travelling experience, and seemed an ideal setting for so romantic a venture as an elopement.

With the germ of her plan in her head new life surged through Phyllida. All at once there was so much to do. Becky was nowhere to be found so she attempted her own packing by stuffing a few unsuitable and ill-assorted garments into a valise.

"Money, I must have money." Phyllida searched through all her purses and reticules. The resulting pile of coins looked very meagre to finance an elopement, but it would have to do. She added a few trinkets, regretting the fact that the fine jewels left to her by her mother were locked in her grandfather's strong box.

"Now all I have to do is to scribble a letter to Gerard and hope that Becky returns soon."

She had barely dried the ink with a little sand and sealed the note with wax when there was a knock on the door and Becky came in.

"Elope with Mr. Lacey? Have you gone mad, Miss Phyll?" Becky's eyes grew large with horror. "Please, miss, I want no part in it. Sir Walter would skin me if he found out that I'd helped you."

"But Becky, who else can I turn to? I must get away at once or I'll be forced to marry Mr. Compton, just imagine how awful that would be."

18

"Would it be awful? He may be a bit on the sober side, miss, but you can't say worse than that."

"Yes I can. He's cold and boring, besides being nearly old enough to be my father. How can I marry him when it's Mr. Lacey that I love?"

"It's only what many other ladies have had to do in the past, and I dare say will have to do in the future," pointed out Becky practically. "Just think what you're doing, Miss Phyll. I'm sure you don't know what you're thinking of. No one would know you any more. You'd never be invited anywhere. And I daren't think what Sir Walter will do. What about when Mr. Lacey's regiment goes to America? Have you thought of that? You'll be all alone."

"Being married to Mr. Lacey, even for a few short days, will be worth all the sacrifices. If I'm with him I don't care about anyone else—except you of course, dear Becky, you are my only friend."

"Oh Miss Phyll, don't say it like that."

"You will take my letter for me please, won't you?"

"I suppose so," agreed Becky grudgingly. "If I don't you'll only give it to someone else and they'd make a right mess of it."

Phyllida hugged her maid until poor Becky was forced to protest.

"Leave me my ribs, miss, or I'll never get there."

The rest was surprisingly easy, only saying goodbye to Becky gave her any pang at all. With her valise hidden by her cloak Phyllida slipped out of the house without being noticed. It never occurred to her to wait for a reply from Gerard. To get away from Barton Hall was her chief thought.

The stage coach from Plymouth reached the crossroads beyond the village at noon, and it was a simple matter to keep to quiet footpaths to avoid being seen. The coach was on time, and she was taken up without comment.

The journey was not a comfortable one. Phyllida had never been in a public coach before, and she found it cramped and stuffy. An unpleasant man, breathing fumes of cheap wine, leaned too close to her for most of the way, but she would have gladly endured far worse for the sake of Gerard. Afraid to spend too much of her little store of money on food and drink she was thirsty and ravenous by the time they reached Exeter.

On her rare visits to that city with her grandfather Phyllida had always stayed at the Bear Inn in South Street, but she had been afraid to suggest that place as a rendezvous in case she was recognised. Instead she was to meet Gerard at the Globe, which she knew was somewhere near the Cathedral. Mr. Robbins, the Vicar of Barton, had often mentioned staying there when he attended diocesan meetings, so it was sure to be respectable.

It was! And respectable inn-keepers do not take kindly to unaccompanied females.

"But I am being met," she protested. "My escort will be here in two or three hours."

The landlord looked at her boldly, clearly showing that he didn't believe a word of her story. She flushed scarlet under his gaze.

"Two or three hours, you say?"

"Yes."

"Very well then, but there'll be no staying the night. And you'll pay in advance."

Phyllida was not at all used to such treatment, and she had to bite back a sharp retort. The landlord led the way into a small, shabbily furnished parlour on the first floor. It looked out over the Green to the vast walls of the Cathedral beyond, and Phyllida ran to look out, but the landlord pushed her back.

"No sitting in the window, mind. I'll have none of those tricks."

Phyllida was not certain of his meaning, but the insult was plain enough, and she flushed again. A wash and a light meal did much to restore her, though, and by the time she had drunk a small glass of wine she felt cheerful again. Here she was, in the middle of an adventure, waiting for the man she loved to come to her. What more could she want? Defying the landlord's instructions she set her chair where she could see the passers-by, and sat down to wait. Below, the Cathedral Green drowsed in the unexpectedly warm spring sun.

At every red-coat that came into view she started. At every carriage that rattled over the cobbles she waited, dizzy with expectation. But Gerard did not come. At first she was not worried. After all, Gerard was a soldier, his time was not his own. Perhaps he had been delayed in starting. But as the shadow of the Cathedral began to spread itself like a dark blanket over the ground the first icy fingers of doubt began to grasp her heart. What if he could not get away at all? Had Becky been able to deliver the note? Had there been an accident? For the first time she began to think how foolish she had been to come without waiting for his reply.

Tense thoughts churned round in her head, as outside the link boys wandered across the Green, lighting the steps of homeward-going citizens. She was tempted to call for candles, but that might have put too great a strain on her slender resources.

"You said three hours and I've given you nearer four. You must leave." The landlord entered, looking far from friendly.

"Please, no! I'm sure there must be a good reason for the delay. My escort will be here soon, I'm certain."

"Half an hour more, then and not a minute over."

Stiffly Phyllida went back to her chair. Doubt had now changed to despair. Gerard was not coming; and alone and bewildered she tried to think what to do.

"I don't think I've even enough money for a night's lodgings." She tried to hold back the tears but they persisted in rolling down her cheeks. "I don't even know where to go. There are my jewels, such as they are, but I won't be able to sell them until tomorrow. I'll just have to find a doorway to sleep in."

The noises of the inn died down, until there was only

a low hum of voices from the tap room. In the Close below, the lights went out one by one, leaving the vast bulk of the Cathedral indistinguishable from the dark sky. With dread she heard the footsteps of the landlord coming nearer.

"Come along, out you go!"

Meekly she picked up her valise, and as she did so a carriage came rattling over the cobbles. Her ears pricked, she heard it come to a halt outside the inn.

"Very well." The innkeeper answered her unspoken plea. "I'll go and see if this is your gentleman."

Sick with anticipation she waited, then footsteps sounded on the stairs, the heavy step of the landlord, and then a lighter step. They drew nearer, coming towards the room. It must be Gerard, it could only be he. She put down her valise, ready to throw herself into his arms. The door opened.

"You've come at last," Phyllida cried and rushed towards the tall figure in the doorway—then stopped abruptly.

"I am sorry to have kept you waiting," Richard Compton said in an even voice. "There was some confusion over the inn, but I am glad to have found you at last. Landlord, some food please at once. A little cold meat or something of the sort for speed, and please have fresh horses for me in half an hour."

The landlord bowed and went out. Already his attitude had changed, he was now all smiles and affability. After he had gone there was a long, long silence. Phyllida was white and shaken, torn between distress that the newcomer was not Gerard and relief at seeing a familiar face.

Mr. Compton casually took off his travelling cloak and draped it over a chair. He looked at the one small candle that she had been forced to order.

"This room is exceedingly dark, I shall have to call for more light," he remarked casually. "Won't you sit down, Miss Phyllida, there is really no need to remain standing."

Automatically she obeyed, still shocked by his unexpected arrival.

"Why did you come?" she asked at last.

Mr. Compton seated himself at the opposite side of the table and gazed across at her. He seemed surprised at her question.

"You did not believe that you could leave home so suddenly without your family and friends being concerned for you, did you? Your grandfather could scarcely come after you at his age, so who more fitting than myself?"

"Oh, I see." Phyllida stared down at the table, unable to meet his eyes. "How did you know where to find me?" She wondered how much he knew of her elopement, had her letter perhaps fallen into the wrong hands? His answer reassured her.

"I enquired at the staging posts. Once I knew that you were heading for Exeter I just followed you here. The difficult part was searching for the right inn—I presumed you would be staying at one somewhere. I—er—presume that you are alone?"

Mutely she nodded, her head still lowered. So he did know that she had tried to elope.

Compton cleared his throat. "Your grandfather seemed of the opinion that you might not be."

Phyllida did not reply, and there was another long silence, broken at last by the arrival of the landlord with the food.

"Please eat something." Richard Compton carved some slices of roast capon onto a plate for her and pushed forward a dish of dressed cucumbers. "We have quite a long journey ahead of us, and you will be faint if you take no nourishment."

"He's so calm," thought Phyllida as she cut her meat into small pieces. "Here I am, betrothed to him, I've tried to elope with someone else, yet there are no rages, no lectures, not even any moralising. He sits there buttering bread as though this was the most normal situation in the world.

23

Even in the comfort of his carriage Mr. Compton spoke little. Phyllida was thankful to lie back in the darkness and think.

"Why didn't Gerard come?" That was the burning question. "Perhaps he doesn't love me enough. Oh no, that can't be it, don't even consider such an idea. There must be some other reason, but what? And poor Becky, how did she fare?"

Tired as she was, these problems kept her occupied all the journey. They arrived at Barton Hall just before dawn, but it could well have been any time, for Sir Walter refused to see her.

"She chose to dishonour my name. She chose to forget that she is a Barton." Sir Walter's querulous voice carried clearly. "She needn't think she can come back here just because her paramour has deserted her. She can get back to the streets where she belongs."

There was the murmur of a quieter voice as Mr. Compton tried to reason with him, but Phyllida could have told him it was useless.

Shaken and dazed, aching with tiredness she began to walk aimlessly along the drive. She tried to think of the future, though it was nothing but a painful blur. She had no home, no money, no friends, and worst of all, no Gerard. There had not even been an opportunity to speak to Becky to find out why things had gone so wrong.

Behind her the sound of horses' hoofs and the rumble of wheels forced her to the side of the drive. The carriage drew up and Mr. Compton got out.

"Won't you get in?" he asked, taking her valise from her.

"In?" Phyllida repeated stupidly, but she allowed herself to be assisted into the carriage. "Where are we going?"

"Have you any friends or relations who would care for you?"

"No."

"Then we will go to my house."

The impropriety of this sank into Phyllida's tired brain.

24

Not that she cared for herself, she felt past any such consideration, but she knew Mr. Compton to be a most respectable man.

"Would that be quite proper?" she asked in a bewildered voice.

"It would if we were married."

"Married!"

"Yes. Why are you surprised? We are betrothed after all.

"But I've done something dreadful. My own grandfather has disowned me. Surely that makes a difference? Don't you want to cry off? No one would blame you."

"I have always been one to honour my pledges. We agreed to marry, didn't we? I see no reason to alter the arrangement."

"Not even after all this?" Phyllida asked in a small voice.

"As to that little episode, there was no harm done really, so I think we had best forget about it. We can be married just as soon as I can get a licence, if you are agreeable."

Phyllida was fighting exhaustion now, but her mind was clear enough about one thing. There was only one answer that she could give.

"I am agreeable, sir." Then as an afterthought. "Thank you, Mr. Compton."

"Splendid. In that case, perhaps it would be as well if you began to call me Richard."

Two

When Phyllida awoke she was not sure where she was. She was only conscious of a vague uneasiness. Then she remembered that she was at Furze House, and memories of Hembury and the strange events of the night came back to her. Her fear had been real enough at the time, but now with the sun shining in the window, and comfortable domestic sounds coming from below it all seemed most unlikely.

"I must have been overwrought," she decided. "What could be going on in a thoroughly respectable establishment like Furze House? Though there is no denying that I get a strange feeling in this house, as though the servants are always watching me." She pondered for a moment then exploded with "Poppycock! It's your imagination again."

One of the maids had already been in and drawn the curtains, so that the warm sunlight made bright pools across the carpet. It certainly looked far from sinister.

How long was it since she had married Richard Compton—five, six days? Phyllida had lost track of time since that quiet early morning ceremony.

"Grandfather won after all," she thought. "I did just as he wanted. I married Mr. Compton, so all of the agony and anguish of my journey to Exeter were for nothing." She had still had no word from Gerard, and the notion that he did not love her lurked painfully in her thoughts. Surely by now he could have found some way of getting a message to her if he'd really wanted to.

"I must try not to think of him," Phyllida whispered. "I must put him right out of my mind."

Brave words, but oh, so hard to do.

Unable to bear lying still for a moment longer Phyllida rose and went to the window. If anything could reconcile her to being mistress of Furze House it was this view. The house stood on the outskirts of Tormouth, a small bustling fishing town. To one side the roof tops of the cob and wash cottages tumbled away down the hillside. But it was the scene in front of her that held Phyllida's interest, for across a small stretch of common lay the pearly expanse of the English Channel. She had never seen the sea before, yet it was there each morning now, right outside her window, and she never tired of its changes of mood and its ceaseless activity.

"I'm sorry madam, I didn't know you were awake."
Phyllida turned her head as the maidservant entered. It
was the grave-eyed young woman who was acting as her
personal maid.

"Come in, Parsons. I will have my chocolate here by the
window."

The maid put the tray on a small table, and as she did
so her eyes followed the line of Phyllida's gaze. A brig
in full sail was edging its way out of the harbour, its
canvas cracking like whips as it rounded the headland,
and caught the prevailing breeze. On its deck two lines of
scarlet figures stood at attention.

With a pang Phyllida thought of Gerard, and wondered
if he could be one of those anonymous dots.

"Poor young men," observed Parsons with genuine
sympathy.

"They are off to America?"

"Yes, madam, more's the pity."

Phyllida crumbled her bread roll, trying not to think
of how Gerard's eyes had laughed at her. He always
seemed to be laughing, and . . . Suddenly she became
aware that Parsons was still there.

"What is it?"

"I brought you this, madam. Master said I was to get
you anything you needed." She held out a fine cashmere
shawl, patterned in delicate greens and pinks.

At once Phyllida was acutely embarrassed, so she
stroked it with one finger, so that she would not have to
look the maid in the eye. She was very well aware that her
wardrobe was scanty.

The servants must be very curious about her, it was
only natural, and she wondered if any of them suspected
the truth. The fact that the new Mistress Compton did
not even share her husband's bedroom must have given
rise to even more interested speculation.

To cover her confusion Phyllida said hurriedly,

"It's very pretty, but where did it come from?"

Parsons slipped the shawl over her new mistress's shoulders.

"It was one of Mistress Compton's, I mean Mistress Maria, the-er- master's first wife." Now she too sounded awkward as she stumbled to find the correct phrase.

"And are you sure that I may have it?"

"Yes, madam. It was the master's last instruction before he went away."

Parsons left the room, and Phyllida sat sipping her chocolate. The shawl was warm about her and smelt slightly of cedar wood. She found herself wondering about the unknown Maria, who had been married to Richard Compton a decade ago. The portrait of her in the Small Drawingroom showed her to have been delicately pretty in a child-like sort of way.

"Very unlike the second Mistress Compton," decided Phyllida.

She had scarcely finished her meal before a servant informed her that Mistress Rouse had arrived, and Phyllida had to summon Parsons back hastily to help her dress.

Mistress Rouse was sitting in the Small Drawingroom feeding cake sopped in wine to a small very overfed dog. Her small rotund figure was swathed in a variety of flimsy shawls that every minute threatened disaster to a collection of figurines at her elbow.

"My dear!" She looked up as Phyllida entered. "Such a beautiful morning isn't it? And here is my poor Choo-Choo simply longing for a walk. And he whispered to me, 'Why don't we invite Richard's little wife?' There, he likes you. I knew he would."

Phyllida bit back a smile at being described as a "little wife", particularly by a lady who barely reached her shoulder. She liked Mr. Compton's aunt. She was lively and warmhearted, so unlike her nephew.

"Thank you. That's a splendid notion."

"Thank Choo-Choo," corrected Mistress Rouse. "After all, we must look after you while Richard is away, the dear boy. It wouldn't do for you to be lonely."

As they strolled along the cliff top at a very slow pace to accommodate Choo-Choo's short legs Phyllida longed to question Mistress Rouse about Maria Compton. She wondered how she might bring the conversation round to it, but she found that there was no need.

Mistress Rouse eyed her shawl and remarked, "How pretty that is. So like one that Maria had—she was dear Richard's first, you know."

"I did know, and the shawl was hers," Phyllida assured her. "Parsons brought it to me this morning. I do hope that was all right?"

"I'm sure Richard will have told her to get you anything you need. I dare say there are trunks of Maria's things still in the closets somewhere. Pity you are so much taller otherwise you might have had them all. A rare lot she spent on them too." She paused to disentangle a trailing drapery from a bush, and Phyllida was afraid that she might change the subject, so she said,

"She must have been very pretty, judging from her portrait."

"She was, if you admire the pale fragile look." Mistress Rouse warmed to her subject. "Poor Richard, he blamed himself for her death."

"He did?" exclaimed Phyllida.

"Not that it was his fault, poor lad. I blame her mother, foolish woman, who encouraged her in her silly fancies. Maria was always imagining that she was ailing. True, she was of a sickly disposition, but in my opinion it was all the physic she took that did more harm than good. Why, when she died the housekeeper and I cleared out her room, and we had to call for Joseph to shift the basket full of her cures and medicines, it was more than we could lift between us. No one needs that amount of stuff. All a body requires is plenty of exercise, and convivial company." Then she added "Plus a little rhubarb if the need arises."

Phyllida felt sorry for the poor ailing Maria. She imagined her longing for sympathy and understanding, but getting little from the frigid man she had married.

"Then Maria took a fancy for taking cures." Mistress Rouse was engrossed in dissuading Choo-Choo from tackling a very elderly bone. "There wasn't a spa in the country where she hadn't sampled the waters, with Richard footing the bill of course. Not just for her gallivanting but for the droves of doctors that she called in. Of course, she wasn't one bit the better for it. Then she would go abroad, to see if foreign waters would work any better than English ones. It was then that Richard put his foot down. Said enough was enough, and though she made his life a misery he refused to give in. It was soon afterwards that she died, and my poor boy has reproached himself ever since. I still say she physicked herself to death. Why the smell of them was enough to make you bilious."

"Poor Maria," thought Phyllida.

"Poor Richard." Mistress Rouse's words were so like her own thoughts that Phyllida jumped. "I've so longed to see him properly settled."

Phyllida felt a twinge of remorse, for this plump affectionate old lady had been one of the witnesses at her wedding, and knew full well that Richard Compton's second marriage did not promise him any more happiness than his first.

They walked on in silence for a while, Mistress Rouse because she felt that she had been somewhat tactless, and Phyllida because she did indeed feel reproached. That Mistress Rouse so idolised Richard was something she could not understand, so much love seemed sadly misplaced when centred on such an aloof man. Still, she had every reason to feel grateful to him, he had married her after all, even though he was at that minute trying to get a reconciliation with her grandfather, no doubt with securing her lost ten thousand pounds a year in mind.

The silence now threatened to become awkward and Phyllida searched frantically for something to say.

"Mistress Rouse," she began diffidently.

"Aunt Rouse," corrected the other.

"Aunt Rouse, there was a disturbance in the house last night."

"There was? What ever caused it?"

"It was Hembury."

"Hembury! Good heavens! Was he drunk?"

"No, he was prowling about the house in the early hours."

Phyllida could have sworn that the old lady stiffened slightly before she retorted,

"I'd scarcely call that a disturbance. Perhaps he was checking the locks or something."

"That's what he said, but he was fully dressed, and—and . . ." Even as she spoke Phyllida felt that her words were foolish. "And I'm sure there was someone lurking in the servants' quarters."

She waited to be told that she was too fanciful, but Aunt Rouse appeared ill at ease.

"I shouldn't take too much notice," she said hastily. "No doubt he had good reason."

"Reasons? To be cooking bacon at two in the morning?"

Aunt Rouse rearranged some of her shawls that had been disordered by the wind.

"I forget that you come from inland," she said unexpectedly.

"I don't understand you."

"It's something that folks from these parts take for granted. Perhaps you should have been warned."

"Madam, you're alarming me. Is there some danger?"

"No. no! You misunderstood me. I'm trying to tell you about the free-traders. The smugglers, if you prefer it."

"Smugglers?" Phyllida was astonished. "Are you telling me that there are smugglers at Furze House?"

"Heavens, what next!" protested Aunt Rouse. "But it is a popular—er—occupation here-abouts, and I dare say that one or two of the servants lend a hand from time to time. I know of some very well connected families who are in league with the smugglers," she said. "Take my advice and ignore strange noises in the night."

Smuggling! Why had not she thought of that before? No wonder the servants viewed her with a wary eye.

"Just the same, why is Aunt Rouse so hot and bothered over the butler smuggling a little brandy?" Phyllida thought. "I wonder if she is more involved than she cares to admit? And if she is, then her precious nephew is certain to be. This is a situation that could well bear watching."

She had little time to dwell on the problem, for as soon as they returned to the house Hembury greeted them with, "The master has returned, madam." Then added in rolling tones, "The Lord shall preserve thy going out and thy coming in, from this time forth and for evermore."

At his words the tall lean figure of Richard Compton emerged from the library. Phyllida forced a smile of welcome, though her heart sank. She still felt awkward in his presence, and if possible she tried to avoid him.

He planted a formal kiss on her cheek.

"You are looking well, my dear."

It set Phyllida's teeth on edge when he called her that, and she tensed beneath his touch. Abruptly he turned to his aunt.

"And how are you, aunt? Did you have a good walk?"

"Yes, thank you, dear boy." Mistress Rouse had to stand on tip toe to return his embrace. "Choo-Choo was extremely diverted, and he has walked so far his little feet are quite worn. Hembury, will you get him a bowl of milk and water with the chill just slightly, slightly taken off, if you please?"

Picking up her pet she trotted after the butler, trailing wisps of lace behind her.

"I should have known better, and asked how the dog was first," observed Richard, with a rare gleam of humour. "Now, my dear, (again Phyllida flinched), we must have a talk. Will you please come into the library?"

32

"You saw my grandfather?" asked Phyllida. Richard poured some wine and offered her a glass.

"Yes, I saw him, but I'm afraid he still refuses to recognise you."

"I knew how it would be. I did try to warn you," Phyllida sighed.

"So you did, but I felt I had to try. He really is a most difficult old gentleman, if you don't mind me saying so. I thought our marriage might have softened him a little, but no."

"And did he mention my inheritance?"

"I'm afraid he did."

"Oh! I assume from your tone that I am still cut out of his will?"

"So Sir Walter gave me to understand."

Phyllida pursed her lips in anger.

"He has no right to do that. Part of my expectations come from my mother, and were nothing to do with the Bartons, but she left such matters in the hands of my father, who let my grandfather see to everything."

"If you feel so strongly about it I will give the matter over to my lawyer to attend to, but frankly I think that there is little we can do."

Phyllida looked at him in some astonishment. This man had married her thinking her to be an heiress to a handsome fortune, yet now that she was penniless he did not appear in the least put out. He looked at her quizzically with eyes that were a surprisingly vivid blue.

"Is something troubling you?" he asked.

Phyllida flushed. There was something about him, an aloofness that made her feel in awe of him.

"I was just thinking," she murmured. "I have come to you empty handed. That must pain you."

"It is not particularly important." He still did not seem distressed, but thrust his hands deep into the pockets of his coat. "Though that must be difficult for you. How stupid of me, I should have thought of that. I suppose you are quite without funds? I will speak to my man and arrange an allowance to be paid to you each month. But in the meantime will this suffice?"

He strode over to a heavy inlaid Chinese cabinet, unlocked a drawer and took out a small leather purse, which he handed to Phyllida. Inside were at least twenty golden guineas. She gasped, for she had never had control of so much money before, then she coloured hotly.

"But . . ." she protested. "I was not hinting . . . I mean, you must not think that . . ."

"I know you were not fishing," Richard interrupted her. "Believe me, if you had been I would never have taken the bait." He smiled, and Phyllida was surprised at the way his long, severe features softened. "But let's forget money for a moment. I was able to bring your things from Barton Hall, and there is something else which I believe will please you."

He rang the bell, and a few minutes later a familiar voice said,

"Yes, sir? You rang?"

"Becky!"

It really was her own dear Becky standing there.

"Oh, Miss Phyll," came the tearful answer, and in a trice they were in each other's arms sobbing. Richard watched them for a moment, a slight smile turning up the corners of his mouth.

"Becky, I think you'd best take your mistress upstairs. I'm sure you have a deal of unpacking to do."

Phyllida half led, half dragged the little maid up the wide oak staircase. She was truly glad to see Becky for her own sake, but she was also eager for news, news of Gerard. At last she would find out what really happened. Once in the privacy of her own room, now littered with trunks and band boxes, Phyllida leaned against the door.

"Now, tell me everything," she commanded.

"Everything, miss?" Becky settled herself comfortably on the edge of a trunk. "Why, he came for me. There I was at home in the kitchen, full of the glooms because I thought I'd never get another place, not a good one anyway, not after being turned off without a character. And then there he was at the door, as cool as you please. 'Becky', he says, 'Would you like to return to Miss Phyllida's service? She is Mistress Compton now, and she has need of you.' Well I didn't need asking twice. I laughed and cried and generally made a guy of myself I was so happy. Fancy, he came all the way to our house to find me, and he knew me too, though our Lizzie was sitting there with me. Wasn't that extraordinary?" Becky's voice had sunk low with astonishment at such attention.

Phyllida stared at her in bewilderment.

"What are you talking about?" she cried at length.

"Why, Mr. Compton, of course. Coming all the way to Stoke Newton to fetch me!" exclaimed Becky, equally puzzled. "And he brought me here in a carriage. So kind he was! He even bought me a mutton pie and some wine when we changed horses."

Exasperated by such stupidity Phyllida gave her a little shake.

"Not Mr. Compton, you silly girl. I'm talking about Mr. Lacey. What happened? Did he get my message?"

"Him?" Becky dismissed the young officer airily. "I went to the camp, like you said, but they'd all gone."

"Gone?"

"Yes, got their marching orders at last. Sent to the war in America, so Farmer Whiddon's cowherd told me. Then when I got back to the Hall there was a rare old to-do. You'd been missed, and Sir Walter was nigh throwing a fit. He was sure that I knew where you were, but of course I didn't. I made sure he didn't get the letter. That was when he turned me off, sent me packing without a word of recommendation to my name."

"My poor Becky, and all for me." A wave of remorse swept over Phyllida and she hugged the little figure to her.

"I was worried sick about you, Miss Phyll. I didn't know if I should hand your letter over to Sir Walter," Becky admitted. "Though the mood he was in I think he'd have killed you as soon as look at you. Then Mr. Compton came to the Hall and insisted that he should follow you. I knew you'd be all right with him, so I kept quiet. Besides by then I was being packed onto the carrier's cart for home."

A weight was lifted from Phyllida's heart, Gerard had not deserted her. That was the secret dread that had hung over her for days, and now it was gone. Becky's news was the first crumb of comfort she had received since the day she had left Barton Hall. She sank dreamily onto her bed, her head filled with thoughts of Gerard, of his handsome face smiling at her, of his light-hearted banter. Now he was sailing across the seas to face heaven-knows what danger.

"My darling," she whispered secretly to herself. "I feel sure that one day I will see you again."

Becky, meanwhile, had been taking in her new surroundings. She wandered round the room, exploring each crack and corner for all the world like a small kitten.

"This is grand, isn't it, Miss Phyll?" Gently her fingers stroked the wall with its pattern of strange birds and flowers. "This is real Chinese, you know, not an English imitation. It must have cost a fortune. And the green brocade curtains go so well. Who ever chose it had taste. Yes, really elegant, I call it."

Phyllida started from her reverie.

"Yes, I expect you're right," she answered, having only half listened to Becky's chatter. Then she collected herself a little. "Yes, I agree it is an uncommonly fine room."

To be honest, she had taken little notice of her new home, there had been too many other things to occupy her mind. Now that she had looked at it properly she had to admit that the furnishings of Furze House were far more modern than those of Barton Hall. The furniture was more spindly and fragile than the William and Mary pieces she had grown up with, the colours of the draperies were brighter, and the rooms more airy and spacious.

"Yet I'd change every stick of it to be with Gerard," she thought.

Becky had still not finished her tour of inspection. "Look, Miss Phyll—I mean Mistress Compton—I'll never get used to calling you that—do you see this cabinet? It's mahogany. We never had mahogany at Barton Hall, did we? And the ceiling, did you ever see such a one? I shouldn't be at all surprised if that wasn't the work of Mr. Adams himself."

Phyllida often marvelled at Becky's knowledge of fashion and good taste. It was far superior to her own. The little maid had once spent a whole season as abigail to a lady in London. She had hated every minute of it, but ever since had been at pains to establish herself as an authority on everything à la mode.

"Isn't this the finest house you were ever in, miss?" the girl insisted.

"I suppose so," Phyllida grudgingly agreed, but added quietly to herself, "I'd like it better if Richard Compton were not one of the inhabitants." Then she remembered his generosity over her allowance and felt ashamed.

"I'm sure you'll be happy here, Miss Phyll. I know I will." Becky flung wide her arms in a gesture of approval. "Who wouldn't in such a house? I'd forget all about Mr. Lacey, if I were you," she advised confidentially. "True he was exceedingly handsome, but Mr. Compton is not at all ill-looking, if only he'd smile a bit more and not look so stern. He has good shoulders, and the way he wears his hair unpowdered is most becoming, though I don't like fair hair on a gentleman as a rule. But he's ever so kind, and very thoughtful. I reckon you've got the best of it, and that's a fact."

Phyllida was aghast, more by Becky's sad want of discernment than by her impertinence in discussing her master in such a way. How could anyone compare Gerard with Richard Compton? It was unthinkable.

"You're a saucy wench," she scolded hotly. "Mind your tongue, do you hear?"

"Sorry, madam." Becky bobbed a curtsy, not one bit abashed. "I'll tell you this, though, Miss Phyll. They fair worship the master below stairs. I just said as how he was a bit quiet like, and near had my head bit off by everyone from Mr. Hembury down. Maybe Mr. Compton is a bit quiet, but I think you just don't know your luck."

Phyllida could contain her anger no longer and hurled a cushion at Becky's head, but with a grin the maid slipped neatly out of the door.

Despite Becky's cheekiness, Phyllida was glad to have her at Furze House. It was more comforting, too, to have her own things about her again. She was disconcerted though when Richard calmly announced,

"We shall have guests to dine this evening. Captain Walters of H.M.S. GRYPHON, and his wife. His ship anchored in the bay last night."

He then returned to reading his newspaper quite unconcerned. Phyllida, on the other hand was horrified. Dinner guests at Barton Hall were few, and when they did come involved much hectic preparation. Now Richard had suddenly presented her with two complete strangers at barely six hours notice. She wanted to protest, to beg to be excused, but did not know how to begin.

Relations between them had been even more strained than usual, ever since she had tried to thank Richard for the money he had given her. His reaction had been most unexpected, almost angry at her gratitude, and now the silences between them grew longer. Some of her alarm at the prospective dinner must have communicated itself to him, though, for he put down the "Flying Post" and looked at her.

"Is something the matter?" he asked.

"This dinner party, how can we be ready in time?"

"It's scarcely a party, merely an acquaintance of mine and his wife. I thought that such a small gathering would be more convenient to you. You have six whole hours, surely that is enough?"

"I have little experience of entertaining," she admitted at last.

"I see. Then this will be a good introduction for you. I

have little liking for formal gatherings, but you will find that I frequently have friends or business colleagues to dine. It is all very simple. First inform Hembury—I will see him about the wine myself. Next see the cook. You will find that she has a fund of suggestions as to dishes. Then all you have to do is choose a suitable gown to wear."

Richard made it all sound so easy, but Phyllida was still not happy.

"I'd best get on with it, though," she decided.

Somewhat to her surprise the servants took the news very calmly, even two extra guests would have thrown the domestics at Barton Hall into a flutter. In no time at all the appropriate dinner service was chosen, the flowers ordered and the seating arranged. The cook soon proved that she was well capable of sorting out a good menu. It was easier than Phyllida had feared.

"That just leaves the worst part, entertaining them," thought Phyllida. "What do I say? I have no conversation at all. Grandfather's guests were always gentlemen, so I withdrew as soon as the port was served. But now I shall have to sit with Mistress Walters, and keep her amused. I only hope she is a kindly sort of woman, someone like Aunt Rouse, then I shall feel at ease."

One glance at Mistress Walters convinced her that this elegant creature who emerged from the sedan chair was not at all like Aunt Rouse. Her much-embroidered gown of gold damask could only have come from one of the best houses in London, and her hair was so powdered and high-dressed that Phyllida wondered how she managed to stay upright in the stiff coastal breezes. She was also sure that every crack in her own elderly blue taffeta was clearly visible.

Mistress Walters floated into the house, there was no other word to describe her movements. At once her hands rose in an exaggerated gesture at her view of the interior.

"Ah, très charmant," she cried in a lisping voice that was blatantly artificial. "And the young bride is waiting for us. How tender, how affecting." She made her curtsy to Phyllida, at the same time producing a wisp of lace with a flourish and wiping away an imaginary tear.

Phyllida was a bundle of nerves, but she did not miss the calculating glance that her guest swept over her, as if pricing everything she wore.

Captain Walters, though, was a very different matter. A bluff hearty man, he had elected to follow his wife on foot.

"Can't abide those chair things," he said frankly, after apologising for the state of his shoes. "They scare the life out of me and make me feel sick."

Phyllida was glad that Richard was monopolised by the beautiful Mistress Walters, for that meant she had to entertain the captain. Her spirits were at a very low ebb, and she felt quite incapable of coping with such a sophisticated lady. The captain, however, sensed her shyness and kept up a cheerful conversation about his travels, to which she gratefully needed to answer only an occasional "How interesting."

Under the watchful eye of Hembury the meal could only have been perfect, but Phyllida watched with growing depression as each cover was removed. The worst of the evening was yet to come.

The conversation at the table was trying enough, with Mistress Walters's arch comments about brides and newly weds. Richard took it all with his customary calmness, but Phyllida felt herself grow hot as more than one jibe reached the border of propriety.

"Neither of us smoke, do we, Walters? So shall we ask the ladies' permission to join them in the Small Drawing-room? Since we are so small a party it would be a pity to separate."

"You can't fool me, my dear Compton." Mistress Walters smiled knowingly at him. "You wish to prevent our exchange of female gossip. You are afraid that your charming bride will confide in me just a little too much. That's it, isn't it?"

Phyllida found herself growing scarlet again.

"A capital idea," said the captain, ignoring his wife. "By all means let us join the ladies, but only if they'll let us bring this excellent port with us, eh?"

In her mind Phyllida had gone over the scores of disasters that might overtake her during the evening, but the truth far exceeded her worst fears. Once the tea and port had been dispensed with Mistress Walters was prevailed upon, with much protesting, to sing.

"No, I declare I'm quite out of voice. Would you shame me, dear Compton, by making me a laughing stock?" But all the time she was edging nearer the spinet.

"Her performance is tolerable," thought Phyllida. "If only she would forget about her gestures and flourishes. Just the same, I hope she continues for the whole evening."

But even Mistress Walters' repertoire had its limits.

"Enough of me," she declared at last. "No, not if you begged me could I sing another note. It is the turn of our little bride. Here, my dear, take my place at the spinet."

Three pairs of eyes turned enquiringly towards Phyllida. Hoarse with embarrassment she mumbled,

"I do not play, I'm afraid."

"Then I will play while you sing." La Walters sat down again. "Which shall it be?"

"I-I-I have no voice either."

This was not quite true, but Phyllida was too terrified to even try.

"Well we shall enjoy your own instrument, what ever it is," put in the captain kindly.

Scarlet with mortification Phyllida was forced to confess;

"I play nothing, sir. I fear I have no music at all."

"None at all?" Mistress Walters looked at her hard, as if to say "How odd."

Conscious of the cold glance that Richard gave her, Phyllida wished that the floor would open and swallow her up. Silently she blamed her grandfather for constantly dismissing her governesses, for never considering her worth educating, and, most of all, for leaving her vulnerable to such embarrassment.

Even the conversation was far beyond her ken, being about concerts and plays, of masques and Vauxhall, mostly introduced by Mistress Walters. Time and again poor Phyllida was forced to admit her ignorance, so much so that she began to suspect that the other woman was doing it on purpose, just to discomfort her.

"But then, of course, for a diversion, I much prefer the theatre. I declare that I could see "The Beggar's Opera" a dozen times without tiring of it, couldn't you, Mistress Compton?" the lisping voice asked sweetly.

"It is not a work with which I'm familiar."

"No? You surprise me, but perhaps your taste is more towards the older theatre. I declare I scarce dare see "Romeo and Juliet", it affects me so deeply. Isn't that so, George? Do you find it affects you, madam?"

Again Phyllida had to say she did not know the play.

"She's doing it on purpose, I'm sure of it," thought Phyllida angrily.

"For myself, I prefer works such as those by Handel," the captain made a kindly effort to change the subject, but Phyllida was growing desperate. The whole evening was becoming a nightmare.

"I agree," she said hastily. "Now the plays of Handel are much more to my liking."

There was a horrible pause. Both men looked awkward, while Mistress Walters gave a supercilious smile.

"You do?" she asked. "And which of Mr. Handel's— er—plays do you like best?"

Too late Phyllida remembered that Handel wrote music. Richard opened his mouth to speak, but he was too late to help her. Humiliated beyond endurance she jumped to her feet.

"Does that satisfy you, madam?" she demanded of Mistress Walters. "You have proved yourself to be superior. It may give you even more satisfaction to know that I've never been to a play, nor a masque, nor a ball.

And as for Sidney Gardens and Vauxhall, they might be in Hades for all I know."

Trying not to see their startled expressions she picked up her skirts and ran from the room. Soon afterwards she heard the Walters leaving, then a much dreaded knock on her door.

"I wish to speak to you." Richard's voice sounded very cold.

She had barely time to wipe away her tears before he strode in. He was very angry. If she had ever wished to jerk him out of his customary calm she had certainly succeeded.

"That was the most appalling exhibition of manners I have ever witnessed, madam." His voice was barely audible. "I will have you understand that no guest in my house is ever to be treated in that way again. Do you hear me?"

"She provoked me," cried Phyllida angrily.

"That has nothing to do with it. She was a guest, and as such was entitled to courtesy. The first thing tomorrow you will send a letter of apology to Captain and Mistress Walters. I have made few demands on you, heaven knows, the least you could do is to be polite to the people at my own dinner table."

And he stormed out, slamming the door behind him. Richard's words had some truth in them, Phyllida had to agree, but that thought only served to make her more wretched than before.

"I hate this beastly place, with its noises in the night," she sobbed into her pillow. "I hate that man and his horrible guests. I hate them all."

It was a long time before her weeping ceased and she fell asleep, but her last thoughts were, as always, about Gerard.

Breakfast next morning was a strained and silent meal, at least on Phyllida's part. Richard greeted her with his customary cool civility, then applied himself to his food. Phyllida was calmer now, and had almost brought herself to the point for apologising for her behaviour, if only a suitable moment presented itself. It was Richard who introduced the subject. Wiping his lips on his napkin he leaned back and said;

"I have been thinking about last night."

Phyllida's spirits at once plummetted to zero.

"Yes," he went on. "I feel that I was unjust towards you last night. Mistress Walters is an extremely silly woman, and you were provoked—not that I condone what you did—but there were mitigating circumstances. I feel that I was largely to blame."

Phyllida, who had been expecting yet another scold, could hardly believe her ears.

"How could you be to blame?" she asked.

"I should have realised how inexperienced you were in all social matters, knowing your grandfather as I do. I must admit, though, that I had not expected your education to have been so limited. Did you have no governesses or masters?"

"'I had governesses certainly, many of them, but none who stayed more than a few weeks. If my grandfather did not dismiss them then they left of their own accord."

"Sir Walter can be difficult, I know, but what of other accomplishments? I thought that all young ladies were instructed in dancing, music and so forth as matter of course, these days."

"That may be so for others, but not for me. Grandfather said that if my fortune did not get me a husband that it was useless trying any other way."

"M-m-m." Richard pursed his lips.

He rose and strode up and down the room, his hands in his pockets, whether because he was distressed or deep in thought she could not say.

"But I've read a lot," Phyllida put in. "Though nothing modern of course, and I do like singing, but I've had no instruction in it. That was why I refused last night."

"I have given the matter a lot of thought," said Richard with deliberation. "And I have come to a decision.

You are an intelligent young lady, and it is quite wrong for you to go through life completely untutored. I consider it my duty to rectify the matter. Therefore, from tomorrow, you are to have lessons."

Phyllida listened thunderstruck by this extraordinary statement.

"Sir, you can't be serious," she said at last.

"But I am. There is an excellent person in town, a Mistress Edmund, who will be the person to attend to your general education. She is the widow of a naval officer and has, I am afraid, come down in the world. She is looking for a post, I know, so I shall contact her at once. She has travelled widely and I should like it if she would instruct you in less conventional matters for a female, such as geography." Seeing Phyllida's astonished gaze he explained. "My guests come from a wide sphere of society. Since many of them are connected with trade and the sea they have knowledge of distant lands. It would therefore be convenient if you also knew something of the globe. My-er-late wife was too delicate to entertain, but when my mother was alive she took a close interest in all such matters, and I would be pleased if you would do likewise. I shall also arrange for you to have instruction in dancing and music."

"Is that all, sir?" asked Phyllida in a deceptively meek voice.

"No, not quite. Any journeying to Bath or London will have to wait for a while, but in the meantime you can become conversant with the latest in modern literature. I subscribe to many publications and my library is large. I shall of course scrutinise any new novels to see if they are suitable reading for you. Now, how say you to such an arrangement?"

Phyllida faltered for a moment, searching for the right words to express her feelings.

"I think," she said at last, "that it is the most preposterous thing I have ever heard. If you think that I am going back to the schoolroom you are very much mistaken." Her voice became angrier as she warmed to the subject. "The whole notion is humiliating and degrading. May I remind you that I am a married woman, not a five-year old child?"

Richard's eyes glittered angrily.

"It is because you are a married woman that I think such measures are necessary. I can think of nothing more humiliating and degrading than for you to be mistress in this house where even the house-maids are better educated and informed than you are."

"May I also remind you that it is not of my own choosing that I am mistress of this house," exclaimed Phyllida, and at once wished the words unsaid.

Richard pressed his lips together in a taut line.

"Madam," he said tersely. "All I ask of you is that you run my house for me, and act as hostess to my guests. I trust that neither task is beyond your capabilities."

Without another word he rang for the table to be cleared and turned his attention to the letters which had remained unopened by his plate. It was as though he had forgotten Phyllida's existence, and with a sinking heart she realised that she was dismissed.

Becky was in the bedroom, bubbling over with excitement.

"Look what's just come, Miss Phyll. Aren't they beautiful? Master had them sent up from the warehouse." She was feverishly unpacking two bolts of silk. "This dull amber is just right for you. It will make a fine formal gown, with perhaps a sack back. Do you see how it hangs so well? And as for the other, this shade of brown is very à la mode up in London, I've heard, and . . . Miss Phyll, what's the matter? You look full of the glooms."

Phyllida sat down on a small brocade-covered chair.

"It seems I am to have school lessons again like a naughty child."

But that was not the real reason for her depression. She was regretting her hasty words to Richard. He was not her ideal choice for a husband, he had clearly been soured

46

by his first unhappy marriage, but she recognised that she owed him much. He had kept to his word and never mentioned her disastrous elopement, nor had he reproached her for her lost inheritance.

"Never mind," consoled Becky. "If it's the master's doing you can be sure it's for the best. After all, I suppose it's not much to ask after he's made you mistress of all this."

"You're right," sighed Phyllida. "But he was very angry. That's twice in two days I've made him lose his temper."

Becky was still experimenting with the lengths of silk.

"Well," she said cheerfully, "at least his set downs aren't as bad as Sir Walter's."

"I'm not sure." Phyllida was surprised how much his rebukes could sting her. "I think that they're just different."

The sight of the coloured silks lying there on the bed added more pricks to her sore conscience.

"I suppose I will have to make my peace with him." She went to her writing table and began to mend a pen for herself. Sometime later she knocked on the library door and then entered. Richard barely raised his head to acknowledge her entrance.

"I have brought this for you to approve," she said quietly, and handed him the letter for Mistress Walters.

He read it carefully, then commented;

"You have a neat hand. I will see that this is delivered." He returned to his papers.

"I have something else to say." It was hard to put into words and his off hand manner did not help.

"Go ahead."

"I had no right to speak to you as I did just now. I wish to say how sorry I am." She took a deep breath. "I have every reason to be grateful to you, I know that. So I will do as you ask and have lessons again. I promise I will try and please you."

Richard's pen scratched its way through a few more words before he replied brusquely,

"I don't want your gratitude. You are not some maidservant on trial in the kitchen. The lessons are for your good, not mine."

"I will attend to them, just the same."

"Very well, please yourself. You'd best let it be known that you are not available for morning calls, in that case."

Phyllida came out of the library feeling just as uncomfortable as when she went in. It was only afterwards that she recalled that during the interview Richard had not once looked at her.

Three

The next few weeks flew by with a speed that astonished Phyllida. At Barton Hall each day had seemed interminable, relieved only by meal times. But now every moment was fully occupied. She still resented having to go back to her school books, but submitted to the indignity with as good a grace as she could muster. Mistress Edmund proved a pleasant person, with a lively sense of humour, so lessons were not as dull as Phyllida had feared.

The dancing lessons were quite amusing, but Phyllida's special joy was Signor Giorgio, her singing master. He was about as Italian as clotted cream or squab pie, having been born plain George Willsworthy in the moorland town of Ashburton, a fact he admitted with the utmost frankness.

When Phyllida teased him about his foreign-sounding title a smile spread over his large good-natured face.

"Pure decoration, m'dear. Seems some folk think a Devon man can't possibly know anything about music, but I've proved them wrong."

He had indeed, for he was recognised as the best music master for miles. On the first morning that his shaggy shambling figure had arrived at Furze House he had endured her fumbled chords on the various instruments that were in the music room, listened to her sing a few scales, then sat back and nodded his head.

"Well, m'dear," he said, "I fancy that with much practice you may become a tolerable performer on the spinet, or perhaps the harp if you prefer it. Your voice, now, that is another matter."

Phyllida was deeply disappointed.

"You mean that it is poor? But I do so enjoy singing. Maybe if I practised . . ."

"I mean," interrupted Signor Giorgio, "that you have a very fine voice indeed. I can't think why you've never had any previous instruction. There is much work to do, of course." His small eyes twinkled as he helped himself to a generous pinch of snuff. "I shall dutifully teach you your instrument, whatever it is, but I shall instruct you in singing with delight."

For Phyllida the arrival of this unconventional music master opened delights that she had not known possible. Starved of music for most of her life she found that now she wanted more and more. She elected to learn the harp, (the spinet still reminded her painfully of her encounter with Mistress Walters), and she spent as much time as she could spare practising.

But free moments were rare. As Richard Compton had warned her, he did little formal entertaining, but there were few days when he did not invite someone to come and "take their mutton" with him. Gradually Phyllida grew more confident, and these small lunches and dinners began to lose their terror for her. She no longer went cold with panic when the small messenger boy from the counting house came panting up with the information,

"If you please, Maister says there be two genn'lmen and a lady to dine."

After a time she even began to enjoy meeting so many people. Merchants, sea captains, passengers from the huge three-masters that called at the port, all found their way to the Compton table, as well as town dignitaries. Richard's visiting list was certainly wide and varied. One person who loved this busy life was Becky.

"I believe you prefer working for Mistress Compton than for Miss Barton," remarked Phyllida one day, when she found her maid singing over some needlework.

"That I do." Becky grinned at her. "Even though I can never remember to call you by your new name. No two days are alike here, not like at the Hall. Why the new faces we see down in the servants' hall you just wouldn't credit, but there at Barton there was just the house servants most of the time. There's always something going on here, even if some of it isn't above board, if you follow me."

"Not above board? What do you mean?"

"Surely you've noticed it, Miss Phyll? There's things that happen here that are a bit on the secret side. I've seen it."

Phyllida remembered her encounter with Hembury. She had all but forgotten about the smugglers, whether it was because there had been no activity lately or because she was tired and slept soundly she did not know.

"What sort of things have you noticed?" she asked cautiously.

"Small things, mostly." Becky did not seem at all alarmed. "Whispering in corners, boots that don't belong drying by the fire, an extra plate served up at dinner. Small things, as I've said. But once or twice I've heard noises in the night."

"Did you go down to investigate?"

"Not me, miss. It's nothing to do with me. Let them get on with it, I say."

"Do you think they could be in league with the free-traders?"

"Smugglers, you mean? What makes you say that, Miss Phyll?"

"Just something someone suggested," Phyllida said hastily, unwilling to expose her informant.

"Could be." Becky snapped off a thread and turned to a fresh bobbin. "As long as it doesn't involve me I don't mind. I haven't seen any kegs or parcels though. They're clever at it."

"Are all the servants involved?"

"So it seems, even Mr. Hembury."

Phyllida was thoughtful for a moment.

"I wonder if Mr. Compton is aware of what is going on?"

Becky chuckled. "I shouldn't be at all surprised. I doubt if Mr. Hembury would breathe out without the master's permission."

That was true enough. Phyllida gave a little smile. It was pleasing to know that her staid husband was not as respectable as he seemed. In fact, she saw little of him, except at meal times, when they were seldom alone. It suited her very well, the less contact there was between them the better she liked it. Grateful as she was to Richard she still did not feel quite comfortable with him. Just the same she marvelled that he should spend so much of his time at the counting house down by the harbour, or pouring over his ledgers in the library. A man of his substance could surely have passed on such work to others. She could not understand him at all.

Phyllida still enjoyed the view from her bedroom window. She sat there a lot, preferring it to her rather dark little sitting room. Although she looked at it every morning the never-ceasing activity of the shipping always gave her pleasure.

"It's almost worth being married to Richard for such a view," she smiled to herself. "Well, almost!"

For several days a small cluster of three-masted barques had hovered at anchor just off the harbour roads. They caught her attention, for frequently she could make out neat lines of tiny scarlet figures drilling on the confined space of the deck.

"Why do those ships never move?" she asked of Parsons one morning.

The maid put down the armful of clean linen that she had been holding and looked out of the window too. Her normally serious expression became even more grave.

"They're transports, madam, bound for America when

the wind will let them. It's been contrary for weeks."

The very word 'America' was enough to bring a pang to Phyllida's heart; she wondered if Gerard had actually reached there yet, and what lay in store for him.

"Poor young men." Parsons spoke almost to herself. "It's a bad look out for them, having to go all that way to fight."

"Have many set sail, then?"

"Not so many really, madam, leastways not from here. The wind has played havoc with the sailings. That's why the camps here-abouts are chock full of red coats. It's sad when they're so sorely needed over there, now that General Washington has forced us out of Boston."

Phyllida was astonished that the girl should be so knowledgeable.

"You're certainly well informed!" she exclaimed.

"Mr. Hembury read it out to us last night after dinner. Master always lets him look at the "Flying Post" after he's finished with it."

Parsons did not seem to think that at all odd, but Phyllida was astounded.

"I know of few servants' halls where they read the weekly newspaper," she commented wryly.

"Perhaps not, madam." Parsons agreed with her. "But then Mr. Hembury has a son in America, and the master knows how worried he gets about him."

"That was a kind action." Phyllida was beginning to acknowledge a grudging respect for her husband. "But I didn't even know that Hembury had a son. Is he in the army?"

"No, madam, he has settled there, somewhere in Maryland I believe. He has married a local girl and has a couple of little ones."

"That must make it very hard for poor Hembury."

New aspects of this war were beginning to present themselves to Phyllida. So far she had considered it only as the dreadful force that had taken Gerard away from her, but now she realised that it was affecting many people deeply in different ways.

"Why, it's almost as though we were fighting his son," she added.

"Yes, madam. He feels it very much. 'Tis a stupid war, the whole of it, if you ask me, madam, putting us against our own kin. I mean, how can the master start thinking of Mr. Henry as a rebel and a traitor, just because we're told we've got to be in this war?"

Phyllida was surprised at this outburst.

"Who is Mr. Henry?" she asked.

"Mr. Henry Compton is the master's cousin, madam. He lives in America, near the town of Harvard," explained the maid. "And a nicer gentleman you've never met—excepting the master of course. I often wonder how he's faring in all this, him and Mistress Compton and their dear baby. I hope their home is far away from the fighting, such a fine house."

"You've seen it?" asked Phyllida in surprise.

"Yes, madam." Parsons' voice was strangely quiet. "I was in America for five years."

"But how was it that you went out to America? Did you go there with Mr. Henry and his family?"

"No, madam, for Mr. Henry has lived there most of his life. No, I was transported."

Phyllida did not believe her ears.

"I'm sure I did not hear you aright. Did you say transported?"

"Yes, madam."

Phyllida sat very still, not knowing what to do or what to say. It was hard to credit that this quiet girl was a criminal.

"I'm sure you must have been falsely accused. Isn't that what happened?"

"No, madam. I did it all right. I'm sorry to say. I killed a man."

Phyllida gave a faint squeal of alarm.

"Does . . . does your master know of this?"

"Yes, madam, but I'm sure he'd never think on to tell you, and I feel that you should know, you being my new mistress and all." Parsons' voice was remarkably calm. "Mr. Hembury said it would come better from me."

"I agree." Phyllida had recovered a little from her first shock. "You had best tell me about it."

"There's not much in it, madam. I was a maid here from being very young. We've always been in service with the Compton family." She said it with unconscious pride. "Then I married, but it didn't turn out well. He drank, and when the drink was in him he was a brute. One night he was worse than usual, and I had to grab something to defend myself with, and it happened to be the meat knife. I never meant to kill him, but in all honesty I wasn't sorry." Parsons had betrayed little emotion, almost as though she was telling about someone-else. "Things would have gone bad for me, but the master spoke up on my behalf. I got five years transportation instead of the death penalty."

"And you came here to work afterwards?" Phyllida found it hard to understand how she could be so unemotional.

"Yes, the master wrote to Mr. Henry about me and got me put with good people, so it wasn't all that bad. It was a deal better than being married to that animal. Being away from my family was the worst part, but the master brought me news of them whenever he came, so that helped."

"Mr. Compton went to America?"

"Yes, madam. He has estates there. Didn't you know? He used to go over every two or three years before all this revolution business. No doubt he'll take you with him when the war is all settled."

Phyllida was still thinking about the maid's tragic story. It was so horrible.

"Tell me, are there any more servants who have been in prison?"

She meant it as a feeble joke, but to her surprise Parsons took her seriously.

"Not many, I think," she said, deliberating carefully. "Mr. Hembury a few times for being drunk and disorderly, that was before he got religion. Master's had to bail him out a few times after Wesleyan meetings too, but that's all. Oh, and Joseph too of course, but then that wasn't really him. It was his father who was jailed for debt and the whole family had to move in with him. It was old Mr. Compton, the master's father, who got them out. That was years ago, and Joseph has been with the family ever since." She thought for a moment longer. "As far as I know that's all, but I wouldn't be surprised if there were more. We're all odds and bobs that the Comptons have collected, God bless them. Mr. Hembury's the one to ask, though, he'll know all about it."

"Thank you I will," said Phyllida faintly.

"Please may I go now, madam, if that's all? I've a deal more linen to sort."

Phyllida nodded. "If that's all?" Was not it enough?

"I've never heard of such an extraordinary household," she thought. "Richard is one of the richest men in the country, yet he works as hard as a ten-shilling clerk, smugglers appear to have free access to the house in the middle of the night, and half of the servants are from jail. This is a mad house!"

For a long time she sat thinking about Parsons and the others, but this was a rare morning free from lessons, since Mistress Edmund had a sore throat. Phyllida did not want to waste her freedom, but before all else she had letters to write. When she had finished she rang for a servant to deliver them. This time it was Joseph who came.

"I want these delivered at once," she instructed.

Joseph looked blankly at the papers in his hand.

"Beg pardon, madam, but the press is out. Would it be all right if I took them later?"

Phyllida did not understand him. She gazed at him, annoyed at his impertinence.

"If I'd wanted them sent later I would have said so.

They are all for the town so they won't take long. Now go at once."

"But, madam . . ."

Joseph withdrew, his swarthy face ill at ease. A few moments later there was a tap at the door and Parsons came in, and Phyllida was not at all pleased to see her carrying the letters.

"It's about these, madam," she began, but a frantic knocking interrupted her.

The pounding was so loud, so insistent, that mistress and maid both went out to see what was wrong. They were in time to see Joseph open the front door. A young man, his face ashen with exhaustion, collapsed into the hall.

"Please . . ." he gasped. "They're right behind me."

With a shock Phyllida recognised young Ned Prettyjohn, one of the junior clerks from Richard's counting house. Before she had time to realise what was happening Joseph had shut the door, and lifting Ned like a sack of grain, slung him over his shoulder.

At the same moment Parsons sped over to the bell rope and pulled it frantically, setting up a fearful clanging in the servants' quarters. Two menservants came dashing out through the baize door. There was no word, no instruction that passed between them, but they knew exactly what to do. They took the half fainting Ned from Joseph and had him out of sight just as a second loud pounding was heard on the door.

Phyllida watched it all open-mouthed. It was obviously a planned operation. Those servants had been drilled in what to do in such an emergency, and they had executed their task with great precision.

"If that's how the smugglers train their men, then I don't give the Preventives much chance," she thought.

The banging continued at the door. Joseph paused for a minute to adjust his coat and take a deep breath to compose himself before he opened it. Outside were a party of men, panting with exertion. They had the look of seamen about them, but they were all armed with short, thick clubs. One stepped forward. He was thick-set and muscular, and his teeth were stained from chewing tobacco.

"Where is he?" he demanded.

"Where is who?" asked Joseph, settling himself in the doorway.

"That run-away who came here. We saw him come, so don't try lying about it, or it'll be the worse for you."

"You wouldn't be threatening me, would you?" Joseph did not seem at all perturbed.

"I'm telling you that we want the scum who ran in here. Send him out or we'll come and get him." The seaman moved forward, but so did Phyllida.

"Joseph, why are these men here?" she demanded.

"They say we are hiding someone, madam."

"He ran away from us, the scum, right in at your front door," shouted one of the gang.

Phyllida drew herself to her full height and glared at them in a way that could not have been bettered by her grandfather.

"I am not in the habit of entertaining—er—scum," she said icily. "Joseph, have you seen anyone answering such a description enter this house?"

"No, madam."

"There you have your answer. Now be off with you."

Some of the men shuffled uneasily, but the thickset fellow was not so easily put off.

"Let me warn you that it is an offence to hinder His Majesty's press gang."

He edged forwards up the steps. At once Joseph moved to prevent him, but Phyllida put out a restraining hand. She glared at the seaman, who was now squarely facing her, and every ounce of pride and authority that she had inherited from Sir Walter shone from her eyes. She did not flinch, even though the man's breath blew rank in her face.

"And let me warn you," she said, "that I will permit no one to enter this house."

For a moment they stood there, then the seaman shuffled back a little.

"We're on His Majesty's business," he growled.

"Then you may inform His Majesty, on my behalf, that I am not even acquainted with scum of any sort, as you so indelicately put it, and certainly would not have such a low person in my house."

Sheepishly the group backed away. They knew there was no way of entering, short of actually attacking Phyllida, and they were not fools enough to try that. As they moved away Phyllida said loudly,

"You may shut the door, Joseph."

As he shot the bolt Joseph let out a sigh.

"Thank goodness for that, madam," he breathed. "Things were beginning to look nasty."

"I mean to find out what all this is about." Phyllida was relieved too, but she was also puzzled. She turned and swept through the green baize door with Joseph behind her.

"Where is the young man?" she demanded. "Those men have gone now, he is quite safe."

"I'll fetch him, madam." Parsons opened the door of a china closet and helped a still shaky Ned out.

"Sit down, Mr. Prettyjohn," Phyllida said. "And when you have recovered you can tell me all about it. Joseph, some brandy for him please."

The young man took the spirits in great gulps, and after a little while the colour began to return to his cheeks.

"I thought I was done for then, Mistress Compton, I really did," he said at last. "I can never thank you enough for saving me."

"But saving you from what? That's what I want to know."

"The press, madam, why, the press." He seemed astonished that she should need to ask. "I'd been to see the master of the FALCON about some faulty kegs of bacon he'd been given. I knew they were about, of course, but I'd only to get from the King's Quay back to the

58

counting house, and that's not more than fifty yards. Then they sprang out on me. I reckon they were lying in wait behind the old store sheds."

"But why pick on you?"

"Because I've two arms, two legs and a head, I suppose, madam. They can't afford to be fussier than that."

"It's no use," said Phyllida in exasperation. "I still don't understand why those men were chasing you."

"They were a press gang, madam. Haven't you heard of them before?"

"Yes, but only vaguely. I think Joseph mentioned it earlier. But who are they?"

"They are a recruiting gang for the Royal Navy."

"But you don't want to join the Navy do you? I thought you worked for my husband."

"So I do, Mistress Compton, and hope to do so for a long while yet. But you see, the warships are terribly short of men, more so now we've a war on our hands, so they are allowed to go through the streets taking what men they need."

"Taking them? You mean abducting them?"

"That's about right."

"But that is barbarous. What would have happened if you hadn't come here?"

"I'd no doubt have woken up in a long boat with a broken head, and found myself part way across the Atlantic by now."

"But what would have happened to your family? You are married, I think?"

"I am, madam, and have a fine baby son, but they would have had to manage as best they could, though my father would have seen to them. But there would be no knowing when I'd have seen them again. We've all a lot to thank you for, Mistress Compton."

"Little enough, I assure you. It was Joseph who did the most. Joseph!" Phyllida suddenly remembered. "Why, I was going to send you out with those letters! That was why you were reluctant to go."

"Yes, madam." The manservant looked rather sheepish.

"You'll not go, of course. Those letters are not important."

"Thank you, madam." There was evident relief in his voice.

Phyllida heard a voice—it may have been Parsons'— whisper,

"There, I said it was just because the missus didn't understand, her coming from inland."

The atmosphere in the servants' hall relaxed, and she had a feeling that in some way she had been tested and come through with flying colours.

"Lor, you should have seen the way the missus stood up to them devils." Joseph was relaying the scene to the cook, who had been unfortunate enough to miss the excitement. " 'I'm not even acquainted with any scum', she said, as cool as you please. You should have seen that fellow's face. I thought I should have died laughing. It's a pity that Mr. Richard wasn't there too, he wouldn't half have enjoyed it."

"I think you are referring to Mr. Compton," Phyllida reprimanded him to cover her own embarrassment.

She chose to ignore his using the familiar title of 'missus' to describe herself. Joseph just grinned, completely unabashed.

I'd best be going now, Mistress Compton." Ned was looking uneasy. "I don't want my wife to be worried. Someone may have seen me running, and told her I'd been taken by the press."

"Do you think it's safe yet?" Phyllida was doubtful. "Hadn't you better wait a little longer?"

"Missus is right," interposed Joseph. "I wouldn't put it past them to be lying in wait for you, especially if they haven't had much luck today."

"Then that's settled," said Phyllida, not waiting for Ned's reply. "You stay here until Mr. Compton comes home, he'll know what to do. And one of the maids shall take a message to your wife. I presume they aren't press ganging women into the Navy yet, are they?"

"Not yet." Ned's face broke into a grin. "I must say I don't really fancy going out there for a while."

"Master'll get you home somehow," agreed Joseph. "Or Mr. Hembury when he gets back from the wine merchant's."

"My stars!" exclaimed the cook suddenly. "I've two mutton pastries in the oven. They'll be burnt to cinders by now." As she dashed off to survey the damage it seemed the signal to the others to return to their duties, and Phyllida withdrew to let them carry on.

"My morning of leisure turned out to be rather hectic," she reflected with a smile.

As Becky helped her to change her morning gown for a more formal one of tabby poplin Phyllida kept thinking of the events of the day. The speed with which Ned had been swept into hiding had made her wonder just how many fugitives had made use of Furze House.

"I would love to know just how far Richard is involved in all this," she mused, but she was careful to keep her thoughts to herself.

She had half made up her mind to sound him out on the subject that evening, to see if he let anything slip that might confirm her suspicions, but Richard was late home. He looked so tired when Hembury opened the door to him that she could almost have felt sorry for him.

"It is typical of him to walk up that steep hill after so warm a day," she thought.

As if he sensed her presence, Richard looked up and greeted her.

"I'm sorry that I'm so late. Tell cook that she can serve in half an hour."

"I hear that you are quite a heroine among the servants," Richard said, almost before he sat down at the table.

"An exaggeration," declared Phyllida hotly. "Joseph did most of it."

"That's not the way he tells it." Richard lifted a cover

to inspect the contents of the dish beneath. "You will be pleased to know that Young Ned reached home safely about half an hour ago, according to Hembury."

"Why do you call him Young Ned?"

"Because his father, who is my chief clerk, is Old Ned, and I stood godfather to the third in line some six months ago, who up till now is known as Baby Ned. I suppose he, too, will enter my service, but it is to be hoped that he has changed his title by then."

Phyllida knew well enough that often two or three generations of one family would work for Comptons. Indeed there was a local saying for the upbringing of boys which went,

"Bear them, baptize them, then put them down for Comptons."

There was no denying that when it came to servants or employees Richard was regarded with a mixture of respect and adoration. He certainly treated them with a greater kindness and consideration than anyone else she knew. How many gentlemen would have helped Parsons in such a way, for example? Thoughts of Parsons reminded her of their conversation.

"I was talking to Parsons this morning," Phyllida said. "Oh?"

"And she told me about her transportation."

"She did? That was very sensible of her. I must admit that I had forgotten all about that unhappy episode in her life."

"Did it never occur to you that I should know that one of the domestics once killed someone?"

"To be honest I never thought of it. But you can't consider Jenny Parsons to be a jail bird, she was just exceedingly unfortunate. But I would vouch for her character at any time. Why, she has been in and out of this house since she was a child, her mother used to be cook here when I was a boy."

"And Joseph, and Hembury? I hear that they have been in prison too."

"Yes, Joseph has, and with Hembury it was more an excess of zeal." Richard suddenly smiled. "Have you had visions of being murdered in your bed? I can promise you that the servants in this house are honest and trustworthy to the ultimate degree."

It seemed a good moment to bait him about the freetraders, then Richard pushed his plate aside with his meat half eaten, and buried his face in his hands wearily. Somehow she found herself saying instead:

"You are tired. You should have had a chair up the hill, or else ridden on horseback."

Richard gave a faint smile.

"It is kind of you·to be so concerned, but I feel that if I don't relish the prospect of walking up the hill I can scarcely expect someone-else to carry me, whether it be two men or one horse."

"But do you need to work so hard? Can Old Ned not do it for you?"

He shook his head.

"There is one chief clerk, that is Old Ned. There is one master, that is me. If things go right or wrong they are my responsibility".

"But why bother?" Phyllida insisted. "You would still be rich even without your trading, surely?"

"I would not be poor, certainly, but there are others to be considered. If there was no Compton Company for example, where would Old Ned work? And Young Ned? And what would be the future for the third little Ned? You see the problem? I am responsible not just for my own household but for upwards of a hundred in this town alone. With the troubles we are having with this war it is a hard task to ensure that those people do not starve. Not to mention the interests of my Aunt Rouse and my cousin Henry, both of whom are major share-holders."

Phyllida was silent. This was a point of view that was foreign to her. Her grandfather had always regarded any-one under him to be there to serve his own needs. It never

63

occurred to him that he might owe them something in return.

"I'm sorry," Richard apologized unexpectedly. "I didn't intend to lecture you on my opinions upon the treatment of the lower classes."

"I find them very different from my grandfather's," Phyllida looked at him carefully. "I believe you are what he would call 'a damned canting radical'."

Surprisingly Richard burst out laughing, a rare thing for him to do.

"I believe you are right," he agreed. "I can almost hear him saying it."

"You mentioned your Cousin Henry. Parsons spoke of him too. I'd no notion that you had connections in the colonies."

"No? I have a plantation in America, which Henry oversees on my behalf, just as I look after his financial interests in this country." The laughter died from his face. "I was in the habit of visiting there as often as I could, for Henry and I are friends as well as cousins."

"This war must bring you great distress as well as inconvenience."

"Distress? That's a small word for it. I worry about Henry and his family, of course, but it pains me to think that we have thrown away a fine and beautiful land. Why, we do not comprehend one fraction of its true worth yet. Once beyond the Ohio River is fully explored there will be even greater opportunities for so many. I fear greatly that King George and his idiot ministers like my Lords Hillsborough and Dartmouth have by their bungling caused a breech that will not heal for many a year." He stopped abruptly. "First a lecture upon social change, then one upon politics. I am sure that this conversation must have little interest to you."

"No, I assure you," said Phyllida politely, but she was struck by the animation in Richard's face as he spoke. "He can be quite human, if the subject is near his heart," she thought secretly.

"I would take you to America if I could, but that is out of the question at the moment." Richard interrupted her thoughts. "But at the end of the month I have to go to Plymouth. I know it is a little late for you to be buying bride clothes, but my Aunt Rouse always extolls the shops and warehouses there. If you would like to come, you may."

Phyllida dropped her knife with a clatter. To go to Plymouth, to see new sights, new places! Would she like to go? She hardly knew how to express herself.

"The entertainments there are not equal to London or Bath, but I feel it would extend your knowledge of polite society. I shall consult Mistress Edmund about what activities she considers would best supplement your education, for I feel that no opportunity should be wasted."

The speech was so typical of Richard, the usual pompous Richard, that she nearly started laughing.

"To think that I almost liked him for a moment," she thought. "So he thinks that he will further my education, does he? Well, no matter. He is taking me to Plymouth, and that is all I care for."

Four

As Richard planned a list of items that would further her education, Phyllida began another that was much more to her liking.

"Aunt Rouse, isn't it splendid?" she greeted the old lady the next day. "We're to go to Plymouth at the end of the month. Now, of all things, I need your help, for I've no notion of the best places to shop."

"What news!" Aunt Rouse clasped her hands with a flourish of lace frills. "I used to enjoy visiting there at one time, but now poor Choo-Choo gets so ill travelling that it is quite out of the question. But I shall enjoy helping you, my dear. Now what do you need first?"

"Shoes," cried Phyllida. "Where do I buy shoes? And laces? I've scarce a decent piece left to my name. Oh, yes and . . ."

"Hold! Hold!" laughed Aunt Rouse. "I can't keep up. I think you'd best write a list of all your needs, then I will write down where to buy them."

"That sounds capital. And will you tell me what to take? I have no wish to appear the complete dowd. Oh madam, I'm so excited. Do you think we'll go to the theatre? And is there anywhere to dance there? Though I suppose Richard does not care for dancing."

"I shall see that he takes you, never fear." Mistress Rouse carefully steered her wide skirts up the staircase. "The Long Room at Stonehouse is the place to go, of course, with concerts and subscription balls. Yes, Richard shall most certainly take you there, you may rely on me for that. I believe that there is bathing there too, at this time of year, but I've never tried it myself."

"And the theatre? Is there a theatre, aunt?"

"Yes, but that is at Plymouth Dock. Still, that is no distance."

Phyllida stopped in her frantic sorting of clothes.

"I've never been to such a place. I've always wanted to do so, to go where there is music and singing and play-acting. And now I shall. I still can't believe it."

"I could almost wish to be going with you, my dear," said Aunt Rouse dreamily. "To be so young—I keep forgetting just how young you are, my love—and to be entering society for the first time. Why, it will be like your coming-out, will it not?"

"With my husband presenting me?" cried Phyllida, and they both started to laugh.

"Perhaps not, then, but the place will be full of elegant people. There's nothing like a war for making a naval town fashionable, you mark my word. But heavens, look at the time, and I've not given you the name of a single warehouse yet! Where shall we start?"

When Richard came home he found them both, ably assisted by Becky, making innumerable shopping lists.

"Between the pair of you and the French privateers I see I shall have little left for my bankers," he commented.

At once Phyllida was conscience-stricken. She was suddenly aware that of course this was his money that she was planning to spend.

"Have I been extravagant? I'm sorry," she cried, and she scored out half a dozen items.

"Shame on you!" For once Aunt Rouse turned on her adored nephew. "The child has been the soul of economy. There's nothing there but essentials."

"I was only joking," protested Richard. "You chide me, Aunt, because I am too serious, then when I try to be amusing you round on me. I can see that I'll never win. Phyllida shall have everything on her list, naturally. I can assure you that we are still some way off the poor house."

"Poor boy." Aunt Rouse relented. "You are attacked from all sides."

"And here comes Hembury, too late to be my ally." Richard turned to the butler.

"Since you are outnumbered sir, I'd give in. It'll come to that in the long run. 'So shall thy poverty come as one that travelleth'," answered Hembury. "Dinner is ready, sir, and I've set another place for Mistress Rouse."

"A particularly apt quotation. Very well, you may serve at once. Come along, ladies, you can plot my financial downfall after dinner."

Richard led the way down the wide staircase, with Hembury dutifully at his heels. The ladies paused only long enough to tidy themselves, but Phyllida was close enough to hear Richard say;

"You are in a fine humour, Hembury. Is it the fine weather?"

"Only partly, thank you sir. I've heard from my boy at last."

"And I gather that all is well?"

"Yes indeed, sir. At least until the time of writing. He's

67

sent his wife and the children inland to stay with her folks. He reckons they'll be safer there than on the coast, so his mind's at ease. 'A wise son makes a happy father!' "

"That's splendid news. It must be a great comfort to you. I'm very glad to hear it."

"Thank you, sir. Such a stupid war, isn't it?" And he was still muttering "So the forcing of wrath bringeth forth strife", as he helped them to slices of plump pink ham.

It was only later that Phyllida began to wonder how Hembury had got news of his son, for there were now few vessels, apart from warships, that plied across the Atlantic. How then had the letter travelled? If the same thing puzzled Aunt Rouse and Richard they gave no sign of it, but concentrated upon the food in front of them.

"Do you really need to return to the counting house so soon?" protested Aunt Rouse, as Richard rose to leave them. "Surely you can have an hour or two without your nose stuck in a ledger? You should enjoy yourself more."

"An excellent scheme, Aunt, if the French will let me."

"Are the Frog privateers still playing havoc with our ships?"

"Yes, and the whole business, what with insurance and the rest, is causing a lot of extra work, not to mention the lost funds."

"Well never mind the French for now. Stay with us and take a turn about the garden for a while. You have a young wife whom you seldom see, and an old aunt who is even worse treated."

Phyllida was not sure that she wanted to be included in this accusation. She would have been very happy to have carried on with her preparations for the trip to Plymouth.

Richard gave a mock bow.

"Since I am accused of such dire neglect I feel I must stay. Old Ned must cope for a little while."

"Now that is sensible," declared Aunt Rouse. "Phyllida, do you take his other arm, then there is no way he can escape."

To Phyllida this was too intimate for comfort, but there was no way of avoiding it. She noted, too, that Richard had mentioned slack trade due to the French at least twice, and she could not help wondering if it was a veiled reproof to her because she had received no dowry. As discreetly as she could she looked at his face, but could detect nothing from his expression. For the next hour she was forced to stroll arm in arm with him, as though they were sweethearts. It crossed her mind that Aunt Rouse had planned it so on purpose.

"If she is scheming to make me fall in love with Richard then the poor lady is doomed to disappointment," she thought. "Even if I wasn't in love with Gerard I'm afraid her nephew is too cold a fish for me ever to feel any affection for him. And I'll wager he'd never want me to."

There was no denying that it was pleasant in the garden, with a gentle breeze from the sea to cool them.

"We shall have no talk of business or war or anything at all disagreeable," decreed Aunt Rouse, picking a sprig of lavender and tucking it in the folds of her lace kerchief. "Gardening we shall talk of, and perhaps a little gossip, but nothing unpleasant."

"What can we do but agree?" said Richard, but his aunt's wishes were soon flouted, for almost at once Hembury came towards them across the lawn of the neatly walled garden.

"Officer Penwill to see you, sir."

"The Preventive Officer? What can he want?"

"He didn't say, sir, except that it wasn't confidential or anything, and sooner than inconvenience you he would come out here to you."

"Very well, show him out."

"Shall we go?" asked Phyllida.

"No, he said it wasn't confidential, so I'll take him at his word. It can't be anything important."

"Then I suggest that we sit down." Aunt Rouse was

already heading for a rustic seat shaded by a trellis of roses.

They had no sooner joined her than a swarthy man dressed neatly in the dark blue of the Preventive service came striding towards them.

"Your service, ladies, and yours, Mr. Compton." He bowed low.

"How do you do, Penwill. It's a hot day, isn't it? Will you take some refreshment to cool you?"

"Most welcome, indeed."

The small man nodded his head vigorously. With his florid complexion and quick movements he reminded Phyllida of a robin, but the glint in his eye was shrewd, very shrewd.

"Now tell me how I can be of use to you?" asked Richard, after they had been served by the ever attentive Hembury.

"A simple matter, sir. In a nutshell, will you hire us a cutter for a few days? I shall need one at once."

"Why, certainly. I've a fancy the old TULIP is free, but you'd best see Old Ned about it. What happened to your SWAN?"

"Holed below the water line. We caught her on something just beyond the head. My guess is that it was that Dutch merchantman that went down a couple of winters ago. I reckon she's shifted. Anyway, I ran the SWAN into Bowyer's Yard, and they say it'll be the best part of two weeks before they've finished with her. I need a replacement urgently, and Old Ned said I must see you." The officer took a long, appreciative sip of his wine.

"Well Old Ned's gone down in my estimations," snorted Aunt Rouse. "Why on earth did he send you all the way up here? And on such a hot day, too. He's quite capable of hiring you a cutter without any help from anyone."

"Quite so, madam." Those black eyes twinkled. "But the freetraders will want notice that we're flying with different feathers."

At the word "freetraders" Phyllida gave a start.

"You are not suggesting that Prettyjohn is in league with them are you?" she asked.

"No, Mistress Compton. At least, not exactly. But the Prettyjohns are a long family, and I dare say quite a lot of them never pay duty on their tea or brandy."

Richard leaned back against the rustic chair.

"I'm glad that business is good for some folks at least, in these troubled times."

"Too good for my tastes." Penwill bobbed his head again. "And the tale is the same all along the Channel. That's why there is no official relief boat for me. But at least we have things better than they do along in Kent and Sussex."

"Why is that, pray?" Phyllida had been watching Richard out of the corner of her eye to see if he was at all discomforted by the conversation, but he seemed quite at ease.

"Here in the West Country the smuggling is more of a family concern, if you follow me. Guns and running fights are rare. If we disturb them the local lads are more likely to abandon their haul and fade into the night, but not so up the coast. There, the gangs are bigger, more vicious. It they're cornered they'll fight, aye, and win as often as not."

Phyllida felt a cold shiver run down her back. There was more to smuggling than she had realised.

"I wonder you aren't suspicious of the madeira in that glass you're drinking," said Aunt Rouse sourly.

Officer Penwill looked at the golden liquid and swirled it gently, then he grinned.

"Unless I'm much mistaken in both Mr. Compton and the excellent Hembury, there'll be a duty stamp on every thimbleful of wine in this house." He took another sip. "Besides, if I worried about whether or not everything I drank had paid its dues to King George I'd be a very thirsty man, especially here-abouts."

"Then you wouldn't expect to find a den of smugglers

in the back cellars of Furze House?" asked Phyllida with great daring.

"A poor opinion I'd have of Mr. Compton, if that was so." Penwill bowed to her over his wine.

"Why so?"

"Madam, your husband has a score of warehouses and yards all over the country. Just supposing he felt the need to go smuggling. Is it likely he'd choose his own home to store the stuff? Particularly now, when he has such a charming bride."

"There, I've emerged without a stain on my character. I'm obliged to you, Penwill," declared Richard.

"Mind you sir, I'm not saying that a little drop of geneva mightn't find its way here on board a Compton ship, from time to time, without you knowing. No, I've a good notion who the ring-leaders are. It's the catching them that's difficult."

"You look remarkably happy for a man with such a hard task," commented Phyllida.

"That's one of my trade secrets, madam," he chuckled. "If I went about looking like the wrath of God then folks would beware of me, so I sits quiet and drinks my ale, then they forget I'm there. That's when tongues begin to wag, and you'd be surprised how much I learn that way."

"That man's a fool," said Aunt Rouse, after the officer had taken his leave.

"He wishes everyone to believe he's a fool," corrected Richard gently. "But I think he's a very able man. One it would be very easy to underestimate."

Phyllida felt inclined to agree with him. There was cunning and intelligence in Officer Penwill's little black eyes, and he was certain that there were no smugglers at Furze House. That was strange, unless Richard and his servants had managed to outwit him in some way. Yet the officer had been so insistent . . . then Phyllida smiled at her own foolishness.

"As if he would voice his suspicions to us," she laughed to herself. But out loud she said,

"If I was a smuggler I'd be very cautious of Mr. Penwill."

"And wise you'd be, my dear," agreed Richard. "But now I have to take my leave of you both. I have matters I must attend to, particularly since we are off to Plymouth so soon. I must speak to Jenkins about overlooking the coach. The road to Plymouth is trying at the best of times, without losing a wheel on the way. We must plan for an early start too, I've no wish to be held up at every toll gate."

"So, you're going by road, eh?" observed his aunt, hitching up a shawl. "That will be a change for you, Richard. I can't remember the last time you did such a thing."

"Don't you normally go by road?" Phyllida was surprised.

"No, I prefer to go by sea, if one of our coasters is going that way. It is more convenient and much less fuss. Besides, our Devon roads are scarcely suitable for wheeled traffic."

His aunt gave an affectionate snort.

"Much less fuss, indeed! Did you ever hear such stuff? What he means, my dear, is that he is glad of any excuse to get on board a ship. Sea fever, that's what he's got. Why, when he was a boy there was no knowing where he might fetch up. He was always pestering the captains to take him along with them. It's a wonder he didn't run away to be a cabin boy."

"That's an exaggeration, Aunt." Richard protested, discomforted by these disclosures. "But I must admit that to be on the open sea with a full spread of canvas above me is very pleasing. All the more so since so much of my life is spent among those dusty ledgers you scold me about."

Phyllida thought of travelling over the waves in one of the vessels she so often watched from her bedroom window. Now that would be an adventure after her own heart.

"And is there no ship bound for Plymouth this time?" she asked, a plan half formed in her mind.

"I'm not sure . . . Come to think of it, the KITTIWAKE will be loaded by then. But since you are coming too I had not even considered it."

But Phyllida was already picturing herself aboard the ship, hearing the crack of the canvas, the wind in the rigging. The whole notion took her breath away.

"But if you'd been alone, you'd have travelled by sea?"

"I suppose so."

"Suppose nothing," chortled his aunt, who could see all too clearly where Phyllida's questions were leading. "He'd certainly have gone on the KITTIWAKE."

"Then why can't we both sail?"

"No, my dear. It is quite out of the question. The trip would be far too dangerous, with the French liable to spring upon us at any point."

"But you would have gone, you know you would. If it wasn't too dangerous for you, why should it be so for me?"

"Please allow me to know best. The whole scheme is far too hazardous."

"Mistress Walters told me she had been as far as the West Indies with her husband, and Mistress Edmund too, she has sailed to many places."

"Yes, and they sailed on men-of-war, a very different matter from a small coaster."

"I don't expect luxury," protested Phyllida, ignoring the dark look on Richard's face. "I wouldn't mind being uncomfortable one bit, if only we can go by sea. You would prefer it, I'm certain of that. Oh, please, Richard, say yes."

"No, there is too much danger."

"The French won't dare to attack so near the shore, surely, so if we kept close in . . ."

"Madam." Richard's voice had an edge to it, his patience was at an end. "I don't think you understand me. I have said that we travel by road, and that is an end to the matter."

Phyllida opened her mouth to protest, but Richard was already bidding farewell to his aunt as though his wife no longer existed. He had shut her out in that infuriating way of his.

"Oh!" exploded Phyllida at his retreating back. "Of all the insufferable, pig-headed . . ." she faltered, unable to think of words dreadful enough to describe Richard Compton.

Aunt Rouse gave a little sigh.

"He may be right, my dear. Those terrible Frenchmen do come very near at times. Only the other day I heard of one of their vessels sheltering right under Roundham Point, as calm as you please."

"But that would never have stopped Richard going by sea, would it?" cried Phyllida angrily.

"Perhaps not, but he only has your interests at heart. He doesn't wish you to be in any danger, that's reasonable, isn't it?"

"No!" declared Phyllida rudely. "All he wishes is to dominate me, without any thought for my preference. I'm no more than his housekeeper."

Aunt Rouse sighed and patted her hand.

"I know that things must be difficult for you, dear," she said gently. "And don't think that I don't understand or sympathize. Your marriage is not to your liking, but if you put your mind to it you could both be happy. And that is my dearest wish. You are right for my Richard, though you may not think so. When my father told me I was to marry Rouse I wept for nigh three days together. I fancied myself in love with the curate, you see, but I soon found that my father had chosen wisely for me. Rouse and I were soon devoted to each other. He's been dead twelve years or more, and I've not seen a man that's his equal, though I've had offers enough. Richard means well, but he is so reserved that often he appears to be abrupt."

For a long time they sat in silence, until Aunt Rouse whispered hesitantly,

"You're not cross with me, are you? I didn't mean to interfere."

"Of course I'm not." Phyllida gave her a swift hug. "Or at least I'm cross with myself because I was rude to you."

"That's all right, then," Aunt Rouse beamed with relief. "Shall we go and finish your list now? There used to be a little embroidress at the back of Notte Street . . ." but she got no further, for they met Hembury coming to meet them.

"The master left a message for you, madam," he said, addressing Phyllida. "He says the KITTIWAKE must sail at seven on Wednesday morning, so could you be ready by then? If so, would you be sure to wear a warm cloak?"

"Oh!" For a moment Phyllida was speechless. They were going to Plymouth by sea! It was too wonderful to be believed. Then she thought of Richard.

"Why is it I'm always furious with Richard, or else full of remorse because I've lost my temper with him?" she exclaimed. "It seems that with him I'm always angry or ashamed."

Aunt Rouse smiled.

"He's a man," she explained philosophically. "What more can you expect?"

The next few days were a jumbled whirl of packing and band boxes, not to mention the last minute appointments with the dressmaker.

"The clothes I order from Plymouth will not be ready for some time, so I must have something to wear during our stay," reasoned Phyllida, when Richard came to query why she had cut short a dancing lesson. "What with Mistress Edmund, the dancing master, and Signore Giorgio, I shall be sailing to Plymouth still in pins."

"Very well," relented Richard. "You'd best close your school books until we get back."

"Thank you," beamed Phyllida, but Richard just walked away.

Phyllida sighed, too used to his brusque manner by now to be upset by it. That was the second time her thanks had received a cold response. When she had tried to express her thanks over his change of mind concerning their sea voyage he had behaved as if she had annoyed him. It was as if her gratitude angered him in some way, but she could not fathom how or why.

Phyllida turned to her last minute preparations. She wondered if she could exist for one more day, the moment of departure seemed so slow in coming.

That night sleep was the last thing she wanted, or so she thought, but within a few minutes of her head touching the pillow she had drifted into unconsciousness.

It was dark when she awoke, and her mind was still full of tangled dreams of ships and waves. Sounds came from below, and half drowsy, she slipped out of bed, her befuddled mind concerned lest Becky had forgotten to wake her, and they missed the seven o'clock tide.

By the time she reached the top of the stairs she was fully awake enough to realise that it was not morning at all, it was the middle of the night. Yet something had disturbed her. At once the sound of movement from the ground floor heightened her senses.

Last time she had prowled about the house in the dark she had met Hembury. This time she decided to be more cautious and dropped to her knees to peer through the carved balustrade. This was a perfect vantage point, with little risk of being discovered from below. Just the same, she jumped at every creak and groan that the house gave.

The sounds below had faded, and all that she could hear was the hum of voices. She could not see the door to the servants' hall from where she knelt, but as she watched a sudden burst of light told her that it had opened. Four men came into her line of vision, their voices low, scarcely more than whispers. The first carried a candle, and at once she recognized the crooked stance of Hembury. At the front door he paused to pull back the bolts, then he turned, and the circle of light from the flame illuminated his companions. There was no mistaking the tall, upright figure of Richard.

"So he does know all that goes on here," breathed Phyllida, then clapped her hand over her own mouth lest the sound had betrayed her.

But the quartet below was too engrossed in its own affairs to look up. Whatever was going on, Richard was very much a part of it.

A movement from the others in the group distracted her. She was sure she'd seen the bulky man in sailor's garb before. His name escaped her, but she'd once met him coming out of the counting house. He was bosun on one of Richard's ships. The bosun edged towards the door. He seemed eager to be away.

Only the fourth man in the party was a stranger to her, she was quite sure she had never seen him before. Of medium height, and dressed in nondescript clothes that made him look like a clerk, he was nevertheless treated by Richard as a guest. Whatever the reason for his visit the stranger was destined to leave with the bosun, for the seaman plucked his coat, as if to urge him away.

The stranger turned to Richard and made a little gesture with his hand, almost as though he was about to salute, then he changed his mind and shook hands instead. Then, surprisingly, he shook hands with Hembury too.

Sudden darkness enveloped the hall as Hembury blew out the candle. For a brief moment Phyllida's eyes were stunned by the blackness, then a wedge of pale light showed where the door had opened.

"I wonder why they are using the front door?" thought Phyllida. "But then it is not overlooked and it is nearer the harbour."

Two shadows slipped through the opening, then all was darkness again. There was a clicking sound, followed by a burst of crimson sparks as Richard relit the candle with a tinder box. He and Hembury were now alone in the hall.

Phyllida was scarcely aware that she was cramped and cold, she was so intent upon the scene below.

"There were no kegs," she thought, "no bundles of any sort."

She wriggled silently into a more comfortable position.

Richard and Hembury were moving again. They were talking together quietly and smiling. They seemed well pleased with their night's work, whatever it had been. Phyllida wished above all things that she could hear what they were saying, but Hembury's gestures were clear enough to interpret. He was asking if Richard wanted some wine. Together they moved towards the library, their solitary candle casting an island of light. For a moment she was afraid they would disappear from her view.

"Come where I can see you," she implored silently.

Tensely she waited for something to happen, then a movement caught her eye. Richard and Hembury may have moved from her line of vision but their reflections were clear in the mirror on the hall wall. Strangely it was Richard who poured the wine, not only for himself but also for Hembury. In amazement Phyllida watched as they raised their glasses in what was indisputably a toast to the adventures of the night.

Phyllida was beginning to feel stiff, but she waited to see what else the night had in store. The library door opened wider and both men came out, Hembury bearing a tray of dirty glasses. The butler turned towards the baize door, but Richard headed for the staircase. Afraid of being discovered Phyllida crept silently back to her own room.

As she listened she heard Richard go along the passage, his footsteps were quiet, little more than gentle thuds.

"He's taken off his shoes," she thought in astonishment. "That proves he's up to no good. Why else should the master of the house creep about in stockinged feet?"

There was a great deal for her to think about, and sleep really was impossible now.

"That stranger, he was the key to the mystery," she decided. "If only I knew who he was. And why he shook hands with Hembury. Lor' I shall never sleep now, I know I shan't."

It seemed only a few minutes later, though, that Becky was pulling back the bed curtains to let in the grey light of an early dawn.

"Come on, Miss Phyll." Becky shook her gently, precariously balancing a tray of hot chocolate and rolls at the same time. "Have you forgotten that we're off to Plymouth today? Master's about already. He says we're to be away within the hour."

Phyllida sat upright with a jerk that threatened the tray.

"I'll never be ready in time," she declared, then with a rush she remembered the furtive happenings of the night.

Everything looked so normal that she could half believe that she imagined it all. That was the trouble with Furze House, during the day it was so ordinary, it was only at night that the atmosphere changed. For a brief moment she considered taking her maid into her confidence, but Becky was too busy to chatter.

With scant ceremony she plumped up Phyllida's pillows and settled the tray on her lap. She then began the task of dragging the trunks and boxes from the dressing room to the hall.

"The boxes have to go right away," she said breathlessly, "so I said I'd push them out for Joseph to take down."

The mood of excitement caught Phyllida, pushing aside the mysteries of Furze House.

"I can bother about them when I return," she decided, as she consumed her food with more speed than was polite. "I'm off on a sea voyage, and I'm going to Plymouth. The smugglers will have to wait. I am sure this is going to be the most exciting day of my life."

Soon she was out of bed and suffering Becky's rapid ministrations. The maid's haste made her clumsy, but Phyllida was too thrilled to pay much attention to pulled hair.

"What's the weather like?" she demanded. "Is it fine? Oh, it must be!"

"Fine enough." Becky craned her neck to see out of the window at the same time as she was pinning up her mistress's hair. "It's coming out sunny and warm, and Mr. Hembury says there'll be a moderate breeze for most of the way, whatever that might mean."

"You don't sound happy, Becky," said Phyllida in surprise. "Is something wrong?"

"It's the sea, Miss Phyll."

"What about it?"

"There's so much of it. Are you sure we can't go by road? The thought of all that water makes my stomach heave even now."

"Think of it as an adventure. You'll enjoy it once we start, you know you will. As for being afraid, why I doubt if we'll ever be out of sight of land."

"Do you think so, Miss Phyll?" Becky sounded more cheerful. "I hope you're right, that's all."

Phyllida was dressed with record speed. It was such a fine morning she wondered if her heavy cloak on top of her wool great-coat dress would be excessive, but decided to be on the safe side and take it too.

"At least the hood will do away with the necessity of wearing a calash to keep my cap on," she thought. "Nasty uncomfortable things. Warm and practical, that's what I'll be."

So saying she tightened the strings of her lace cap under her chin.

Richard was waiting for her in the Small Drawingroom, engrossed in some list he was compiling. It was a long one, and Phyllida wondered with a chuckle if it was of all the educational visits he planned for her. But even that could not dampen her spirits this wonderful morning.

"You are prompt, my dear." Richard looked up as she entered. "I shall be with you directly. I must finish these last minute instructions for Old Ned. Why do you smile? Have I said something amusing?"

Phyllida shook her head.

"I'm just excited," she said hastily.

While he finished his work she looked through the window at the sea. It was pale aquamarine, and the little gusts of wind were capping each wave with white lace.

"I shall be out there soon," she thought. "A part of all that excitement and movement."

Richard straightened from his task and looked at her.

"The wind will die once we are round the head," he assured her. "But just the same, are you still sure that you don't want to change your mind? The coach can be round in a few minutes."

"No!" Phyllida's reply was most emphatic. "No thank you," she repeated more politely. "I would like nothing better than to travel by sea."

"Good. I am looking forward to it too," Richard put aside his pen. "If you are ready we can go now."

His face was as stern as ever, but Phyllida got the impression that he was pleased.

It was planned that they should go on horseback to the harbour, the narrow hilly streets were unsuitable for the carriage on such a short journey. As the little cavalcade wound its way down the slope Phyllida was so excited that she could hardly sit still on her mount. Only the apprehensive face of poor Becky, who was up behind Joseph, struck a glum note. Even Richard seemed to be in holiday mood as he rode ahead with the groom.

Although it was still very early the little harbour was bustling with activity. Small boats criss-crossed the smooth stretch of water that was enclosed by the high granite walls of the quays. The horses had to pick their way through the barrows and carts that were piled high with silver fish. Now and then they had to avoid a string of pack ponies, baskets of whiting destined for "up country" slung over their pack saddles. And all about them dodged the fisherwives, with striped aprons spangled with gleaming scales. It was noisy, smelly and slippery, but Phyllida loved it all. Already she could see the KITTIWAKE moored in the deep water at the far end of the quay.

Ahead of them a platoon of red-coated soldiers waited patiently for one of the fleet of gigs to ferry them to a transport waiting beyond the hard. As she looked at them Phyllida felt herself grow cold, for there was something painfully familiar about the officer in charge. It was there in the way he stood, in his manner of holding his head.

"Gerard!" For a moment Phyllida was afraid that she had spoken aloud. Then the officer turned, and with a sinking heart she saw that it was not Gerard at all.

"Are you all right?" asked Richard, turning in his saddle.

"Yes, thank you," she replied. "My horse stumbled."

She recovered her composure quickly, but the incident opened a wound she had thought was beginning to heal.

"Come along." Richard's voice broke through her thoughts. "You are holding every-one up."

Guiltily Phyllida urged her horse forward and followed him, but she could not help her eyes stealing towards the group of soldiers waiting on the quay.

Five

Phyllida had little chance to brood, for Richard was already by the KITTIWAKE, waiting to help her dismount. The vessel was compact and sturdy, shallow-draughted enough to lie right alongside the quay wall. At once Phyllida's spirits began to soar again. Her adventure was beginning, and not even painful thoughts of Gerard could dim the thrill entirely.

"Ooooh, Miss Phyll, I don't like this at all." Becky's

voice quavered as she balanced along the gangplank. She still viewed the whole expedition with trepidation, and made no bones about saying so.

"Go along, maid, you'm not started yet," chided a gruff voice, and a tiny man with a face as tanned as old leather appeared at the top of a companionway.

He caught sight of Richard and a great beam split his face, showing a assortment of ill-coloured teeth.

"There you be, maister. Did you'm get lost then?" He greeted him with more affection than ceremony.

"Come along now, Bowden, we aren't late." Richard was not put out by this familiar greeting. "My dear, this is Captain Bowden, the best skipper on the coast, and the greatest rascal."

"How be 'ee, missus." The little man held out a gnarled fist. "You'm proper welcome, I'm sure. It's high time the maister brought you along. Now do 'ee want to go below or stay up here?"

"Up here, please." Phyllida did not know whether to be amused or affronted by his lack of respect.

"That's just 'andsome then." Another hideous grin spread across Bowden's face. "For I've fixed up a liddle ole cubby 'ole for 'ee on the forrard deck, where 'ee'll be snug and not get stepped on."

He seized her hand and half dragged her to a small canvas shelter that had been rigged on the deck. Phyllida allowed herself to be propelled into it, at once laughing and outraged. But Bowden had clearly gone to a lot of trouble on her behalf, and she was touched by his consideration.

"Now I'll just shift that bit of canvas, it's just there so your petticoats and fall-lalls won't get messed, and I reckon ee'll be as right as ninepence in there."

Bowden surveyed his handiwork with satisfaction.

"It's splendid thank you. I'm sure I shall be comfortable. I'm looking forward to this very much."

Bowden's face shone, and his fringe of whiskers showed up like hoar frost.

"We'm proper pleased to 'ave 'ee, missus, and that's a fact. I'm glad too that the maister's got company for once and not going about all lonely."

Phyllida was saved from replying to this extraordinary comment by the sound of Richard's voice.

"So this is where you've hidden Mistress Compton, then."

If anything Bowden's smile grew wider.

"Just seeing as 'er's comfortable," he assured him. "And I suppose you'll be wanting to take my ship off me as soon as ee can." In a mock confidential voice the old skipper remarked to Phyllida, "Maister's a good seaman spoilt by money; if only 'e'd not been born a Compton 'e'd 'ave made a fine captain. Any excuse to go to sea. Always been the same." In a louder tone he said, "I'd best get us on our way, then, since I'm to be a gentleman of leisure for the rest of the trip." And he scuttled his way aft.

Phyllida watched him go with some amusement. She wondered at her grandfather's reactions if one of his people should ever speak to him in such a fashion. The rage he would throw would be truly monumental.

"But," she reflected to herself, "for all his ranting and raving he's not served half so well as Richard."

At that moment Richard spread a warm rug across her knees. Having done so he sat down beside her.

"We'd best keep out of the way until the KITTIWAKE is clear of the harbour."

"Do you really intend to take over the ship?"

"Surely, but, believe me, Bowden will be watching all I do with an eagle eye. It was he was taught me all I know about sailing and seamanship, so he will have no scruples about telling me if I'm wrong.

Phyllida found it hard to imagine Richard enjoying the vigorous life of the sea, he still seemed such a staid and stern person, but she did not have long to ponder on the matter for the activity on the KITTIWAKE began to increase. The vessel cast off her moorings then gave a slight shudder as she took up the rhythm of the wind and tide. Slowly at first, then gaining speed the ship drew away from the granite quayside. Phyllida felt a quivering beneath her feet, then she saw the little town of Tormouth begin to recede behind them. They were at sea at last.

Minute by minute the hills slipped away in the distance until they were no more than blue smudges. Never in her life had Phyllida felt such pleasure. The brilliance of the light on the water, the keening of the wind in the rigging, this was all a new and wonderful world to her.

She felt the tang of the salt spray on her lips and knew that her complexion would be ruined, but she did not care, not even if she had to spend the rest of her life smeared with cucumber juice.

"No need to ask if you'm enjoying yourself." The small figure of Bowden came up and sat beside her unbidden.

"It's—it's wonderful." Phyllida struggled for a word that would describe her enjoyment.

"You and maister'll make a good pair, then," grinned Bowden. "He's sent me about my business long since, so I've naught to do but see that you'm happy."

Phyllida glanced aft to where Richard was in charge of the wheel. The difference in him was so staggering she could scarce believe it. He was totally absorbed in steering a course through a fleet of russet-sailed fishing boats, and as she watched him Phyllida wondered at the change in him. Richard, who was so precise in matters of decorum had discarded his jacket, and stood at the wheel in his shirt sleeves. She noted with amazement that this fastidious man who in the past had been known to change his shirt three times in one day because the cuffs were soiled, was now unaware that he had a streak of pitch on one sleeve, and that lace hung loose from the edge of the other. His hair was untidy from the wind, but it was his face that puzzled her the most, it looked so changed. It was some time before she realised that this was because the tight frown that so often furrowed his brow was gone. He looked younger, and much less forbidding.

"Maister's 'appy now." Bowden's voice spoke in her ear.

There was affection in his tone. Hastily Phyllida turned round, discomforted at having been caught staring, but Bowden chuckled.

" 'e looks a different person at sea, doan 'e? It's grand to see him that way for a change." He patted Phyllida's hand. "And I think it's grand the way you share 'is likes too. Now Mistress Maria, 'er'd puke something awful as soon as 'er'd set foot on board."

Phyllida stiffened haughtily at his familiarity, but Bowden did not seem to notice.

"Poor maister." He spoke sadly. "Life 'asn't treated 'im well. She wasn't the one for 'e. Oh, pretty as one of they chiney ornyments, she was, but who wants to be married to one of they? What with Mistress Maria and 'er tantrums, then the old maister and missus dying so close, within a week of one another—that was a blow to 'im I can tell 'ee."

Bowden suddenly saw that Phyllida was looking at him with disapproval. Unexpectedly he chuckled.

"I've been speaking out of turn again, 'aven't I?" He patted her hand again. "Well maybe I've a right, seeing as 'ow I've fished the maister out of the water more than once with my boat'ook through his breeches. That was when 'e was a lad, mind. I wouldn't care to try it now."

Phyllida tried to keep the haughty expression on her face, but the thought of Richard in such an undignified position made it very difficult. A small snort of laughter escaped her and Bowden grinned again.

"I don't mean to be disrespectful, missus," he assured her. "I just speaks as I find, and I can tell you there's nothing I wouldn't do for the maister."

Once again Phyllida noted the deep devotion which Richard inspired in all who served him. Perhaps it was only with his social equals that he was so cold. A small note of curiosity surged inside her. Richard never spoke about his parents, and she found it hard to picture him as the member of a family, instead of the rather solitary figure she had grown accustomed to.

"You served old Mr. Compton?" she asked.

"That I did. Rare broke up when he died, I can tell you. It was so sudden, you see. Everyone thought the missus would go first, as'er was in such bad health—not that she ever played up to it—but it was the old maister who collapsed suddenly and was gone within the hour. Then five days later the missus went too, just 'adn't the 'eart to carry on without 'im. They was a close family the Comptons. Thought the world of one another. What with one thing and another. I just reckons the young maister's got out of the way of enjoying 'isself, but now 'e's got you to put that right, missus."

"You are glad you chose to sail?" Richard's voice made her jump.

"Yes indeed." Phyllida wondered how much he'd overheard.

"You are not feeling indisposed, then?"

"I've never felt better, though I believe poor Becky is in misery."

"Missus is a proper un, and no mistake." Bowden broke in. "Taken to it in the manner born, 'er 'as." He rose and gave his place to Richard. "Now you stay 'ere and 'ave some vittals, maister, and I'll see after the ship. After all I doan want ee enjoying it too much or I'll be out of a job."

And he hurried away.

"Do you want to eat now?" asked Richard.

"Indeed I do. I've suddenly realised how hungry I am. I only hope Hembury has packed enough."

Richard opened the wicker hamper and revealed a staggering array of pies, meats and fruit.

"Splendid!" he exclaimed. "Hembury knows what sea air does to the appetite, so I think we'll fare well. Shall we serve ourselves, or shall I call Joseph?"

"We'll manage well enough, I think. Besides, I don't think I can wait a moment longer for something to eat."

She handed him a crisp white napkin, and cut him a generous slice of cold game pie. For a while they ate in silence, then Richard leaned back with a sigh of contentment.

"This is the life, far away from bills and receipts and dusty offices."

Phyllida was surprised.

"But I thought you enjoyed that sort of thing?"

"It's well enough, but not what I'd have chosen had I been free."

"And were you not free?" It had never occurred to Phyllida that he would wish another way of life.

"Not really. My grandfather and father built up the business long before I was born. I was the only one to take it over, since my cousin Henry was in America by then. Someone had to take charge and there was only me. But sometimes I would change it all to be at sea, with all its dangers and discomforts."

Phyllida selected an apple from the basket and took a bite. For a brief minute she had a picture of a younger, happier Richard, unhampered by all his worries and responsibilities. Unexpectedly she felt a twinge of sympathy for him.

The afternoon sun blazed down, and Phyllida felt her eyes closing. She was angry with herself, for she did not want to lose a single second of this voyage, but excitement and her disturbed night took their toll and soon she was asleep. When she awoke the sun was lower in the sky and the coastline seemed much nearer. Ahead of her she could make out a break in the line of hills.

"Plymouth," announced Bowden with relish. "We'll be in the Sound within the hour."

Phyllida was sorry that the journey was over, but she was quivering with excitement at the prospect of setting foot in a new town.

Saint Nicholas's Island slipped by, then the point of Mount Batten. As they inched their way into Sutton Harbour she could hear the steady chant of the rope walkers on the hill above. Then at last they reached their moorings.

Phyllida had always considered Tormouth harbour a busy place, but it was nothing compared with this. Flanked by great warehouses, the cobbled quays rang with the clatter of hoofs and the rumble of carts. The air was sharp with the smell of fruit and wine, overwhelming even the everpresent fish.

She was dazed by so much bustle and was glad when Richard took her arm and led her to the waiting carriage. Joseph was already attending to the luggage, and one of the crew of the KITTIWAKE followed, carrying Becky. Poor Becky, who had retired below before they'd even been out of sight of Tormouth, and had spent the entire journey in misery.

"Sickest thing I ever seen," remarked the sailor, as he lifted her into the carriage.

Becky gave a groan as the carriage lurched then set off away from the harbour.

"I think I'm dying, Miss Phyll," she said weakly.

Phyllida patted her hand.

"Never mind. It's all over now."

"No it ain't, Miss," wailed Becky. "We've got to go back the same way, and I'll die. I know I'll die."

"We'd be sorry if that happened," said Richard, without the hint of a smile. "But if it's as bad as that perhaps you could return by road. If your mistress can spare you, that is."

Becky opened her eyes.

"Thank you, sir," she said fervently, and the look she gave him was one of utter adoration.

"One more servant who is devoted to Richard Compton," thought Phyllida drily.

Their journey was short, too short for Phyllida, who wanted to look out onto the streets of Plymouth, but she was delighted to find that their inn was in the centre of town, just off Whimple Street, and almost within sight of the Guildhall.

"A trifle noisy, perhaps. I usually choose somewhere

nearer Stonehouse, but you no doubt wish to be near the shops." Richard's tone was clipped and precise.

A change had come over him the moment he had stepped upon dry land, or so it seemed, for he was once again the dour Mr. Compton. But Phyllida did not mind, anymore than she heeded the din rising from the streets below. In fact she enjoyed the hustle and bustle that they could see from their parlour window.

She looked out and was reminded with a pang of the last time she had surveyed the passing scene from such a window. Those memories of waiting at Exeter for Gerard brought a flush of pain to her cheeks even yet, and she was glad that Richard had retired to his own chamber, and was not there to comment upon it.

There was a garrison at Plymouth, as well as naval docks, so the streets were thronged with uniforms, and half unconsciously she found herself watching out for Gerard.

"You must stop this," she scolded herself, not for the first time. "Gerard is across the Atlantic by now, and even if he were not, what then? You are married, and there's an end of it."

These thoughts were full of sense, but in spite of them Phyllida could not prevent herself from keeping a watchful eye open for a familiar figure in uniform, for a handsome officer with dark eyes that were always laughing.

The next few days were packed with activity. Richard spent much time away from her, attending to business matters, but she was not dull, not with so many fascinating shops at hand. She had to admit that he was generous and made no protest about the amounts she spent at the silk merchant's or the glove maker's, or any of the dozen or so other tradepeople she patronised. This list that she and Aunt Rouse had so carefully made together was all but ticked off when she discovered that Richard had not forgotten his own list.

"I have completed the bulk of my affairs," he announced unexpectedly one morning. "So, my dear, I am free to escort you round some of the sights. I think you would benefit from taking in some of the antiquities of the area. Then, too, I know that Mount Batten is a model of taste, that must improve your judgment in such matters. We will return home by ferry, and, I hope, will be in time to attend the concert at the Long Room. Now I have obtained the programme for you, so that you may have a chance to study it before we go, if you have time."

"If I have time!"

In any other man she might have thought it a joke, but she knew all too well that Richard was serious. In vain she protested that she had an appointment with the dress-maker. Richard had made up his mind to take her on a tour, so on a tour they went.

She soon found out that on successive days Richard had planned other outings:—to explain the defences of Plymouth, for example, an exhaustive examination of a collection of paintings, plus a tour of the major architectural exhibits of the dockyard. Nothing seemed beyond his scope, and at night Phyllida limped back to the inn, footsore and weary.

"This is not at all what I planned to do," she moaned, but Richard's reply of;

"It's for your own good," was unanswerable.

There were subjects she enjoyed though, even some on Richard's itinerary. Observing the ships at anchor in the Hamoaze was one, noting their places of origin, guessing their cargoes. She had no idea why Richard thought such an occupation had any value for a fashionable young lady, but she knew better than to argue. It was very amusing just the same, particularly when Richard hired a spyglass for her to gain a closer look.

It was the social life that Phyllida really longed for, and somewhat reluctantly Richard indulged her. They attended concerts at the Long Room, subscription balls at the Fountain Inn.

"Did you ever hear such music," she cried more than

once. "I can never get enough of it. Please may we go again?"

On several occasions they went to the theatre, and Phyllida found herself in agreement with the hated Mistress Walters that it was a most wonderful diversion. Despite Richard's attempts to widen her horizons Phyllida still managed to enjoy herself at Plymouth. Her only dread was that it would be time to return to Tormouth before she had accomplished half that she wished.

One Sunday morning they attended morning service at Saint Andrew's, which pleased Phyllida, for she enjoyed looking at the many fashionable ladies in the congregation.

She was confident that she was looking her best, in a now gown of blue and gold striped Italian silk, finished in record time by the Plymouth dressmaker. Her hair was high and powdered, and topped by a wide hat trimmed with matching plumes.

"How many people you know," she whispered to Richard, after having bowed for about the twentieth time on their way to their pew.

"Mainly business acquaintances," he whispered back.

Just the same, she had to own that it was very pleasant to be acknowledged on all sides. After the service was over she looked forward to spending the rest of the day strolling among the people of quality in the meadows at Stonehouse, or perhaps on the famous Hoe. Richard, however, shattered her plans with a few words.

"You take the carriage back to the inn, and dine without me. I have someone I must see at Plymouth Dock. You will have Becky and Joseph to escort you."

"Will you be long?" asked Phyllida, hoping that her walk among the fashionable would perhaps be only delayed.

"There's no knowing." Richard bowed in greeting to a plump man in an outmoded bag wig. "I shall of course be as quick as possible, but I have much to discuss."

"And what am I to do in your absence?" snapped

Phyllida. "I can scarcely go out alone. Am I to stay cooped up at the inn?"

Richard looked at her coldly, a look that was very familiar.

"I am sorry if I have inconvenienced you." His voice was angry. "It was unavoidable. I doubt if spending two or three hours in our rooms will be so great a hardship when you consider we've hardly been there this last week. If you are at a loss, then I suggest that you find something to occupy you from among the books that were delivered yesterday."

So saying, he abruptly handed her into the carriage, then got in and sat beside her.

"I shall ride part of the way," he informed her. "I trust you do not object to an extra ride?"

"It is your carriage, sir." Phyllida was equally polite. "I suppose you may take it where you please."

Very much out of temper Phyllida sat in silence as the carriage bumped its way over the cobblestones on its way to Plymouth Dock, which was now a thriving settlement that had sprung up beyond the old town. Richard read his newspaper, ignoring her completely.

"Put me off here," commanded Richard when they reached the top of Fore Street. "I will walk the rest. Now you take your mistress back to the inn."

"Shall I come back for you later, sir?" asked the coachman.

"No, I shall walk or take a diligence."

"Having come so far we may as well take you to your friend's door," snapped Phyllida.

"I will walk," insisted Richard firmly.

"Shall I not come and wait while you talk to this person?" Phyllida resented being left alone.

"I have no idea how long I'll be. Joseph, see your mistress safe back to the inn, now."

"Yes, sir," Joseph jumped down from his place on the box of the hired carriage and opened the door for Richard to alight.

As he did so Phyllida caught a look that passed between master and man. What was it? Caution? A warning? Or just a look of commiseration from the servant because his master's wife was in a temper? No, Richard was a lenient man with domestics, but he would never have permitted insolence. The look troubled Phyllida, but was not enough to make her forget her angry mood.

"If I'm to return to the inn, then it will be by the longest route," she decided. Aloud she commanded, "I want to go back within sight of the sea. Take which roads will give me the best view."

"Very good, madam." Unseen by her the coachman exchanged a shrug of resignation with Joseph.

She knew she was being unreasonable, but that did little to soothe her temper. She was very disappointed that even one day of this precious stay at Plymouth should be wasted.

"It was inconsiderate of Richard to be engaged on a Sunday too. Whatever can he be up to today? His principles are far too strict to allow him to conduct business on a Sunday, so why was it important? He was secretive too. There is some mystery here." Then Phyllida interrupted her own thoughts. "You are finding shadows and secrets in everything, these days. Now be honest, there is no reason why Richard should tell you where he's going, and as for not wanting the carriage, what's so odd in that? He often goes weeks at a time without ordering it out at all." She then had an engaging idea. "There are some low places in the district, I believe. Perhaps he has gone to indulge in a little debauchery for an hour or two?"

To be honest, she had only the vaguest notions of what constituted debauchery, but she was aware that it involved the over-painted, frowsily dressed females who frequented the waterside. The idea of fastidious Richard in company with such creatures was enough to raise a smile.

"All I need now to get me completely out of the doldrums is to watch the sea for a little while," she decided, much cheered. "It's a pity it's a Sunday, for there will be fewer ships, but there is bound to be something of interest."

The carriage wove its way through the Sunday crowds that thronged the narrow streets. It left the Plymouth Dock area behind and made its way along the banks of Millbay, and then it was forced to little more than a crawl among a tight press of people. Looking out Phyllida saw that on one side of the road there was a row of small cottages, and on the other was a high stone wall, on top of which a militia man was idly surveying the people below. A vast crowd was making its way through a large gateway in the high wall.

"Why have we stopped?" Phyllida demanded. "What are all those people doing?"

"We're stuck in the Sunday market crush, madam," the coachman informed her. "We'll be out directly."

"The Sunday market, what's that?"

The coachman had his work cut out controlling the horses among such a crush, so Joseph answered.

"It's held there, madam, in Mill Prison, where they keep the American prisoners, aye and Frenchies too."

"And what do they do?"

"Just sell the bits and bobs the prisoners make, madam. It earns them an extra few pence."

She examined the crowd. There were some gentlefolk among it, mingling with the throng of town and country dwellers who were making their way in. It was not as fashionable as Stonehouse Meadows of course, or as elegant as the Hoe, but it would be more diverting than sitting alone at the inn.

"Stop the carriage," she demanded. "I wish to go to the market."

Oh no, madam," Joseph was horrified. "If you'll pardon me," he added hastily, "but it's that crowded. You'd not enjoy the crush."

"Kindly don't presume to tell me what I will or will not enjoy."

"No, madam. Sorry, madam. But you get all sorts

there, pick-pockets, cut-purses and a lot worse."

For a moment Phyllida's decision wavered, but Joseph put the seal on things by adding rashly,

"Master wouldn't like it at all."

That was all she needed to make up her mind.

"Hand me out," she stated. "I'm going to the market."

His burly face crumpled with worry Joseph jumped down, opened the door and unfolded the steps.

"If you're sure you're set on going then you'd best let me go first, madam. And please keep hold of my belt. Becky, my girl, stick close behind your mistress. And another thing, hold tight to your purses." With a final "What will the master say," Joseph edged his way into the crowd.

Within a moment they were being swept along into the yard.

"I don't like this, Miss Phyll," wailed Becky, from the rear.

Phyllida was unused to such a crush, and felt the first murmurings of panic at being so hemmed in. Already she was regretting her whim. Clasping firmly to Joseph's leather belt she was carried along through the gate and into the open court beyond. At the far side of a further wall rose a huge grim building, the like of which she had never seen before. That must be the prison, she decided.

The visitors were only allowed in the outer courtyard, and once through the gate there was more room. She was able to look about her. At the sides of the yard small stalls were erected selling all manner of trinkets of wood and bone. They were a miserable collection, but the men selling them were even more pitiful.

Their faces were grey and haggard, their clothes in rags, and many were so thin that their bones seemed about to pierce their skin. Phyllida drew in her breath, aghast that men should be brought so low. These, then, were the rebel Americans.

"Well if that aint disappointing," a petulant voice behind her protested. "They look just like us. I was sure they'd be different. You'd take 'em for Christians."

"Damned rebels, that's what they are," a stout farmer exclaimed. "Hanging's too good for them, going against their king like that." And he shepherded his brood of equally stout daughters round to show them what rogues looked like.

"They seem more half starved to me," piped up Becky from behind her mistress's skirts.

"Don't they just," agreed a small sprightly woman with bright cheeks. "I've a boy in America the same age as some of those. Can't think of them as enemies, somehow, not like the Froggies." She raised her basket in front of her and gave it a shake. "I'm always afraid I'll find my Jan here, him sailing on board an American barque, like, so I come most weeks with a little bit of something, just in case." She lifted the corner of the white cloth to show its contents. "Just some lardy cakes today, but then Jan always was fond of them. And if he aint here, then they'll find a good home with some other poor boy."

The old woman pushed ahead, her basket held aloft like a banner.

"Now my son is here," remarked a neatly dressed man to no one in particular. "This'll be the first time I've seen him in seven years. Strange how things turn out, isn't it? But for this war I might never have seen him again."

"Most of them are a rabble," a high voice declared. "Indentured servants and low farming folk."

Phyllida heard the talk without heeding it. She was stunned by the sight of the miserable prisoners.

"Those poor men," she kept saying. "Those poor, poor men."

In her distress she lost her hold on Joseph, and at that moment a fresh wave of newcomers swept through the gate, taking her with it.

"Joseph!" called Phyllida in alarm.

"Let's go from here, Miss Phyll," cried Becky.

"I don't think we can."

Phyllida turned to see if there was any escape, and at

once was pushed off balance. Flinging up her arms to save herself she was sure that she would sink beneath those oncoming feet. Becky screamed and clutched at her, but she was too late. Then, just as Phyllida was sure that she would go down, an arm grabbed her round the waist, and hauled her out of the way of danger. Half fainting Phyllida let herself be led to a seat. It was no more than a wooden box, but she sank down onto it gratefully. She looked a sorry sight, her fine new striped gown was crumpled like a rag and torn in two places, her hair was coming down, and she had lost her wide hat altogether.

"Miss Phyll, are you all right?" Becky had somehow managed to battle her way across the sea of human bodies and practically threw herself at her mistress.

"I'll be better in a minute," said Phyllida weakly, and grasped her hands, feeling her dizziness gradually recede.

She closed her eyes to recover herself, and when she opened them again she saw a pale face gazing at her in concern.

"Are you feeling better now, madam?" asked a voice with a faint, unfamiliar accent.

"Yes thank you."

A smile of relief spread across the young man's face, softening his haggard features.

"I was worried about you for a moment," he said.

"But for your quick help I should be in very sorry straits." Her voice was still shaky but she was able to sit up.

"I suggest that you remain here for a while and rest. This crowd will be gone soon, the crush will not last long. Or would you prefer me to call the officer of militia? He would escort you to your carriage, a service I'm afraid I am not able to perform for you."

It then dawned on Phyllida that she had been rescued by one of the rascally Americans. She was recovered enough to take in more of his appearance. His face was pleasant enough, had once been handsome perhaps, but now it was gaunt and haggard, with dark circles beneath the eyes. The way his cheek bones showed beneath his skin was proof that he had not eaten well for the last few months. But there was still a sparkle of humour in his eyes.

"You've been more than kind already," said Phyllida. "I don't know how to thank you. My man is out in the crowd somewhere. I would like to stay here until he is able to get back to me, if I may."

Still shocked, a shiver ran through her, and at once the American removed his jacket and slipped it round her shoulders. Phyllida looked down at the blue coat with the gold braid, now much tarnished and torn.

"You are in the navy?" she asked.

"I am, madam, or was. May I introduce myself? I am Captain Henry Merritt, from Newburyport, in Massachusetts at your service."

"My husband has an estate near Harvard. Is that close to your home?"

"It is indeed, madam. By American standards at least. Harvard is a fine town, I have been there many times."

"My husband speaks highly of the country. He thinks it very beautiful."

Phyllida was feeling rather awkward. Conversation was difficult for her at the best of times, and she had never addressed an enemy before.

"Though it is hard to think so of this young man," she decided.

But Captain Merritt was speaking again with some animation. He was talking about his home.

"It is most beautiful in the fall, I think, when the leaves turn colour. There are fine woodlands near our house, and when I'm home I go there a lot with my boys, hunting."

"I need not have worried." Phyllida listened to the captain. "The poor fellow just wants to talk of his home and family." And she felt sorry for him, in this awful place, and so far away from all that he loved.

She learned a lot about the captain and his wife, his

two growing boys and the little girl who had been born to them just before he left America. Behind his talk Phyllida could sense the dreadful unspoken question that haunted him—would he ever see them again?

Captain Merritt suddenly stopped and gave a wry smile.

"You must forgive me, madam," he said ruefully. "I fear I have run on and on, and bored you to extinction about my family. It is so rarely that I get such a sympathetic listener."

"But I'm not bored," Phyllida assured him with sincerity. "I appreciate how distressed you must be, parted from your family."

"I am used to partings, being a sea-faring man, but it is the lack of news that worries me the most. In here there is no knowing how the war progresses at all. It may be right near my home, it might be hundreds of miles away. All we hear are rumours, rumours, rumours."

"You can have no newspapers or broadsheets?"

"They are not allowed, and of course letters are very few indeed."

Phyllida thought of Richard's copy of the "Exeter Flying Post," still on the seat in the carriage.

"There's one in my carriage," she said. "If we can only get it in here."

"Joseph is coming at last," cried Becky, noticing the familiar figure battling towards them. "Perhaps he can do it."

A flushed and perspiring Joseph struggled forward.

"Thank heavens you're all right, madam," he puffed. "A rare fight I had, getting through all those folks. I got carried clean over to the other side of the yard."

"I'm quite safe, thanks to the captain, here, but I wish you to do something as soon as you have recovered your breath. The master left his newspaper in the carriage. Do you think you could get it and bring it here? But secretly, mind, for it is forbidden."

Joseph looked up at the walls. Militia men, fully armed, were watching the market crowd with bored eyes. Suddenly he caught the gaze of one of the guards, who surprisingly gave a knowing wink and turned the other way.

"It's all right," said the American. "Fortunately the Regulars are not on duty today, they are too vigilant by half, but the Militia men are a good set on the whole, and willing to turn a blind eye."

"I'll be off then, madam," said Joseph.

"Very well, and tell the coachman to bring the carriage round to the gate. The crowd is thinning so we will soon be able to leave. You say the Militia men turn a blind eye?" Phyllida added, turning to the captain.

"Sometimes if someone wants to smuggle in books, or go over the wall."

"Over the wall?" she dropped her voice. "You mean escape?"

"I do indeed. We've had many of those, and some have got clear away. But you need friends on the outside to help. Most who go do so for the money."

"I don't think I understand."

"A reward of five pounds is paid for capturing an American prisoner, so sometimes one of us will arrange to escape and be recaptured by a certain guard. Then they both split the bounty money."

"That is the most extraordinary thing I've ever heard," gasped Phyllida.

"Aye," chuckled the captain. "There are one or two prisoners who have almost made escaping into a profession. But it's wisest to do so when the Militia are on duty, as I've said. Their officer is a most gentlemanly fellow, who has spoken up on our behalf on more that one occasion. He even got us an extra ration of cheese once when the meat was unfit to eat."

"You were served bad meat?" Phyllida wrinkled her nose in disgust.

"That's not rare, believe me!"

"But don't you get proper rations?"

"I think we do. I understand that the British Admiralty

allow us quite adequate provisions, but we rarely see them."

"But where do they go?"

"First they are sent to the keeper, and he is very loath to part with them."

"He keeps your food?"

"Yes, and our coal for heating. No doubt he makes a pretty penny selling it again to the local merchants."

"But can't you complain? Is there nothing you can do?"

"Many have tried, but it is a hard thing to prove. Besides the Admiralty is in London, and that is a long, long way from Plymouth. If it were not for the good friends we have in the town and elsewhere we would starve, there is no doubt of that. That is why we hold our market, selling the small things that we make so that we can buy extra provisions. Aye," Captain Merritt spoke thoughtfully. "There have been grass and cabbage stalks eaten here ere now, and a good deal worse."

Phyllida was horrified. She could hardly believe that men could be kept under such conditions, yet she had the proof of her own eyes in the pallid gaunt figures of the prisoners who were still standing at their stalls.

At that moment Joseph returned. There was no sign of the newspaper, and she wondered if he could not find it.

"The coachman is turning the carriage round at the bottom of the street," he announced, a little louder than was necessary for the benefit of the guards. "And he will be here directly, madam."

"I must go now." Phyllida rose to her feet and returned his jacket. "I thank you for your prompt assistance."

The American bowed over her hand.

"Thank you, madam, I shall never forget your kindness."

"But I've done nothing," protested Phyllida. "It is I who am in your debt."

"You have spoken to me as a friend," answered the captain. "And listened to my boring monologue about my family as though you were truly interested. You can have no idea what that means to someone in my situation."

Moved almost to tears, Phyllida whispered,

"I hope you are soon with your loved ones, sir, and I am truly pleased that we met, though I could have wished that it was in happier circumstances for you."

Joseph gave a polite cough.

"Would you do me the honour of shaking hands to say farewell, sir?" he asked surprisingly.

"Surely," answered the captain.

As they did so Phyllida saw her servant ease a piece of paper from his coat sleeve, and push it into the cuff of the American. The movement was swift and neat, and clearly well practised. Then Phyllida remembered Joseph's childhood experience of the debtors' prison.

"I couldn't manage it all, sir," hissed Joseph, "so I just brought the bits concerning the war and America. I thought that's what you'd want."

"Many thanks, Joseph. That will mean so much to the men in here."

"Now, madam". Joseph turned to his mistress. "Had we better go now? That is if you'll pardon the liberty. This lot'll be leaving soon, then we'll be in the thick of it again."

"Very well. Good bye, sir," she said to the American.

Then on a sudden impulse she opened her reticule and emptied a shower of coins on the table among its collection of home-made spoons. "I only wish it could be more."

Before he could comment she hurried away to the gate, with Joseph and Becky trotting in her wake.

"Beg pardon, madam," said Joseph, as he handed her into the carriage. "But do you think you'd best not tell the master anything about all this? You came very near to getting hurt, and if the master knew I'd not looked after you properly he'd have my hide."

Phyllida was less convinced about her husband's concern for her welfare, but Joseph looked so worried that she smiled and nodded.

"I doubt if it would be so bad, but I agree. I won't say a word to Mr. Compton."

It was a relieved Joseph who took his place on the box as they drove away.

Phyllida sat deep in thought for the rest of the journey, fretting all the time about the plight of those unfortunate prisoners. She half considered telling Richard about them to see if he could help them. She knew he was influential enough, and was always concerned about those in trouble, but she had promised Joseph not to mention the visit to Mill Prison. She regretted her promise, but it was given and there was little she could do about it.

Her quarrel with Richard took on a very trivial light now, compared with the troubles of Captain Merritt and his friends, and Phyllida felt ashamed of her former ill-humour.

"There I go again," she thought with exasperation. "At one minute I'm in a fury with Mr. Richard Compton, and the next I'm full of remorse. It's most disconcerting."

Six

Phyllida was thankful that Richard had not yet arrived at the inn, and therefore did not see her disreputable state. Of her new finery most of it was past redemption.

"I don't know what I can do with this, Miss Phyll." Becky held up the blue and gold dress, now torn and begrimed beyond recognition. "Though perhaps it'll wash and make over into a petticoat or a drape."

"If you can make anything of it you can have it." Phyllida had lost interest in the dress. "But for goodness sake have me looking improved before Mr. Compton gets back."

She was in just as bad shape as her clothes, with her

hair dishevelled and a smudge on one cheek. Whisking away the damaged finery Becky set to on her mistress, and when Richard eventually arrived back he found her finishing her solitary dinner, dressed neatly in a cream chintz gown and a muslin kerchief.

"I am sorry I was so long. I trust that you weren't bored?" he asked.

"No thank you. I managed to keep myself amused."

Richard made no reference to her early bad humour. That was one of his better attributes, he was not one to rake over old coals.

"Have you dined?" she asked.

"I have, thank you, but if that is coffee you are drinking I will join you."

He sat opposite her at the table as Phyllida poured him a cup.

"You know that we must leave here in two days time?" he continued. Phyllida nodded. "Well I have been making arrangements for our return."

"We're going on the KITTIWAKE?" she asked eagerly.

"No, I'm afraid not. I have ordered a post chaise to take us."

"A post chaise?" Phyllida was aghast, and her coffee cup wavered precariously in the air. "Why, sir? Is there no ship going back to Tormouth?" She set the cup firmly in the saucer.

"I have not even looked into the matter. I have heard talk—reliable talk—that the activities of the French privateers are on the increase. I think it is most unwise to travel by sea, so we must go by land."

His tone was full of his customary finality, but Phyllida ignored that. She had so looked forward to repeating the exciting experience of their previous journey.

"French privateers!" She flung up her head in an obstinate manner. "What do I care for them? They would never dare to attack so close to land. I'm not afraid of them even if you are."

Richard sighed. "Yes they would dare. Last week they

sank a brig off Cawsand, well within sight of the shore. It is not cowardice but prudence which prompts me. We will return by road. It is arranged."

Phyllida opened her mouth to protest again, expecting him to turn from her in his usual manner of ending an argument, but he said unexpectedly,

"I am disappointed too. The voyage here gave me more pleasure than anything I have experienced for years." Just for a moment his expression softened, and he was the carefree Richard she had glimpsed on the KITTI-WAKE.

An all too familiar wave of remorse swept over her. After all, he had given in to her when they came. Instead of protesting she said meekly,

"I am being unreasonable, I know. Becky and I will be ready to go by road."

"Thank you, my dear. Now if you will excuse me, I have matters to attend to."

Phyllida had no ally in commiseration in Becky.

"We're going by chaise, Miss Phyll?" The girl's face lit up with relief and joy. "I've been that worried about you going back by sea. I know the master said I could go by road anyway, but I wasn't easy in my mind about letting you go alone. I mean, supposing you'd wanted something on the voyage?"

Phyllida was forced to suppress a smile. Becky, as she remembered it, was in no fit state to wait upon anyone during the journey coming to Plymouth. But then Richard returned, and with a quick bobbing curtsy Becky left them. He was looking rather ill-at-ease. Phyllida glanced at him in puzzlement.

"Do you want something?" she asked.

Richard coughed. "I wonder if you would like to walk on the Hoe after evensong?" he asked. "I know you were disappointed this morning, but the weather is still pleasant, for all the hour will be late."

Phyllida beamed. "I would enjoy that very much," she said.

She recognised that he was trying to make amends for her frustrations of the day, for normally he disliked going out in the evening.

"Perhaps you would care to wear these, then."

He put a flat leather-covered box on the table. When Phyllida opened it she found a string of pearls. They were beautiful, not large, but carefully matched and delicately tinted. They were far, far better than any other jewels that she had. For a brief spell she was too astonished to speak.

"They were my mother's favourites. I brought them to Plymouth to have them cleaned and restrung, for they haven't been touched since her death. I was going to give them to you when we returned home, but if you would like them you may have them now."

"Like them?" Phyllida could not imagine there being any doubt. "But they are the most beautiful pearls I have ever seen. How can I thank you?"

At her thanks Richard immediately lost his diffident manner.

"They are always given to the wife of the eldest son in our family," he said brusquely. "So they are yours by right."

Turning on his heel he walked quickly out of the room.

"Why does he resent my thanks?" Phyllida wondered, aware that unintentionally she had upset him once again. "Really he is the most difficult man to understand, but these pearls are indeed magnificent."

She put them on and gazed at her reflection in the mirror. She twisted her head this way and that so that the soft lustre of the pearls glowed against her skin.

"But if these are a family heirloom why did he never give them to Maria?" she wondered.

The morning of their departure dawned dull and drizzling, quite in keeping with Phyllida's attitude of mind, but as the journey lengthened so the weather brightened and her spirits lifted accordingly. The countryside was unfamiliar and caught her interest, and in addition she had the pleasing prospect of showing off her Plymouth finery to the ladies of Tormouth.

Before long the steady rocking of the carriage had a soothing effect and her eyelids began to droop. It was the noise and clatter at the posting inn that woke her. At first she was too comfortable to stir, then with a start she realised the reason for her comfort. Her head was against Richard's shoulder and his arm was about her, shielding her from the jolts of the journey.

"You are awake at last?" He looked down at her.

"I think so. Did I sleep for long?" She straightened up and slowly, almost reluctantly he let her go.

"Half an hour or so." He flexed his shoulder. "Long enough for me to get stiff."

Before Phyllida could reply the innkeeper came to entreat them to sample his wine, and their moment of intimacy was gone. She had found his closeness strangely disturbing, And equally strange was his behaviour. It was incredible that he should do anything that resembled affection, at least towards her.

The rest of the journey was uneventful and when they arrived at Tormouth, Furze House looked particularly trim and neat. Hembury was obviously glad to see them.

"Welcome home, sir and madam." His greeting was respectful and formal, but then he burst forth with,

"So He bringeth them unto their desired haven. Oh that men would praise the Lord for His goodness."

"Thank you, Hembury. It's good to be home again." Richard calmly handed his hat and cane to the butler. "All is well, I trust?"

"Yes, thank you, sir. Old Mr. Prettyjohn sent up an account of all happenings since you went away. It's on your desk, and there are letters and messages beside it. Mistress Rouse came up this morning and did those, madam," he added as Phyllida sniffed appreciatively at a bowl of roses.

Aunt Rouse was their first visitor, and by the warmth of her greeting Phyllida knew that the old lady had missed them sorely. Richard, hurrying to keep an appointment, had time to do little more than kiss his aunt in passing.

"I will leave you to give your approval of all Phyllida's Plymouth grandeur. I'm sure I will only be in the way there. But you will eat with us won't you, so that I can greet you properly?"

"How well he's looking," beamed Aunt Rouse as Richard closed the door. "In better looks than I've seen him for many a day. That's your doing, my dear, seeing that he doesn't work so hard. But what of you, child? Why, you have become quite a beauty, but I wish you were a little more plump."

Phyllida was well used to Aunt Rouse's hints, and shook her head.

"Ah well, time enough," sighed the old lady. "But what's this? Those pearls, are they . . . ?"

"Richard had them restrung at Plymouth before he gave them to me." Phyllida finished her question for her.

"My dear sister-in-law had many jewels, but none that she valued so much. They were far and away her favourites." Aunt Rouse's smile positively glowed. "And Richard has given them to you. That shows how fond he is of his little wife. But this is splendid. I am so happy that your marriage is going well."

She would have had cause to doubt her assumption if she had heard Richard and Phyllida after she had gone.

"I have seen Mistress Edmund," Richard informed his wife, in very unloverlike tones, "and she will resume your lessons on Monday morning."

Phyllida pulled a face.

"Do I really have to go back to my school books? I feel I have been very patient and suffered them long enough."

"And I feel that there are still serious gaps in your education. Your tastes are far from being fully formed and you still need much instruction. However," he stated in the manner of one making great concessions, "I am aware that changes may be necessary. I noted that at the subscription balls at Plymouth you showed an aptitude for dancing. Therefore there is no need for you to have dancing lessons. I suggest that tuition in drawing might be of benefit."

"Let my extra lessons be with Signore Giorgio," pleaded Phyllida. "I'll spend any amount of time with him, but drawing lessons will just be a waste of your money. I have as much art in me as a left-handed pig."

"All the more reason for the lessons. Then your knowledge of painting and the allied arts will be increased. I noted that you were woefully ignorant on the subject when we were looking at that exhibition of the works of Sir Joshua Reynolds."

"Did you indeed!" cried Phyllida indignantly. "I must say that I am heartily sick of being educated. Sir Joshua seems to have prospered very well without my approbation. I have no talent for drawing, and I have no wish to develop one. I will consider extra music, and of course Mistress Edmund, but that only because she sorely needs the post. But drawing, no!"

"Your drawing lessons will begin on Wednesday morning," replied Richard blandly. He was in his most infuriating mood.

"Why does he treat me like a child?" exploded Phyllida in the sanctuary of her own room. "He makes me so angry. He didn't even listen to a word I said."

"The master means well, no doubt," Becky consoled her.

"That's what everyone says about him—he means well. It's what he does that makes me so angry."

"But he's a good enough gentleman at heart." Becky persisted. "He has his funny ways, of course, but then what gentleman hasn't? And they could be a good deal worse, like Mr. What's-his-name up at Grange Manor who keeps his light o' love on the top floor, or old General Brigsby who insists upon drilling his whole family and servants just like when he was in the army. Terribly trying they must be."

"I sometimes think that Mr. Compton would have

made a fine general, with his 'Do this', and 'Do that'," Phyllida grumbled.

Just then a maidservant came to announce that a visitor had called.

"For me? I'm not expecting anyone?"

Curious to see who it was, Phyllida went down to the Small Drawingroom. The thin angular figure gazing out of the window looked very familiar.

"Mr. Robbins!" she cried.

The Vicar of Barton swung round, and the apprehensive look on his face melted into one of pleasure.

"Miss Phyllida! My dear, you have no idea how glad I am to have found you."

"To have found me? I don't understand."

"Why, I have been so concerned for your welfare. Did you think you were quite without friends, my dear child? If only I had not been away at the time of your quarrel with your grandfather. I blame myself. I suppose you never thought to go to the curate for aid? No, I thought not. Worse than useless that man, I'm afraid. But when I heard that you had gone and no one knew quite where, I assure you I suffered many sleepless nights on your behalf." Mr. Robbins' rambling speech came to an end, and Phyllida found herself blinking back tears.

"I am gratified," she said in a trembling voice, "to know that I have such friends. There were times when I believed I was all alone."

"Tut-tut, poor child," clucked the vicar, sympathetically, as he handed her a handkerchief to dry her eyes. "I have spoken sharply to your grandfather, difficult old gentleman, not at all the Christian thing to do, you being so young. I made enquiries about you, but no one was quite sure, so I came here, but you were away. You are married I trust?"

Phyllida nodded and he gave her a fatherly pat on the shoulder. She was used to his blunt ways, and knew that he spoke in all sincerity. Few men would stand up to her grandfather, but Mr. Robbins was one of the hardy few. Some of his outspokeness was no doubt because he did not owe his living to Sir Walter, but to the Bishop of Exeter, who was cousin to his wife, but he was also an honest man who would not shirk anything which he deemed to be his duty.

"I need not have worried." Mr. Robbins gave a shrug that tilted his wig askew. "Mr. Compton is a worthy gentleman, the whole country knows that, and he is much respected. Splendid to see you mistress of such a house as this, splendid indeed. Came to reassure myself that you were not forced into anything, easily happen in the circumstances, but could have saved myself the bother." He gave a toothy grin. "No need to ask if you are happy. Can see it in your face. Never seen you looking better. Splendid!"

Phyllida could not reply for Richard chose that moment to walk in unexpectedly, his cool blue eyes sweeping over their ungainly guest. Phyllida was flustered, wondering how much of his earlier haughty humour remained.

"Mr. Robbins, the Vicar of Barton, has called to see me," she informed him. "Mr. Robbins, this is my husband."

The Vicar extended a thin bony hand and made his bow.

"Servant, sir, trust you will make allowances for my calling to assure myself of Miss Phyllida's well-being. Told her grandfather he'd behaved badly, difficult gentleman. Glad she's so well married."

Phyllida took a deep breath and waited for Richard to give the Vicar one of his set-downs. If there was one thing he hated it was any sort of prying into his private life. For a second he stayed absolutely still, his features set, then his face softened.

"I am glad that my wife has friends with her welfare so much at heart," he said, then turning to Phyllida. "Perhaps Mr. Robbins would like some refreshment? Please ring for Hembury."

Relief flooded through her, she knew he'd recognised the Vicar's genuine concern.

"Glad you understand, sir." The Vicar too was relieved. "Delicate matter, but felt it my duty to come."

"Quite so." Richard didn't seem at all put out. "Now, sir, will you have madeira or sherry?"

The Vicar's visit lasted half an hour, but the time sped so quickly. It dawned on Phyllida that apart from Becky he was the only contact with her old life that she had seen in months, and she was surprised at how eager she was for news of her former home. She had thought herself done with the place for ever, but her ties were still strong. She was even glad to have news of her grandfather. Richard, too, was at his most affable, and pressed the Vicar to dine with them.

"Thank you, but no. Promised to be home, so long a journey, my wife worries so." His large teeth flashed in a grin. "She'll be glad to hear that you're so well settled, my dear. The girls will be glad too."

Phyllida had always envied the Robbins girls. Their devoted parents had made innumerable sacrifices on their behalf, so that their lives were full of incident. Their talk had been of trips to Exeter or even Bath, places of which Miss Barton of Barton Hall had known little or nothing. Phyllida was human enough to be pleased that Mr. Robbins' report on her situation would be so glowing. She was glad too that she was looking every inch the mistress of a prosperous establishment, in her elegant damask gown.

Mr. Robbins kissed her hand with warmth, if not grace.

"Perhaps I may write to you? News of Barton and Sir Walter? And if you ever need an independent person to mediate on your behalf, at your service always, don't mind tackling him." Then more warmly. "So glad you're happy, my dear."

He squeezed her hand, bowed to Richard, then departed with his customary long strides.

Mr. Robbins' visit had an unsettling effect upon Phyllida. It was his constant assertion that she was happy that troubled her. As she dressed for dinner she reflected upon his words carefully.

"I may not be happy," she thought. "Not in the blissful way I was happy with Gerard, but I can't say I'm unhappy. No, not unhappy."

This new idea was a revelation to her. It was something she had not considered before. For so long it seemed that misery had stalked her life, first under the lash of her grandfather's tongue, next, the loss of Gerard. It was scarcely possible that her wretchedness had disappeared. True, she still loved Gerard, but even the sharp pain of her loss had dulled. Mr. Robbins's visit had also called to mind the alternatives that she might have suffered. If Richard had not rescued her, what would she have become? Where would she be now? On the streets? In the poorhouse? At best a drudge at some inn. Even Richard's overbearing manner and the strange happenings at Furze House paled by comparison to these. Such strange notions stayed with her throughout the night, and left her restless the next morning.

Her music lesson over, she had no inclination to stay indoors. Outside the brightness of the late summer sun was warm on the flowers, and she decided to take a turn about the garden. With some agitation she paced through the neat geometrical patterns of the borders, trying to wear away her restlessness. On through the fruit garden she went, past the stiffly trained fans of trees. Without realising it, her wanderings brought her to the kitchen plot, backing as it did upon the servants' entrance.

A plump, rosy-cheeked girl in a calico apron was delivering a basket of fish. When she saw Phyllida she gave a startled bob and was gone, leaving her wares in the arms of the little kitchen maid. She stood there, clasping the basket in arms that might have been made of wood.

Aware of the effect that her sudden appearance had had

upon the child, Phyllida smiled, to put the maid at her ease, and said,

"I see we are having turbot for dinner, and are those lobsters I see, too? I think of all things they are my favourite dish."

She looked in the basket, with its cool green lining of ferns. A piece of paper protruded from the shell of one blue-green lobster.

"Is that the reckoning? Let me see it, please."

"The reckoning, madam? There's no reckoning. That comes up this evening." A stupid expression fixed itself on the girl's face.

"What's the matter with you? Of course there is a reckoning. That piece of paper, there!"

She stretched out her hand to take the note, when suddenly the maid dropped the basket. Fish, lobsters and ferns all cascaded on to the path. With an exclamation Phyllida jumped back to avoid her shoes being spoiled.

"I'm sorry, madam! I'm sorry!" The stricken look on the maid's face dissolved into tears as she frantically scrabbled on her hands and knees, picking up the basket and its contents. Suspiciously Phyllida watched as each item was replaced, but there was no paper.

"You put it in your pocket," she accused. "What was it? Give it to me at once, you wicked girl."

"I arn't got it, madam!"

The wails of the girl were reaching the pitch of hysteria.

"Is something wrong, madam?" The calm tones of Hembury broke through the noise. "Now stop that row at once," he admonished the girl in quite a different voice.

"There was a note among the fish." Phyllida spoke angrily. "And this creature will not give it to me. She declares it does not exist, but I'm sure she has put it in her pocket."

"Did you see what was on the note, madam?"

"No. That was what I wanted to find out."

"Do you hear that, you ungrateful girl? What have you

116

done with the note? Remember, 'Lying lips are an abomination unto the Lord.' "

"Mr. Hembury, sir, there was no note." The answer came in gulping sobs.

"There is just one thing to do, madam. I will go through the girl's pockets."

Hembury stooped and turned out the pockets on the maid's apron, and on her print skirt. As he did so Phyllida could have sworn that he gave the culprit a wink. For a moment Phyllida was taken aback. Surely she had been mistaken. She watched more keenly.

"There, madam. As you see there is no paper."

Hembury straightened up, but not before Phyllida had noticed a flash of white at his cuff. That was just the way that Joseph had smuggled the newspaper into Mill Prison. Phyllida was about to protest, but then changed her mind.

Hembury was bound to deny it, then what could she do? Helplessness welled up inside her. Hembury and the kitchen maid were certainly in this conspiracy together, and for Phyllida to persist would surely end in an undignified wrangle.

"Very well," she conceded, tight-lipped. "We will say no more about it for the moment."

As she swept along the garden path she made up her mind about one thing.

"I must consult Richard about this. Things have gone too far, smugglers or no smugglers. I won't have the servants ganging up against me in this way."

But the opportunity to talk with Richard did not present itself too easily. For one thing, he was very late home, and when he did arrive it was with a pile of books and papers that accompanied him even to the table. Conversation was non-existent.

"I shall just have to be blunt about it," thought Phyllida, then without more ado she began.

"I think the servants are in league with the smugglers," she blurted out, "and Hembury is the ring leader."

If she expected this announcement to cause some

violent reaction she was doomed to disappointment. Richard continued to scrutinize the list of outstanding debtors, and contented himself with answering,

"M-m-m-m, and what makes you think that?"

"Lots of things that I've noticed, but today there was something . . . Richard, you are not heeding me at all! Kindly put aside your work for once and listen!"

Reluctantly he marked his place with one finger and looked up.

"I assure you that I am paying attention."

"Good! Something happened today that I found most disturbing. There was a note of some sort with the fish, but the kitchen maid denied it. Then Hembury came along and sided with her. But there was a note, and they were deliberately keeping it from me."

"That hardly seems enough to constitute proof of smuggling, now does it?"

"What was the note, then?"

"Probably no more than a billet-doux for one of the maids. It may even have been for Hembury himself, if we still get our fish from Dawson's. I believe he once had quite a fondness for Mary Dawson."

"Be serious, Richard. You don't expect me to believe that someone is so love-sick for Hembury that they send him sonnets inside the lobsters. I want to know what it's all about, and why Hembury sided with the girl. Oh, and he slipped the note up his sleeve. He didn't think I saw that, but I did."

Richard sighed. "Seemingly your day was much more diverting than mine, for I still have much work to do. Now to clear up this business—I have no idea what Hembury was up to, but I am sure he had excellent reasons. I will question him on the matter, though, and as for the kitchen maid, I think we can safely leave the domestic managements to Hembury. I fancy, though, that much of this episode stems from too much imagination on your part. It will be as well when next week comes and you resume your lessons." He rose and pushed back his chair.

"Now, if you will excuse me, I have work to do." He did not wait for her reply, but left the room.

Phyllida was furious. " 'Too much imagination, indeed.' How dare he. And why does he always walk away and leave me angry? There was a letter. I saw it, and it is useless of Richard to pretend otherwise. He's covering up, that's what he's doing."

She considered his reactions. He had been calm, too calm. What would an innocent man do if his wife accused the butler of smuggling? Scoff, most likely, or laugh at her. He might even lose his temper, but Richard had done none of these things. The more she thought of it the more she was convinced that Richard had been forewarned of the little disturbance. He had been expecting her complaint, and had his reply ready, too ready.

She was almost prepared to confront Richard again, but she got no chance. As she walked out into the hall he was already striding towards the front door, his hat under his arm. He looked at her coldly.

"If I am needed I shall be at the Coffee House for most of the afternoon, at a meeting of the Harbour Commissioners." He gave her the briefest of nods, then addressed his next remark to Joseph, who was holding open the door. "Any messages for me can be sent there."

With that he stalked out. Phyllida tapped her foot angrily, but she had no time to waste in useless anger, for she had an appointment in town with Aunt Rouse. The little draper's shop had announced the arrival of a new consignment of gloves, and she had promised the old lady to go with her to buy some.

It took her longer to dress than she expected, and so she had to hurry down the long steep hill into town, for fear she would be late. At the foot of the slope Phyllida turned away from the harbour, towards the narrow cobbled main street. As she did so a group of people caught her eye.

"What's the matter over there, Miss Phyll? An accident

do you think?" asked Becky, who had been trotting respectfully in the rear.

"It seems so." Phyllida craned her neck as they drew near. "I hope that no-one is badly hurt."

The crush was so great that she could make out no details, but then she heard a familiar voice shrieking and wailing,

"My poor missus, she's dead, she's dead!"

Phyllida and Becky stared at each other in horror.

"Sally!" they exclaimed together.

There was no mistaking the strident voice of Mistress Rouse's abigail. At once they pushed their way to the front of the crowd, and there, stretched out at their feet, looking pale as death, was the old lady. Kneeling beside her was her maid, Sally, who was wailing and wringing her hands.

"Stop that, you silly girl, or I'll slap you," said Phyllida sharply as she sank to her knees beside the still figure. "Now tell me what happened."

"It was a cart going by piled high with wooden boxes," Sally ceased her wailing and gulped a reply. "One fell off and hit my missus. Look!"

Sure enough a huge bruise discoloured Mistress Rouse's forehead.

"This place is all wrong for wheels," grumbled someone. "Said so all along. Should stick to pack ponies, like we've always done.

Phyllida was not interested in details. She tried to staunch the bleeding from a cut on the old lady's cheek with her muslin kerchief.

"Stand back, everyone, and give her air," she commanded. "Becky, fetch your master at once. He's at the Coffee House. Will someone find a blanket and something to use as a stretcher?"

"The dragoons have gone for an 'urdle from the cattle market," a voice informed her.

Phyllida looked down at Aunt Rouse with some concern. If only she was not so still. Not even her eye lids had fluttered. The crowd fell back, and Richard arrived.

"Poor Aunt!" he exclaimed: "Let's hope to heaven that it isn't a serious injury."

His face was drawn with distress, but at once he took charge of the situation. In no time he had dispatched one messenger for the doctor, and another to Furze House to have a room prepared.

"For she must stay with us, where we can care for her," he insisted.

"Here comes the dragoons," called someone in the crowd, and the people fell back again. It seemed as though a small tide of scarlet uniforms surged into the middle of the throng, as some soldiers led by two officers hurried in, carrying a wattled hurdle between them.

Perhaps it was the movement of being lifted on to it that disturbed Aunt Rouse, for she opened her eyes. At the sight of Richard she smiled weakly.

"Such a silly thing," she whispered. "Just a bump on the head."

Then she drifted back into unconsciousness again.

"It would have been a deal worse but for those officer gentlemen," protested Sally, in her shrill voice.

"How do you mean?" Richard, with Phyllida's help, was tucking a borrowed cloak over his aunt.

"Why sir, she nearly fell under the wheels. These gentlemen caught her just in time, and it's a miracle they didn't go under too."

"We did nothing, sir." One of the officers spoke up. "We are just glad to have been of some small service."

At the sound of his voice Phyllida felt as if she had been turned to ice. She had been mistaken once before, but this time surely she could not be wrong? Hardly daring to breathe she lifted her gaze to look at the officers for the first time. She found herself staring into a pair of dark eyes that were usually full of laughter. Now they were wide with astonishment. There was no mistake this time.

"Gerard!" she whispered.

Seven

It was fortunate for Phyllida that there was so much activity, for no-one noticed her shocked expression. All attention was focused upon Aunt Rouse. All that is except Gerard's. For one eternal moment he too was paralysed, but quickly he recovered, bending over the old lady to hide his emotions. With a superhuman effort Phyllida forced her eyes away from him, and she too turned towards the injured woman.

Richard, Gerard, and his companion, helped by Young Ned Prettyjohn, carried the improvised stretcher up to Furze House. Phyllida walked beside them on trembling legs. She was thankful to be silent, for Becky had gone with Sally to fetch some belongings for Aunt Rouse. Once in the house, Richard lifted his aunt in his arms to carry her up to the room awaiting her. She stirred.

"Why am I here?" she askd vaguely.

"You are here so that we may take care of you until you are well again," said Richard gently. "Now, no arguments."

But shaken as she was, his aunt did argue.

"My Choo-Choo! I won't leave him."

"Choo-Choo shall stay too." Richard consoled her. "Joseph has him in care now."

"Splendid." Aunt Rouse relaxed. "He likes Joseph."

Phyllida listened to it all as in a dream. Nothing seemed real. She longed to raise her head and look at Gerard, to take one long lingering look at him, but she dared not. Instead she kept her head bowed.

"Parsons shall attend you until your own woman comes," Richard told his aunt. "I'm sure that Phyllida will provide you with anything you need until them. Phyllida!"

His voice made her jump.

"Yes, Aunt dear, I shall come with you." Phyllida had not heeded any of the conversation.

"But will you lend Aunt anything she may need?" insisted Richard.

"But of course. I will go now."

Reluctantly Phyllida was forced to precede him up the stairs, every step taking her away from Gerard. At the foot of the staircase Richard paused, his aunt still in his arms.

"Gentlemen," he addressed Gerard and the other officer. "I hope you will stay long enough for me to express my gratitude. I will be back directly. Hembury, attend to my guests if you please."

So saying he carried Mistress Rouse up to the waiting bedchamber.

Feverishly Phyllida sought out a nightgown and cap, a shawl and some slippers. She wished so much to be downstairs, but she knew her place was with Aunt Rouse. She did not want to be callous, she was truly sorry about the accident, but the shock of seeing Gerard again had left little room for other emotions, particularly now that it was obvious that Aunt Rouse's injuries were not serious. Phyllida was so afraid that Gerard would leave before she had a chance to speak to him, or take one more look at him. Waiting upon the elderly lady she felt that the delays were interminable, yet in truth Parsons had scarce got her comfortable in bed, swamped in Phyllida's night gown, before the doctor arrived.

His examination was swift but thorough.

"No serious injury, Mistress Rouse, but I advise a sound rest. Shock can be a distressing experience to a lady of your years."

"A lady of my years! Impudent fellow!" scolded Aunt Rouse in a voice that proved she was feeling better. "Now when can I return to my own home?"

"Mr. Compton wants you to stay here, and I must say I agree with him. It is best that you are where you can have every comfort, and be surrounded by people who care for you."

"I shall feel better when Choo-Choo is by my side in his basket."

The doctor was not at all in favour of this arrangement, but was soundly over-ruled by his patient, and since he was an old acquaintance, he gave in with good humour.

Phyllida stood by in a daze, not heeding the half-hearted arguments between Aunt Rouse and the doctor. Mechanically she instructed servants, arranged matters for the comfort of her unexpected guest. There were delays when Aunt Rouse's Sally arrived, in floods of tears, still convinced that her mistress was at death's door. The abigail was comforted, Aunt Rouse's packing seen to.

"This will never end," thought Phyllida, her nerves at breaking point. "I shall have to stay here forever. I shall never get away. Oh, Gerard!"

Even the little ormolu clock on the mantel seemed to beat out his name. But at last order was restored. With relief she saw the doctor administer a sleeping draught to Aunt Rouse and heard him say,

"A good sleep, madam, will be of more benefit than all the physick in the world, so I suggest that we all leave you in peace."

"I can go now," thought Phyllida in triumph. "I can go."

Again, though, there was a delay. Tearfully, Sally declared that nothing would induce her to leave her mistress. It took more time for the doctor to assure her that she could stay, but only if she remained very quiet.

Phyllida found that she was shaking with suppressed emotion. When at last they took their leave of a drowsy Aunt Rouse, Phyllida found that she had to force herself not to run down the stairs. She reached the hall as Richard was bidding farewell to the two officers.

"My dear, you are just in time to say goodbye to our guests," Richard said affably.

Goodbye so soon? How could her first words to Gerard

after these months of waiting be goodbye. She heard herself say, in a remarkable calm voice,

"But won't they dine with us?"

"Your husband has been kind enough to ask us already." It was Gerard's companion who spoke. "But, unfortunately, our duties prevent us."

"I hope you will both do us the honour at a later date," suggested Richard. "Perhaps when my aunt has recovered. I know she will be eager to thank you yourself. But what am I about? My dear, I have not introduced you to these gentlemen to whom we are so much in debt. May I present Lieutenant Parker and Lieutenant Lacey. Gentlemen, my wife!"

The strange young officer bowed and kissed her hand, then she turned to Gerard. He did not dare to look at her, but murmured hurriedly,

"Your servant, madam."

At the warmth of his fingers and the soft brush of his lips on her hand Phyllida felt as though her whole being was aglow. How could she have imagined that her pain for Gerard had dulled. Nothing had altered. Her love for him was as burning as ever.

She barely heard Lieutenant Parker answer,

"We'd be delighted to accept your invitation, sir. We look forward to it."

Then the door closed upon them. Phyllida was still trembling. Surely Richard must notice the change in her, how could he help it?

"They seem excellent fellows." Richard guided her into the Small Drawingroom and poured wine for them both. Incredibly, he noticed nothing.

"Yes, excellent." What could she do but agree?

"I shudder to think what might have happened if they hadn't been there. Poor Aunt! What a blessing her injuries aren't worse."

"Yes, it's a relief."

To her own ears Phyllida's replies sounded stilted, but

she found it hard to answer him when half her mind was engaged elsewhere.

"I have not thanked you yet for the help you gave, too. I know how much you did to make Aunt comfortable before I came—Sally told me all about it. It was well done, my dear, very well done."

At once Phyllida became aware that Richard was standing very close to her. As she looked up at him he suddenly bent and kissed her, not one of the cool pecks that he usually gave, but full on her mouth, and with surprising warmth.

Phyllida did not move. Her lips were cold and un-resisting, astonished by his unexpected behaviour. At her lack of response Richard released her and took a step back. His face was set and hard once more.

"I have to ride over to Salbridge to look over that new barque," he said abruptly. "I must go."

Without another word he left.

"Richard!" Phyllida whispered after he had gone. In a daze she put her hand to her lips that still could taste his kiss. "What of Richard?"

In her surge of love for Gerard she had forgotten one important factor. Now she was married!

"What am I to do?" she wondered. "Surely I can't have found Gerard only to be parted from him again? Fate would not be so cruel. I love him, but I'm Richard's wife." She rocked herself backwards and forwards, her arms wrapped about her body for comfort. For a long time she wrestled with her problem. What was she to do?

"It's no use," she said at last. "I must see Gerard again, if only to explain how I came to be married. That can't be wrong can it? Not when I love him so?"

She hurried to her sitting-room and began to write him a note. A dozen times she began, only to tear it up again. There was so much that she wanted to express, but she knew that she had to be discreet. Her final draught was less emotional, more direct.

"Be at Mulberry Cove tomorrow
afternoon at 3. Must see
you.

P."

With hands that shook she folded the page and sealed it with wax.

"Becky shall take it," she decided, and rang for her maid.

When she came Phyllida handed her the note and said,

"I want you to take that to Lieutenant Lacey. I don't know which is his camp, but I'm sure you'll find it without much trouble."

To her surprise Becky stared at the letter for a moment as though it was some loathsome object, then with more candour than was proper in a maidservant said flatly,

"No!"

"Did I hear aright?"

"You did, Miss Phyll. I said no." Becky spoke more gently. "I carried a letter for you once before, remember? And a right kettle of fish that landed us in. But it would be nothing to what would happen if you were found out this time."

Phyllida's own conscience stirred within her, and she gave vent to her feelings on poor Becky.

"You saucy thing!" she exclaimed hotly. "How dare you speak to me so! I should box your ears! Just you do as you are bid."

"No, Miss Phyll." Becky was adamant. She put her hands behind her back as though to remove them from temptation.

"Things are different now, don't you see? You are married. I know it's the fashion for ladies to have their paramours, but them's London ways, and won't do here."

"Come, come, Becky." Anger had put a sharp edge on Phyllida's voice. "You spend much of your time trying to make me à la mode. I'm surprised that you should kick at this."

"There's fashions and fashions," quibbled Becky. "The master would be real upset, you know."

Phyllida looked surprised. This was an unexpected argument.

"I very much doubt if Mr. Compton would care, one way or the other. But besides, you are making too much of the whole thing. I only want to meet Mr. Lacey once. After all, we were forced to part very abruptly. Would you grudge me that? I'm not planning an elopement this time. Mr. Compton will never know."

"He's a nice gentleman, the master. He took me in when I hadn't a character. There's not many would have done that."

"You are grateful to him because of your wretched situation," cried Phyllida. "You have no loyalty to me any more."

"He took you when you had even less to recommend you." Becky spoke before she had time to think.

This struck home too close for comfort. In a fury Phyllida lifted her hand and struck her maid hard across the face. There was a second's complete silence. In horror Phyllida saw the crimson weals left by her fingers begin to form in Becky's cheek.

"Becky, oh my dear Becky. I didn't mean to do that! I'm sorry."

In floods of tears she put her arms round the maid's shoulders.

"I didn't mean to hit you, truly I didn't! But I must see him. We've been parted for so long, and it means so much to me. I had put all my hopes in you, and now you refuse. But I've no one else. You shall have my pomona green jacket, the one I bought in Plymouth, if you will take the letter for me, just this once. Please."

"I don't want the beastly jacket," wailed Becky. "But I will go for you, if only you'll promise never to ask me again."

"I promise, dear, dear Becky."

Phyllida was suddenly elated. Tomorrow she would

see Gerard, and at that prospect everything faded into insignificance.

After that Becky was soon back, and this time with an answer.

"Mr. Lacey said yes, Miss Phyll. That was all. No other message. I found him easily enough, him being camped just beyond the New Road."

Phyllida did not think it possible that time could go so slowly. The whole of the day dragged and the night was little better.

"I shall see Gerard in fifteen—fourteen—thirteen hours time. There's so much I want to tell him. So many explanations. I have to tell him why I married. I wasn't being disloyal to him. Surely he will understand, especially when I assure him that I had no alternative."

Phyllida went over the coming meeting a dozen times, anticipating what she would say, how Gerard would greet her, how he would take her in his arms.

The fateful day, when it did arrive, brought a change in her attitude. The doubts that she had suppressed so successfully now made their way to the surface.

"You are married to Richard Compton. What business have you seeing another man?" whispered one furtive voice within her. "What if you're seen? Tormouth is a small place, the scandal would spread quickly," whispered another.

These voices of her conscience grew so loud that by mid-morning she had half made up her mind to stay at home. Her morning lessons were a fiasco because she could not pay attention. For her drawing master's disapproval she did not care a fig, but when even kind Signore Giorgio frowned, tut-tutted and said quite sternly,

"This will not do, m'dear. Your wits are not with the music at all," she burst into tears and fled from the room.

Finally she determined to keep her tryst with Gerard, "Just this once." Phyllida took a long time to pick out a suitable gown. She wanted to look her best for him, to be beautiful, so that his dark eyes would light up at the sight of her. After much deliberation she chose an Italian robe in pale blue silk, much flounced and embroidered. Becky watched the proceedings in disapproving silence.

"Are you sure that's what you want to wear, Miss Phyll?" she asked dourly, crimping the gauze ruff that went with it between her fingers.

"Of course I am," Phyllida stared at her. "It's most becoming, isn't it? What's wrong with it?"

"For taking tea with the mayor's wife, nothing! But for a married lady going to meet a gentleman who isn't her husband, everything!" Becky's fingers crimped with greater determination. "You'll stand out like a beacon light in that. By evening there won't be a soul down by the harbour who doesn't know where you've been and who with. And . . . " She paused for dramatic effect, "by nightfall the master will know too."

"Oh don't, Becky!" Phyllida sat down suddenly on the bed, a sick feeling in the bottom of her stomach. The bright silk gown slid to the floor. "I don't think I'd make a very good conspirator. I don't think of the practical side. What do you suggest?" Then seeing Becky's disapproving face, "Help me, please, Becky."

"It's not for me to say, Miss Phyll. Or should I say Mistress Compton?"

Biting her lip, Phyllida went to her clothes press and took out a riding habit in dead-leaf brown tabinet.

"There," she said hesitantly. "Does that suit you better?"

"It'll do, Miss Phyll." Becky gave a grudging nod.

Her appearance was not as modish as Phyllida had hoped, but by the time her hair was dressed and powdered, and a round hat set at a rakish angle, Phyllida felt more at ease.

The walk to Mulberry Cove was quite a long one. As she made her way through the gorse-spattered heathland she forgot the fashionable mincing steps she tried so hard to cultivate, and instead took her customary long strides, leaving poor Becky puffing in her wake. She made the way even longer by insisting upon great detours to avoid meeting other walkers.

"No one must see me," she hissed to a protesting Becky.

The cove lay in a small valley, secluded and with slopes clothed in beech and oak. It reminded Phyllida of the woods above Barton Hall, where so often she had escaped to just such a meeting. She was early, she knew, and the little cove had a deserted air about it. Furtively she settled herself in the shadow of some rocks, prepared to dodge into their shelter if some stranger should come.

It was the clatter of pebbles that warned her of his coming. Many times she had imagined this moment, with all its joy and happiness, but inexplicably she was stricken with shyness and unexpected doubts.

"Suppose he doesn't love me now? Suppose he has found someone else?"

Gerard too was hesitant, for he made no move towards her, but just stood gazing at her.

"Phyllida, can it really be you?" he said at last.

Then as if to prove it he stretched out his arms to her. In a flash she had run towards him and flung herself into his embrace. Everything was all right!

"My darling, my darling," she half whispered, half sobbed. "I was so afraid you had forgotten me. How long have we been apart?"

"Forgotten you? Never! How could you believe such a thing?" He held her close, tenderly kissing away her tears. "But I had almost given up hope of ever seeing you again."

"I hadn't," said Phyllida. "I knew that one day we would find each other. I always looked for you. Everywhere I went I looked."

"And we were so close all the time. You've no idea how much it broke my heart to leave without sending you a message, but our marching orders came very suddenly. We had to leave at an hour's notice and no-one was allowed off the post. I did try to let you know."

"I'm sure you did, my darling." Her tone was tender.

"I suppose it was after I'd gone that your grandfather forced you to marry Compton. Indeed I nearly fell down when I saw you yesterday. You were the last person I expected to see. The last, but the most welcome."

With a shock, Phyllida realized that of course he had no idea of all that had happened since their last meeting. Her world had been turned upside down, her heart had been broken, and Gerard knew nothing of it.

"It did not happen quite like that," she said softly, and as well as she could she told him the whole sad story—of her grandfather's anger, of her letter that was never delivered, her nightmare trip to Exeter, and finally her marriage to Richard Compton.

Gerard listened to it all in horrified silence.

"What you've been through, my poor, poor darling," he said at last. "If only I'd known. Of course I would have come to you, then it would have been me that you married, instead of him. How much you have suffered and all because of me. If only we'd been married . . . but then we would have still had to face the heart-break of parting."

"You are sailing soon?" Phyllida did not even dare to think of the bliss that might have been hers.

"It could be any time. We should have gone long since but for these contrary winds. The sailings are all weeks behind."

Phyllida thought of the soldiers bound for America that she so often watched from her window. How close Gerard had been to becoming one of their number. How close she had been to never seeing him again. She shivered at the awful thought, and Gerard held her more closely.

"You are cold, my love?"

"No, not really."

For a wonderful eternity they stood in each other's arms, content not to speak, happy with each other's presence, but abruptly Gerard let her go and sprang back.

"What the!" he exclaimed.

"What is it?" Phyllida whispered in alarm.

"There is someone watching us, there in the trees."

She looked towards the trees, her heart thumping, then gave a sigh of relief as she caught sight of a familiar striped petticoat against the foliage.

"Becky," she said. "It's only Becky."

At once Gerard turned back to her, his features relaxed.

"She gave me quite a start," he admitted with a rueful smile.

He slid his arms about her waist once more, but Phyllida noted that he kept a watchful eye on the path.

"How is it with you?" he asked at length. "Are you well treated? Is he good to you?"

"Well enough. He is generous."

"Do you have a fondness for him?" Gerard asked hesitantly.

"For Richard? Of course not. He is too cold and reserved." Despite her critical words she felt guilty at discussing Richard in that way, so she hurriedly added,

"I love you, don't you believe that?"

"Yes, but he has so much to offer you, with his money and position. I have so little."

"Gerard, you mean more to me than every penny of the Compton money. You must believe that."

"I do. I am very conscious of all the difficulties about us, though. There seems so little future for us, I would do nothing that might prejudice your happiness."

"But you are my happiness."

"Yet I must be gone from you soon. The only merit in going to America is that I might improve my situation, get promotion. But then what, my love? What can we do? You would still be married."

"But I did not wish to marry him."

"That does not alter things, does it? True, if you had not married Compton you would not be here now, and we

133

would never have met again. It has been such joy, here with you. Oh Phyllida, what I am trying to say is that we must not meet again."

"Not meet again?"

Phyllida looked at him in disbelief.

"I don't understand. Why shouldn't we meet? Please, what have I done?"

"Nothing! Nothing, my sweetest one. But you have so much to lose. Supposing someone should see us together and the word reaches Compton. The consequences for you would be terrible. I love you, but I want to consider your good name and your happiness. There are no risks for me, but for you . . . ."

"But if we are careful no one will see us. Richard need never know. Gerard, without you there is no happiness for me." She was panic-stricken that they would never see each other again.

"You have to spend the rest of your life with this man. What would your position be if he found out about us? Think of that, dearest. You have a fine house, you have wealth and position. I cannot let you throw it all away for me. Compton seems a decent fellow, but I fancy he could be pretty nasty if provoked. He could make your life very miserable indeed. How can I risk that, even for the joy of seeing you?"

Gerard's voice was gentle but determined, and Phyllida was terrified that he might go.

"Please don't leave me," she begged. "I know it is for my sake, but please stay. I need you." She desperately grasped at anything that would change his mind. "My husband," she said frantically. "He may appear respectable but he's not. He's involved in illegal things."

Gerard looked at her quizzically, holding her at arms' length.

"My dear what are you saying?" He smiled gently. "Everyone knows that Compton is a by-word for respectability."

"He's not. He has secrets. Things go on at Furze House."

"Be sensible, darling. You don't mean he holds a gambling hell in the cellar?"

"It's no joke, it's all true. He has something to do with the freetraders. I know, because I've seen things."

"Tell me what you've seen, then." Gerard's tone was still incredulous as he folded her in his arms and kissed her neck. "I wouldn't be surprised if his servants helped the smugglers a little, that happens often enough, but Compton . . . That is too much!"

"But he does. Strangers come in the middle of the night, then go secretly. I've seen him with them—well one of them—and there are secret messages that I am not to see, and his servants are suspicious even of me."

"This stranger you saw, why couldn't he have been someone calling on business?" Phyllida thought that Gerard's arm tightened about her just a little.

"In the middle of the night? When the man left with the bosun . . ."

"The bosun?"

"Yes, he was there too. I don't know his name but he definitely sails on one of Richard's ships. When the man and the bosun left together Hembury blew out the candle, so that no one could see them go."

"So Hembury was there as well?"

"Yes, and Richard removed his shoes to come upstairs, so that he made no noise."

"It certainly is strange. I don't like to think of you being so close to danger. What sort of a man is Compton? I mean, is he a radical sort of a man?"

Phyllida was surprised.

"Yes, my grandfather called him an out and out Whig once. But what have his political views got to do with it?"

"If his views are so much against the present government he may have no scruples about disregarding any law it might make, such as those concerned with Customs and Excise. Do you follow me?"

"I do." Gerard's reasoning was sound. "And he is very much against the government, you should hear him on the subject of this American War."

"It is as I thought." Gerard nodded his head pensively. "Afraid as I am for your reputation I cannot leave you alone in such a household, that's for certain. I must be near at hand if you need help."

"Then we will meet again?"

"We will indeed, but we must be so careful. I would not have you hurt in any way, my dearest."

Phyllida returned his kisses with gratitude and longing.

"You have no idea how wonderful it is to be with you," she said. "To know that you care about me."

"Poor darling Phyllida, you've been alone for so long. But now I'm here to protect you. There is nothing to fear."

Safe in the encirclement of his arms, Phyllida was sure that she would never be afraid again.

"We will meet here?"

"No, best be prudent and go elsewhere."

"The lane by the ruined mill, then. That place is never visited now."

"Very well. By the mill. I'll soon find the place."

"Tomorrow?"

"No, I'm officer-of-the-day tomorrow. Better make it the day after. And Phyllida, if anything strange happens again, tell me and I will try to find a way to deal with it."

As they parted Phyllida was almost giddy with happiness.

"Becky, Becky," she cried blissfully. "He still loves me as much as ever and we are to meet the day after tomorrow. Isn't that wonderful?"

Her words brought a reproachful look from Becky.

"Miss Phyll, you said it'd only be the once," she cried accusingly.

"There's no need for you to come, I can go alone." Phyllida was at once on the defensive. "It will probably be the last time. Mr. Lacey's regiment expects to sail any day now, then I shall never see him again. You don't blame me for snatching what little happiness I can, do you?"

"I suppose not, Miss Phyll." Becky gave in grudgingly. "And I'd better come too. Who else would you get? Jenny Parsons? A right mess that'd lead to. Very well, I'll come, but I only hope it is the last time."

Becky's remonstrance had stirred up Phyllida's uneasy conscience, and now it troubled her all the way home. While she had been with Gerard it had lain quiet, but now she was in a torment again. She was desperate to see Gerard again, but she knew how angry Richard would be if anything approaching a scandal was to touch his family.

That evening she scarcely touched her food, and looked so white and drawn that Richard said,

"Are you quite well, Phyllida? You look out of sorts."

"I'm well enough, thank you," she answered swiftly, afraid lest he'd noticed the way she had jumped at the sound of his voice. "I—I think I'm tired, that's all."

"Delayed excitement after our Plymouth trip, perhaps?" Richard's tone was full of concern. "Yes, you have really had little time to recover have you? In that case I think you should have a rest from your lessons for a while. Spend more time in relaxation. Since the weather is good why not take the carriage and explore the country-side? Enjoy yourself."

His unexpected consideration was too much for Phyllida in her tense state of nerves. She dashed from the room in tears, knocking over her chair as she ran.

Eight

Phyllida was doomed to a sleepless night of tossing and turning, which should have left her limp and weary. Instead she found herself full of restless energy that would not be still. She was heartily grateful that her lessons had been cancelled for the week, for she could never have endured sitting still for all those hours.

A long walk over the cliff-tops might have provided some solution, but the morning had brought with it a steady and persistent rain. Desperate for some activity Phyllida looked about her sitting-room.

"This chamber is uncommonly dark in bad weather," she complained to Becky. "Perhaps if we moved that chair to the window so . . . and now the table beside it."

"But now you can't open the drawers of your escritoire, miss."

"Oh dear. Nor can I. That must go over by the door there."

In no time at all they were both engrossed in a mammoth session of rearranging the furniture, with the help of Parsons, who had been summoned from the kitchen. After changing her mind several times, Phyllida was at last reasonably satisfied with the result.

"There is one thing that this room lacks, and that is a chest of drawers. I am so cramped for space to store things."

"Perhaps there is one in some other room?" suggested Becky. "Shall I go and see?"

"We'll all go, for I'll have to go to make sure that it is suitable. Parsons, you lead the way. You will know the most likely places to look."

There was a slight delay while Parsons went to the housekeeper for the keys to some of the rooms, then she led Phyllida and Becky to the east wing of the house. This part was seldom used, only when there was a large number of guests staying. On the way, Phyllida stopped at a door near her own sitting-room.

"What's in there?" she asked.

She had been taken on an inspection tour of the house when she had first arrived, but that was no more than a jumbled impression of holland covers and empty chambers.

"I'm sure there's nothing suitable in there, madam,"

said Parsons quickly. "I seem to remember something that might do in the Red Bedroom."

"Very well, we'll try there first."

They trooped along to the room, but as soon as they went in Phyllida knew that they had wasted their time.

"Where is the chest?" she asked, gazing about her.

"Here, madam." Parsons removed a dust cover to reveal an old-fashioned coffer chest.

"But that's not what I want. Silly girl, don't you know the difference?"

"Sorry, madam. I made a mistake."

Clicking her tongue with annoyance Phyllida stalked out. Parsons showed them through a bewildering number of other rooms, all neatly kept, but nevertheless little used. None of them had a chest of drawers.

Phyllida was surprised at Parsons, she had always considered the sad-eyed maid to be an intelligent girl, but now, as she led them through room after room, her mistress began to doubt her judgement. In all their tour they did not see one single piece of furniture that was at all suitable.

"This is ridiculous!" exclaimed Phyllida. "There must be a spare chest of drawers somewhere in a house this size."

"I'm worn to the bone," complained Becky, but not loud enough for her mistress to hear.

They had come back to the inhabited part of the house when Phyllida saw the door she had noticed before.

"What did you say was in there?" she asked.

"That was Mistress Compton's room—the master's mother, that is, madam."

"We may as well look in there. It's the only place we haven't seen."

Parsons had some difficulty in unlocking the door, but at last she managed to turn the key.

At first the room was in darkness, but when the holland blinds were raised light flooded in, making them all blink. When Phyllida grew accustomed to the brightness she gasped with pleasure, and looked about her with delight.

"But this is beautiful!" she exclaimed. "So bright and gay. It's much prettier than my own sitting-room. And the view! Just look at the view, Becky!"

From its corner position the windows looked out dizzily over the harbour, and beyond it to the English Channel.

"This room belonged to the master's mother, you say?" Phyllida turned to Parsons, who had apparently recovered her usual alertness.

"Yes, madam. It was her favourite room. She used to have her chair pulled up to the window, and sit there by the hour after her health failed, poor lady. She liked to watch all that went on down in the harbour, but most of all she liked to see the Compton ships coming and going."

"I would like to see all of it," Phyllida declared. "Let's have all the dust sheets off, shall we?"

Deftly Parsons and Becky whisked away the covers, exposing the furniture that had been shrouded underneath. Phyllida was not disappointed, the furnishings were as beautiful as the room itself. The wood was a soft golden walnut, and though the fabrics of the upholstery were a little faded, the colours were warm and had been chosen to blend with the room. Seldom had Phyllida been in a chamber that had appealed to her more. She loved everything about it. It had a friendly atmosphere. Already an idea was forming in her mind.

"Did the master have the room shut up after his mother died?" she asked, wondering why such a beautiful place was never used.

"No, madam. He was very eager for Mistress Maria to have it, but she would not. She said it was too bright and gave her a headache, and the view from the window made her suffer from vertigo." Parson's voice registered faint disapproval.

Phyllida wondered at the mentality of anyone who

140

could prefer her dark, shaded sitting-room to this.

"Would Richard mind if I moved in here?" She spoke out loud unintentionally.

"Beg pardon, but the master would be delighted, I'm sure. He hates having it closed up and getting all faded." Parsons flushed under Phyllida's astonished gaze. "I'm sorry if I'm taking liberties, madam, but the master makes us polish and dust here twice a week, and have a fire regularly in the winter, just to keep it nice."

"I see. Thank you." Phyllida smiled. "I must admit that the more I see the more I like it. I think I'll have a really thorough look."

Most of the furniture was uncovered by now, and only one settee was left half-shrouded. She leaned across to pull back the dust sheet, and as she did so her foot caught against something and sent it spinning across the floor with a clatter.

"What on earth . . . !" she exclaimed. "Whatever was that?"

"Here it is, Miss Phyll."

Becky bent down and picked up an earthen ware bowl, one such as was used in the servants' hall. Its sides were stained with what appeared to be soup of some kind.

"Who has been having meals in this room?" Phyllida demanded.

Parsons had gone white.

"I don't know, madam."

"Someone has, that's for sure. There's a spoon too. It's there, under the table. It must have rolled there when you kicked it, Miss Phyll," Becky pointed out.

"You are not going to suggest that Mr. Compton brings bowls of soup up here, are you?" asked Phyllida.

Parsons hurriedly retrieved the spoon, as though anxious not to have to face her mistress.

"No, madam," she answered at length. She seemed at a loss for words. "But—but maybe one of the younger maids came up here . . . for a prank."

"Come come, Parsons. Are you suggesting that the

servants in this house are so in need of a diversion? Besides, why choose the only unused room in the house that is regularly visited?"

"I don't know anything about it, madam. But there is no knowing how long the bowl has been there."

Phyllida sniffed gingerly at it.

"It is fresh," she announced. "It does not smell at all rancid. Why, it could have been brought here just today." Then she stopped.

Had it indeed been brought in this very day? Had someone been hiding in the room? Pensively she gazed at the settee. Two cushions were propped at one end, as though to support someone lying there. Had that someone been brought the soup, finished it, then put the bowl beneath the settee, out of the way?

But where was that person now? Then she remembered Parson's vague behaviour earlier.

"Was that why she had led us on a fool's errand all over the house? So that the mysterious person could be removed before I saw him—or her?"

The more she thought about it the more probable it became. Parsons must have gone downstairs, not just to get the keys, but to give warning that the mistress was going round the house. All of the maid's confusion between chests was mere subterfuge. Phyllida suddenly realized that the girl was still standing before her, her face pale with anxiety.

"Very well, Parsons," she said mildly. "I shall have a word with Mr. Hembury about the matter. We can't have the junior servants wandering about at will. They might bring candles up here and set the place alight. I only hope that the episode wasn't prompted by hunger. You do eat well in the servants' hall, I trust?"

"Very well, thank you, madam." Parsons had difficulty in keeping relief out of her voice.

"Good. Then it can only have been a prank, as you said. You can take the bowl and spoon away now."

Phyllida dismissed both servants, and wandered back

to her old sitting-room. She looked at it with some disapproval. It was elegantly furnished, true, but compared with the other room it was gloomy.

"Secret visitors or not," she decided. "Nothing will turn me against that room. I shall ask Richard about it this evening."

Parsons had been telling the truth in one respect at least. Richard seemed very pleased when Phyllida made her request.

"You like my mother's old room? Why certainly you may have it, if that is what you prefer. After all, you are the mistress here." A slow smile lit up his countenance. "We must see about having it redecorated for you. I noticed the other day that the wall-paper was sadly scuffed, and no doubt you will want to choose new draperies for yourself."

She was surprised that he still visited the room, for sentimentality was not an emotion she had ever recognized in him. She had deep pangs of conscience too, at his generosity. If only her love for Gerard did not overwhelm her so, she could have been tolerably happy with Richard. As it was, he was just an obstacle in the way of her complete joy.

When she met Gerard, later in the day, all her torments of doubts fell away, and she was aware only of being with the man she loved. Their meeting was short, painfully short when compared with all her anticipation. Gerard was late, and Phyllida waited, damp and shivering, in the early morning mist.

"My love, I was afraid I would never get away." Gerard swept her into his arms by way of greeting. "Did you think that I had forgotten?"

"No," lied Phyllida. "I knew you would come when you could."

"There was pandemonium at the camp."

"You haven't heard . . ." she cried in panic.

"No, no," he soothed her with kisses. "There is still no news of our sailing. We are moving camp nearer to town, that's all. We are taking the place of the Regiment of Artillery, who have already gone."

"But that must surely mean that you will sail soon?"

"I fear so, my darling, but let's not think of anything so dismal, let's change the subject completely. How have you passed the time since we have been parted?"

"Only in ordinary things, though I have picked out a new sitting-room for myself. Oh yes, and such a strange thing happened." And Phyllida told him all about the discovery of the bowl.

"So you think someone has been hiding in there, do you?" he asked when she had finished.

"What other explanation is there?"

"Yes, I agree. You must take no risks, darling. Do you think you are in any danger? For if so I will contact the Preventive men at once and have the whole matter exposed."

"No, I'm certain that there is no danger to me. I am just uneasy that so much should be going on so close to me. Besides, Officer Penwill is sure that Richard has no connection with the smugglers. I've heard him say so."

"You are wonderful, darling Phyllida." Gerard gave her a long lingering kiss that left her breathless. "You are so brave. I don't like leaving you, but as you are so confident of your safety . . ."

"Leave me?" broke in Phyllida. "You can't mean to go now?"

"I don't want to, I assure you. There is nothing I want more than to stay here with you and tell you how great my love is for you, but I must get back. I shouldn't be here at all. Parker is covering for me, and if my absence is noticed we shall both be reprimanded."

"But I will see you again?" said Phyllida, biting back her tears.

Gerard began to shake his head, but she caught his arm.

"Please!" she begged.

Then he relented. "I feel it is not wise, for your sake, but of course we will meet. Not until next week, though."

"Next week?" She was dismayed. So much could happen in that time. What if he received his sailing orders?

"I shall be away, my pet. Just for a few days. We are on an operation to assist the Preventive men further down the coast. I fancy it is an exercise to stop the men from getting bored, but I must go."

"Of course you must." She gulped back her distress. "I know you have your orders to obey."

As Phyllida walked back along the stony lane her heart was very heavy. Their meeting had been so short and strangely unsatisfactory. Now she looked back to it, they had talked so little of love, though the taste of Gerard's long lingering farewell was still on her lips.

She had the unwelcome task, too, of telling Becky that she had planned yet another meeting with Lieutenant Lacey. The maid was sheltering against a thicket, and already Phyllida imagined she could see the condemnation in Becky's eyes.

"I meant this to be the last." She justified her actions to herself. "I truly did, but when I am with Gerard I know I can't part from him, not just yet. Not until he has to leave for America."

In the days that followed Phyllida kept herself busy, to pass the interminable days until she saw Gerard again. There was plenty to occupy her, for the decorators had moved in, and were busy in her new sitting room. She changed her mind a dozen times about colours and materials, only to settle for the shades and brocades nearest to the originals.

Phyllida spent much time at this, but even so, at their appointed hours, her tutors arrived to give her lessons. Music was still her greatest joy, her favourite of them all.

"Quite delightful, my dear," Signor Giorgio would say at the end of each lesson. "You have made remarkable progress. If you were not married to Mr. Compton I could assure you of a comfortable career as a singer."

"If only I'd known earlier," she thought wryly, re-

145

membering those awful days when she had almost found herself destitute. "My life would have been so very different."

The decorators went, and it only remained for the cloying smell of paint to disperse before the curtains could be hung, and the new carpet laid. Then Phyllida could move in. Eager to hasten the process she collected a large bowl of pot-pourri and took it upstairs. For a moment she was startled to find someone already there. Her mind flashed back to the hidden stranger, but these figures—there were two—proved very familiar.

"You caught us at our task." Richard straightened up, an air of embarrassment about him. "I hoped that we would have finished before you came." He turned to Hembury, who was with him. "If you will adjust that screw to make the whole thing rigid . . . There, it is ready. I hope it pleases you," he said, turning to his wife.

Now Phyllida could see a brass cylinder set on top of a tripod.

"A spy-glass!" she cried. "Of all the wonderful things!"

Richard plunged his hands deep into his coat pockets.

"I remembered how intrigued you were with the one at Plymouth," he said, "so I thought you might like one of your own."

"You mean it is mine? Just for me? I shall be able to watch the harbour and the ships and all that happens!"

Beside herself with excitement at her new toy, she flung her arms about Richard. At once he stiffened, then coldly disentangled himself from her embrace.

"Hembury will inform you about the ships, if you so desire," he said icily. "Or if his duties prevent him, I think Joseph is knowledgeable in such matters."

With that he turned and left the room.

Her cheeks scarlet at this brusque rebuff, and furious with herself for her impetuousness, Phyllida turned her attention to the telescope, and Hembury who stood by tactfully ignoring her discomfort.

"There you are, madam," he said, showing her how to

146

focus on a small cutter that was making its way against the wind. "With this spy-glass you can see for miles. 'Even all the kingdoms of the world in a moment of time'."

"Surely not that far?" She tried to joke, to soothe her ruffled feelings, but already she was becoming absorbed in all the sights she could see in the neat round eye of her new plaything. Hembury stood there, patiently giving her the names of the ships that she caught in the sweep of her spy-glass, and respectfully joining in her amusement at seeing the tiny, doll-sized figures that scuttled along the quay. At last he begged leave to go and supervise the preparations for dinner.

"Yes, of course," Phyllida assented, dismayed at the late hour. "I should not have kept you so long. But before you go, open the window, please. The smell of paint is making my head ache."

As Hembury did so the sounds from the harbour swelled up and filled the little room. Abruptly the regular clanging of a bell cut across all other sounds, and a deep voice bellowed out a message in a harsh monotony. The distance and the heavy local accent defeated Phyllida.

"What is the bell-man calling?" she asked.

Hembury bent his head to catch every phrase.

"Some American prisoners escaped from Pymouth are thought to be in the area. The crier says there's five pounds reward for each of them."

Phyllida shivered, remembering that day at Mill Prison, and poor Captain Merritt, who had been so grateful for such a little kindness. Now some of his friends were being hounded like animals. It was a terrible thought.

"Who can blame them for wanting to escape from such a dreadful place?" she whispered.

"Yes indeed, madam." Hembury fixed the window sash, then made his bow, but as he left she thought he murmured something about "Deliverance to the captives", but she could not be sure.

Richard's mood of cool reserve had undergone a swift

change by the time he returned home. He thrust his hat into Hembury's waiting hand as he came through the door, and his footsteps rang on the marble floor in a hard forceful way.

For one agonized second Phyllida's uneasy conscience made her wonder if he had found out about Gerard, but at the library door Richard turned and snapped at the butler,

"When Officer Penwill comes you are to show him in at once."

With that he stalked into the library and slammed the door. Unaware that he was under scrutiny, Hembury made a face at his master's hat before putting it on a side table, then he began his way back to the servants' hall, but before he had reached the green baize door the Preventive Officer had arrived, and was shown straight into the library.

Relieved at not being the cause of Richard's anger, Phyllida hovered on the stairs. She had been on her way to get a book, but she had no intention of facing her husband while he was in such a mood. Puzzled at what could have caused him to get in such a rage, she crept back up to her new sitting-room, intending to amuse herself with the spy-glass until the light faded. The windows were still open, and unwittingly she found herself eavesdropping on the conversation below.

"I want to know the meaning of it all." Richard's voice was as cold and as hard as steel. "Why my ships and no other? Do you realize that for the last week every one of my vessels that has entered or left port has been searched by your men?"

"I'm sorry about it." Penwill did indeed sound regretful. "But what can I do?"

"Being sorry is no good. What the devil do you expect to find? You said a few months back that you were certain I wasn't involved in any smuggling. Do you think I've suddenly taken to hiding brandy in my coal and tea, in my bales of kersey?"

"No, but I have to obey my orders."

"Your orders are all very well, but what about my reputation? Do you think that every harbour rat hasn't noticed that your men go for my ships and my ships alone? It's not doing my business any good at all, and heaven knows, things are bad enough at the moment. I can't afford loss of confidence in my good name."

Phyllida had been imagining the little Preventive Officer sitting on the edge of his chair in an agony of nerves, but she was mistaken. Penwill was not intimidated by Richard's onslaught, for his voice rang out firm and decisive, very unlike the clownish character she had met in the garden that day.

"I'll tell you straight, Mr. Compton, I don't expect to find so much as a sniff of contraband on board any of your vessels, but if I did I'd lay a guinea to a China orange that you had no knowledge of it. But as I've said, I have to obey orders from the Collector at Plymouth, and they are that not one of your ships is to pass unsearched."

"But why?"

"That's what bothers me. There's something here I don't like. I've not been told what to look for, whether it be East Indian goods, geneva, or what. All I know is that information has been received that your craft need looking at." He paused for a moment before he added, "Tell me, sir, have you any enemies, or someone who wishes you ill?"

There was a deep silence, so complete that Phyllida could hear her own heart pounding in her ears. At last Richard replied in a voice that sounded carefully calm,

"None, so far as I'm aware."

"I must say that I've never heard anyone speak ill of you, but that still doesn't alter the fact that someone has informed against you. Someone with influence too, for I've heard—unofficially, mind you, but from a source that has proved reliable in the past—that this information, whatever it might be, was passed on by the military.

There's no knowing where they got it from, of course, but I'll do my best to find out."

"The military?" Richard sounded baffled.

"As I say, if I thought that you were involved with the freetraders, Mr. Compton, I'd be at you like a shot, despite the fact that you are such an eminent man, but I'm sure you're not. That's why I'm giving you this warning. There's a very nasty smell about this whole business, sir, and I think you should be on your guard."

"I thank you for your frankness and your advice." There was more warmth in Richard's voice now. "And I apologize for my harsh words earlier. I see now that you had no alternative. It is a situation that places both of us in difficult positions."

"No offence taken, sir." There was a scraping of chairs as Penwill obviously stood up to leave. "In my line of duty you get used to having brick-bats thrown at you from time to time. If it's of use to you, I could put it about that this information against you is just a ruse on someone's part to draw my attention from the real culprits. How would that do? It should help a bit."

"I'd be most obliged to you."

Their voices were growing more faint as the men went out of the room, but Phyllida was just able to hear Richard add,

"I'm concerned in case this matter reaches the ears of my wife or my aunt. It might worry them."

From below there came the mumbling sound of voices in the hall, followed by the thud of the front door closing. Richard's steps sounded on the stairs as he went up to his dressing room to change for dinner, but Phyllida did not stir. She sat immobile, a feeling of sick dread inside her, as she considered all that she had heard.

Gerard must have passed on the information she had given him, there was no other explanation. Yet she had expressly said that she did not want the Preventive men to hear it. That enemy of Richard Compton's was none other than his own wife!

Visions of him imprisoned or transported came into her head, and made her clench her fists in horror. She had no love for her husband, but she could not see him in conditions like those at Mill Prison, or worse. After his kindness about the room and the spy-glass her betrayal seemed particularly despicable. Even though Richard must be a freetrader, in spite of what Officer Penwill thought, she still did not want him punished. She had to meet Gerard and get the whole matter sorted out. She knew she would not be easy in her mind until then.

For a whole day she had to wait. A whole day of agonized self-reproach, before she saw Gerard again. With his customary caution Gerard had chosen a small copse as their rendezvous, he was still against their meeting twice in the same place.

As she rested against a tall sycamore Phyllida hoped desperately that she had come to the right place. She shuffled her feet in the dead leaves on the ground, wanting him to come and reassure her that he loved her. There were other things she wanted reassurance on too.

"Darling!" His voice made her jump. She had not heard his approach. "You were miles away." His brown eyes smiled at her in the way that she found so attractive. "I only hope your thoughts are of me."

She held her face up for his kisses.

"Of course," she answered. "I think of you every day."

For a long time she was content to stay in his arms.

"No hurrying away today?" she asked.

"Not today. All my attention is for you."

How long they were together she did not know, time had no meaning for her when she was with Gerard, but she knew she had to tackle the question of the searches with him, and the thought made her uneasy.

"What is it, sweet? Something is troubling you, isn't it?" Gerard looked at her questioningly. "Has something happened to alarm you?"

"Not alarm me exactly." She made her head more comfortable against his chest. "But I find it disturbing."

"Tell me!"

"The Preventive men have been searching all of Richard's ships lately, and he's very angry about it."

"And you think the Preventive men may be suspicious of his connection with the smugglers?"

"I don't know, but I heard Officer Penwill tell him . . ."

"Penwill? The Preventive officer?"

"Yes. Why do you look so startled? Richard called him in because he wished to complain, and I overheard them talking. Penwill said that someone had informed against Richard. Gerard, you didn't tell anyone about my foolish ideas, did you?"

"They are foolish ideas now are they? Don't you believe your own eyes any more?"

"Of course I do, but I don't want anything to happen to Richard. I don't want him put in prison or anything, and I did ask you not to tell the Preventive men of the strange things that happen at Furze House."

"What do you want, then? You seem very concerned about Compton all of a sudden." Gerard looked hurt.

It occurred to Phyllida that he was jealous, and of Richard too.

"Darling, don't look like that," she cried. "Of course I don't love him, but I have reason to be grateful to him, you know that, so I don't want him harmed."

"I see!" The pained light faded from Gerard's eyes and an expression of understanding took its place.

"You only want information, proof, if you like, against him. Then if he did find out about us you could threaten him with it. By Harry, that's clever. That's a splendid plan. He'd never dare to cut up rough with that hanging over him."

Such a plan would never have entered Phyllida's mind, not in her wildest dreams. For a moment she could only regard it with disgust, but Gerard was so full of admiration for it that eventually she nodded.

"Then we'll continue to search for definite proof, and no more accusations about informing the Preventives, eh?

Do you know, I've a notion how Compton may be involved with this business. He may be a sleeper."

"A sleeper? What's that?"

"He's the man who put up the original money to finance the smuggling operations. The Frenchies want paying for their cognac, after all. Compton would be in an admirable position to do that. He would not be involved with any of the details, would probably never even see a keg or barrel. Yes, with that man of his, what's his name? Hembury? Yes, Hembury as his go-between he would be in a very nice way of business."

"You could be right." His arguments sounded very convincing to Phyllida.

"I know I'm right, my love. It takes a shrewd man to be a successful sleeper, and I'm sure your husband is very shrewd indeed."

When they parted, Phyllida left in a glow of happiness, she was to have another meeting with Gerard—that was more than she had dared to hope for—and all of her former worries were stilled. Only as she neared Furze House did she realise that Gerard had never actually denied being the informer.

Nine

"I hope you have no evening arrangements for Friday," said Richard one morning at breakfast.

"No. I'm sure I'm free. Why?" Phyllida was engaged in spreading a slice of bread with apricot conserve.

"I have invited some people to dine, that is all."

"Then it is all one whether I have a prior engagement or not," she thought, indignantly. Aloud she said, "Who are they, pray? Do I know them?"

"Two you have met. Those officers who were so useful to Aunt Rouse when she fell."

Phyllida went cold. Gerard at Furze House! To be

153

treated as just another guest! It was unthinkable!

Richard carried on speaking, not noticing her changed expression.

"I thought to invite their commanding officer too, and his family. He has a wife and two—no, three daughters. Aunt Rouse will come too of course, now that she is fully recovered. Ah, yes, and an old acquaintance of mine who is in town awaiting passage to Plymouth, and his son in law."

There was a silence as Richard obviously expected some reply from her.

"A good balanced table." She babbled the first thing that came into her head. "Yes, very good. Six ladies and six gentlemen. Do you want me to order anything special from cook?"

She was amazed at her own calmness. She could actually discuss the practicalities of the dinner, knowing that Gerard would be there.

"I shall leave the details in your capable hands, my dear."

From his tone it was clear that Richard had lost all interest in the dinner party for the moment, as he turned his attention to his usual pile of early morning messages.

There was no such detachment for Phyllida. Her heart was pounding as she wondered how she could bear to be in the same room as Gerard, and not betray her love for him in some way. She was in an agony of terror one minute, and an ecstacy of excitement the next. Somehow she summoned the cook and Hembury to plan the menu and organise the table. Somehow she instructed the gardener about flowers, but it took a superhuman effort on her part.

Becky was in her element. It was rare that she had the opportunity of preparing her mistress for such a gathering, dinners at Furze House seldom exceeded eight at table. She spent her time in a happy flurry of smoothing and crimping tongs. Phyllida found it difficult to share her enthusiasm, the whole dinner party was threatening to become more and more of an ordeal as time went on.

When at last the evening came, she was reluctant to go and dress, as though by delaying her preparations she could lessen the trial before her. At last, after many urgent entreaties from Becky, she made her way to her dressing room.

As she passed the dining-room the servants were putting the final touches to the table, under the eagle eye of Hembury. A maid was placing folded napkins of spotless linen at each place, a footman was straightening candles in gleaming silver sconces. Such activity made her dread the evening even more.

"You'll never be ready in time, Miss Phyll," Becky scolded her. "I still don't know for sure which gown you want, you never said. So I've put out the rose pink gauze. I hope that was right."

She did not wait to find out, but began undoing the laces of Phyllida's bodice, and fairly wrenched the day gown from her.

"Ouch," protested Phyllida, as the laces became entangled with her hair. "Don't be so rough!"

"I'm sorry, Miss Phyll." Becky did not sound in the least sorry. "But I've a deal to do if you're not to greet your guests in your shift." And she pulled at Phyllida's petticoats with just as much vigour.

Phyllida resigned herself to Becky's ministrations, suffering herself to be pushed, pummelled and laced into a fashionable shape. Becky painted her face for her, darkening her eye brows, rouging her lips and cheeks, until it was a lady very much à la mode who stared back at Phyllida from the mirror. She refused point blank, though, to let Becky dress her hair as high as she wanted.

"No," said Phyllida firmly. "You've spent over an hour and a half on it, you've teased it, you've pomaded it and you've padded it. Any more and my neck will break. Just add the powder and be done."

"You should have called in a proper coiffeur, by rights," Becky muttered rebelliously, as she twitched the powdering gown over her mistress, and set to work with a vengeance, sending a fine white cloud all over the room.

"I prefer the way you do it," said Phyllida, as well as she could.

That left only the gown to be put on. It was one she had bought in Plymouth, but never worn before, and as Becky tightened the laces Phyllida could not suppress a thrill of excitement. It was indeed a beautiful gown, of rose pink gauze over silk, trimmed with silver lace. The trailing lines of the sack style suited her tall slender figure, and it was cut fashionably low, so that it scarcely covered her breasts.

"Wait till the master sees you," breathed Becky, with approval. "Fair knock him over, you will."

But it was Gerard's eyes that Phyllida longed to see light up as she approached.

The elegant figure reflected in the cheval glass was a far cry from the dowdy country miss who used to run through Barton Woods.

There was a gentle tap on the door, and a respectful voice informed her,

"Master's compliments, madam, and he's waiting for you in the White Drawingroom."

Startled out of her reverie, Phyllida took up her fan and swept out of the room, hoping she looked composed and regal, because in fact she was far from feeling either. Richard was standing near the fireplace when she entered. She waited a second, wondering what his reactions to her gown would be. He raised his head and took one look at her, then sharp lines of disapproval etched his face. At once Phyllida stiffened, ready to take the rebuff that was sure to come.

"Is that one of the gowns you bought in Plymouth?" Richard asked. "I do not recall having seen it before."

"It is indeed." Phyllida's reply was crisp. "This is the first time I have worn it."

"It is a charming colour, but surely the neckline is most immodest?"

Phyllida looked down at her offending decolletage. "It is most fashionable," she informed him. "By London standards it is almost prudish."

Richard's face softened not at all.

"Thank heavens, then, that we live hundreds of miles from London, both in distance and in manners. No matter what may be the thing at Vauxhall Gardens I cannot allow you to appear in company so exposed. The gown is most unsuitable, kindly go to your room and change it."

Phyllida stared at him aghast.

"You can't be serious!" she protested.

"But I can!"

"You have no notion of fashion, besides, have you any idea what it cost?" She knew her voice was rising in anger, whilst Richard's remained maddeningly calm.

"Neither the fashion nor the cost have anything to do with the matter. You surely have others. There were bandboxes enough that came from Plymouth."

"Of course I have others in my clothes-chest, and that's where they'll stay." She was shaking with anger. "I refuse to be ordered about like a child. I will not change my gown."

"If you were a child then the situation would not arise, but as it is, you are my wife. And while you remain in such a situation I will not have you appearing before my guests half naked. Either go of your own free will or I shall, most reluctantly, be obliged to carry you up myself."

His voice had not risen, his face had not changed, but she knew that he meant every word. She longed to flout him, but that would only be followed by humiliation. Tears of anger poured down her cheeks as she shook with rage. At last she burst out with the best argument she could think of.

"There's no time, the guests will be here at any minute."

Richard glanced at the French clock on the mantel.

"Then go to your abigail and get a scarf or a shawl or something to wrap round you."

With that she was dismissed. He turned away from her as though she no longer existed, in that maddening way of his. Phyllida stared at his back for a furious minute, searching for something cutting to say, though she knew it was useless. He would give no sign that he had heard.

A sudden clatter of hooves outside was the signal that the first guests were arriving. With a dismayed gasp Phyllida fled up the stairs.

Tut-tutting with vexation Becky flatly refused to spoil the lines of the gown with a shawl. Instead she swiftly stitched a shade of silver gauze in the offending neckline, then turned her attention to Phyllida's smeared make-up.

"It will have to do, Miss Phyll," she commented, gazing intently at her handiwork.

Feeling drained and exhausted, Phyllida descended the stairs once again, sure that this was a disastrous beginning to what was certain to be the most taxing evening of her life. She no longer even had the assurance of knowing she looked her best to give her confidence.

Although Phyllida did not realize it, her emotional outburst had heightened her colour in a way that was far more flattering than Becky's carmine pot. Also, her determination not to be beaten by Richard's disapproval made her hold her head up defiantly, and move like a queen. When she entered the White Drawingroom she looked really beautiful.

Richard registered no emotion, but there was genuine approval in the eyes of the two men who rose to make their bows.

"My dear," Richard greeted her. "Pray let me introduce an old business acquaintance of mine—Mr. Wilson, and his son-in-law, Mr. Rogers. They are bound for Plymouth soon on the KITTIWAKE, with Captain Bowden."

A portly gentleman, in the sober dress of a cleric, kissed her hand, then after him a smaller, younger man who was almost as somber, made his obeisance.

Phyllida must have spoken to them for they were all

smiles and affability. She was vaguely aware of a conversation about their trip to Plymouth, but her attention was not with them at all. She was too keyed up with the thought of having to face Gerard with her husband beside her—the thought made her quite giddy. There was a further diversion when Aunt Rouse arrived in a flutter of feathers and trailing lace.

"Am I late?" The old lady bustled in, unhitching a frilled cuff from the door knob as she did so. "Isn't it naughty of me? But Choo-Choo wouldn't eat his supper. He knew I was coming out, you see, and he didn't approve one little bit of being left behind. Richard, my dear boy." She paused long enough to lift her face up for a a kiss. "I wonder you invite me. It's not five minutes since I left your guest room, and here I am again. Phyllida, my dearest, you are in very good looks tonight. I hope that Richard appreciates you, that's all. He has said how pretty you look? No? I thought not. Shame on you, Richard." She did not wait to be introduced to the guests. There was obviously no need, for she held out her hand to the portly gentleman. "My dear Wilson. So long since I saw you. You are well, I trust? And your good wife? And this must be your son-in-law, of whom we have heard so much."

Phyllida, who had no previous knowledge of the silent Mr. Rogers, and was quite unaware that Aunt Rouse knew Mr. Wilson well enough to address him with such familiarity, was grateful for the tidal wave of conversation that followed the old lady. It gave her time to compose herself.

"If I can ever be composed again," she thought.

When the dreaded moment came it was not so fearsome as she expected, for Gerard did not arrive alone. Instead, the remaining guests all arrived in one large party, which caused enough confusion for her bright colour to pass unnoticed. Gerard had time for no more than a squeeze of her hand as he bent to kiss it before her attention was claimed by Lieutenant Parker, and Gerard, himself, was swept away by Aunt Rouse.

Colonel Wood was a pleasant jovial man who had brought with him his equally pleasant jovial wife, and their three exceedingly pretty, flaxen-haired daughters. As Phyllida welcomed the ladies she watched Gerard out of the corner of her eye. Never had she been so grateful for Aunt Rouse's steady stream of chatter that kept his attention carefully pinned down. He looked so handsome in his scarlet dress uniform, bright with gold braid, that she feared her love for him must be obvious to everyone. However, Mistress Wood, who had just embarked upon a detailed description of their former home in Hampshire, did not seem to notice anything amiss.

The announcement that dinner was served should have been a relief, but somehow it was not. Phyllida had spent many anguished hours wondering how she would react to meeting Gerard here, at Furze House, but she had never stopped to consider how he would behave. Natually she expected him to appear cool even off-hand. What she did not anticipate was that he should flirt outrageously with Amelia Wood, the eldest and prettiest of his colonel's daughters.

At the far end of the dining table Gerard and Amelia sat together, seemingly delighted with each other's company. Unable to tear her eyes away, Phyllida watched him crack walnuts for the pretty Miss Wood, peel oranges for her, pop bon-bons into her small red mouth. All the time Miss Wood's china blue eyes were gazing at him in utter adoration.

Mistress Wood noticed the flirtation too, and smiled fondly. Leaning across the portly figure of Mr. Wilson, she hissed in a stage whisper,

"Young Lacey and my 'Melia seem pretty thick, don't they, madam? Of course, having three gels we get the young gentlemen at our door all the time, worse than puppies they are. Mind you," and she became more conspiratorial, "I must say that young Blood is the pick of the bunch. A regular favourite with us all. He has all the attributes we favour, looks, address, breeding. All but money." She heaved a sigh for this major shortcoming. "Who is to say what this American campaign might bring him. There's all sorts of openings for a young man of ambition and goodness knows he's got enough of that."

Phyllida mashed her fruit mould into a pulp, knowing that to swallow any would choke her. So Gerard was well known at the Wood house, was he? With a shudder she wondered if he had visited there while he'd been stationed at Barton. A terrible picture formed in her mind of Gerard leaving her, and dashing off at once to try to win the favours of Amelia.

With desperate intensity she turned her attention to the general conversation. She would never let Gerard see that she was so distressed by his behaviour. Mistress Wood's mention of America had caught the ear of the whole table.

"Do you think you will be sailing soon?" Richard asked the colonel.

"Without a doubt. Should have been there long since, of course, but that's politicians for you. Never send the ones who'll do the job." The colonel quartered his apple with energy, as though he was already addressing the foe.

"You have no sympathy for our kinsfolk across the Atlantic, then?" asked Mr. Wilson mildly.

"Sympathy!" Colonel Wood spluttered over a mouthful of apple. "Heaven above, sire, no! Of course not! Disloyal to His Majesty, that's what they are. Traitors the lot of them!"

"I believe that there are some who are not in favour of independence," cut in Richard's quiet voice.

"True, true," conceded Wood, "but as for the rest, hanging's too good for them. We'll soon put a stop to those dashed Colonials and all their nonsense."

"But surely you do not condemn a country for wishing to trade where it chooses, to raise its own taxes and to determine its own future?" It was Mr. Rogers who spoke. They were almost the only words he had uttered all evening. At first Phyllida had considered him terribly shy, but then she began to wonder if he was feeling well. There was a chalky pallor to his skin, and perspiration glistened on his brow. He was also painfully thin, yet she noticed he ate very little, declining the richer dishes that were offered to him.

Colonel Wood suffered from no such disability. He had just noticed a particularly fine cheese that he had not sampled, and helped himself to a generous slice before answering.

"What country is it that you speak of, sir? America? There is no such nation. Just a collection of plantations and colonies that will be at each others throats before you can say knife. No, my chief fear is that it will all be over before we get there. Already I heard that my Lord Howe has all but blockaded the whole coast from North Carolina to Rhode Island. New York is already in our hands. Why, it'll be finished by Christmas, and we'll all have been sea sick for nothing."

"I hope the beastly war will be over soon," announced the youngest Miss Wood pertly, her eyes fixed on the good-natured face of Lieutenant Parker. "I think it's wretched to have our dear Lacey and dear Parker taken away from us. We shall be desolate without them."

"Well, you aren't wishing your beaux much favour, that's all I say," admonished her father. "They've both got their ways to make in the world, and when did a soldier ever prosper in peace time? By the by, I didn't notice you included your poor papa among those who would be torn from you by this rebellion. That's modern youth for you," he cried in mock despair. "No time for the older generation."

Among the laughter that followed Mistress Wood cried, "Then let's hope for a successful campaign, and death to all rebels."

"How blood-thirsty you are, madam," laughed Gerard, "but I will drink to your sentiments."

He lifted his glass, and for a moment, one brief

wonderful minute, his eyes met Phyllida's. Caught up in the spell of that one glance she too raised up her wine glass.

"A successful campaign and death to all rebels," she echoed.

She did not notice that only the officers and the ladies of the Wood family joined her in her toast.

Gerard shared no more secret moments with her. For the rest of the evening there were no more glances between them, no brief touches of fingertips. Gerard appeared completely captivated by Amelia's blue eyes. In an agony of jealousy Phyllida threw herself into her role of hostess, chatting to the ladies, teasing Colonel Wood and Mr. Wilson, and flirting with Lieutenant Parker, much to the annoyance of the younger Miss Wood. But Gerard did not seem to notice.

In the large, formal White Drawingroom, after dinner, Gerard still made no attempt to come near her. All about her the conversation buzzed, but Phyllida was growing more and more unhappy, yet she realised that she was being completely unreasonable.

"You don't expect him to flirt with you right in front of Richard, do you?" she asked herself. "He's being cautious for your sake."

But that did not stop her feeling pain every time he looked at Amelia Wood. Richard was deep in conversation with the pale Mr. Rogers, but after a while he turned to Mistress Wood.

"Madam," he said with his customary courtesy. "Can we prevail upon one of your daughters to entertain us? I am sure that such charming young ladies are bound to be very accomplished. We have the spinet or the guitar, as you see, and there is also a harp."

The good lady flushed up with maternal pride.

"They've all had masters, of course, but I think my Amelia is the best performer. A pleasant little voice, she's got, though I shouldn't say so."

"Then will Miss Wood be kind to us all, and give us all pleasure?"

Amelia blushed and looked reluctant. At last, though, she gave in.

"But only if dear Parker will play for me," she insisted. "I do not feel at ease, playing in company, and he does it so well."

"Of course I will." The kindly Parker crossed over to the spinet and sat down.

"If Parker has the privilege of playing for Miss Wood then I demand the right to turn the music," declared Gerard, springing to his feet. "Then I can stand near you and admire you at the same time," he whispered, but loud enough for the whole room to hear.

Mistress Wood settled herself more comfortably in her chair next to Phyllida.

"My, isn't he a caution?" she giggled behind her fan.

The bright smile on Phyllida's face grew stiff as she forced herself to watch Gerard bend low over Amelia's head, ostensibly to help her choose her music.

"A folk song, I beg of you. Nothing suits your voice so well, my dear Miss Amelia," he demanded. "Ah, here is the very one, 'Sweet Nightingale'. That is my favourite above all others."

"Very well," agreed Amelia. "But pray, sir, stand further away. You are putting me off."

With obvious reluctance Gerard moved away a little, and after a nod from Parker Amelia began to sing. She did indeed have a sweet piping voice, but her performance was full of halts and stumbles, with Parker manfully keeping pace in his accompaniment. It was poor comfort for Phyllida though, who by now felt as though her false smile was stretched across her face for ever.

Amelia was persuaded to sing an encore, and at every phrase, every note she uttered, Gerard watched her with loving attention. Phyllida's agony was increased when Mr. Wilson, who was at her other side, whispered in her ear;

"Charming to watch them together, isn't it, madam?

Always a delight to see young love."

At last Amelia sat down among polite applause, and Gerard followed at his heels. Lieutenant Parker rose too, but was shouted down with requests for him to play alone. He played well, and with much feeling, so that Phyllida listened with genuine enjoyment, but not even the music could soothe her smarting heart.

"Madam." Parker bowed towards her. "I have heard that you sing. Could we have the honour of listening to you?"

"Only if you will accompany me, sir," she replied. As soon as she began to sing she knew at once that she had everyone's attention. She chose a song by Mr. Handel, one that suited her range and quality of voice to perfection. As the last of her notes died away there was a moment's rapt silence before the burst of applause. Phyllida needed no convincing that she had completely eclipsed poor Amelia's performance.

"Superb, Mistress Compton. I declare I've never heard better." Lieutenant Parker's admiration was warm and wholly sincere.

"If it had been Gerard who praised me . . ." thought Phyllida, and glanced towards him. As she did so her eye caught the expression on Amelia's face. Poor Miss Wood, though smiling bravely, was clearly embarrassed, only too aware that her own singing had been so greatly inferior.

At once Phyllida felt a wave of shame sweep over her. Memories of that terrible dinner party when Mistress Walters had humiliated her so terribly came back with a sickening clarity. Now she had done just the same to poor Amelia.

"You did it quite deliberately," she told herself. "You set out to hurt her, and after all she's not to blame if Gerard flirts with her. How could you do such a thing?"

"Please, madam, may we hear more? It was Mr. Wilson who spoke, pleasure beaming from his plump cheeks.

"Yes, indeed." The cry was taken up on all sides.

"Very well," Phyllida agreed at last. "But we have had a deal of singing. May I play the harp instead?

To murmurs of assent she sat down at the instrument with great deliberation. Signor Giorgio had forecast that she might be a tolerable performer at it, but in this case he had been over optimistic. Phyllida was still a long way from any sort of mastery of the harp. The jig by Bach that she played came out as a series of jerky twanks that only vaguely could be recognized as tuneful. Though concentrating on her music she was aware of the mixture of amusement and embarrassment from her audience. When at last it was over and the polite applause had finished she saw that Amelia was smiling again, her discomfort all gone.

"Thank goodness for that," thought Phyllida. "After all, just because you're angry with Gerard there is no need to stoop to the level of the Mistress Walters of this world."

She felt almost happy that her self-imposed humiliation had been so successful, but it did nothing to divert Gerard from flirting with Amelia.

The long evening dragged on, but at last the guests got up to leave.

"Surely now he will make some sign," Phyllida thought, but Gerard's lips merely brushed her hand coolly in farewell, then he dashed away to ensure himself a place next to Amelia in the carriage going home.

The atmosphere in the White Drawingroom was flat and dull, even Aunt Rouse had departed. Only Richard stood there, winding the French clock. Although Phyllida had dreaded the evening so much, now she was reluctant to end it. She wandered about the room listlessly.

"Come along, my dear. Why are you lingering?" Richard was waiting for her.

"I don't feel like going to bed yet." She trailed her fingers along the top of a sideboard. "I suppose it's the excitement."

"A most successful evening, I thought, thanks to you.

Your singing was particularly good." He made no mention of the fiasco with the harp. "A pleasant evening altogether."

"Yes, very pleasant," she echoed, although those were not her true sentiments.

"But the servants have had a very long day and must be tired. We mustn't delay them any more. You may come in now, Hembury," he called to the butler who had been hovering in the hall. "You may let the servants finish now and go to bed. They can clear up in the morning."

"But the dining-room is not tidy yet, sir."

"Leave it just the same, but make sure the candles are all properly extinguished. Your mistress will have breakfast in her room, tomorrow, and you can bring something on a tray to my dressing room for me. That should keep us out of your way."

"Thank you, sir. That will be much appreciated. May I go and dismiss the others?"

Richard nodded and Hembury withdrew. Phyllida watched the scene with some annoyance.

"How typical of the man," she thought. "So considerate towards his servants, yet it never occurred to him to consult me about my wishes concerning breakfast."

"Come along, Phyllida."

There was a note of impatience in Richard's voice. Reluctantly she picked up her fan and went into the hall. Already the sounds from the servants' hall were fading, and only Hembury remained, carefully extinguishing all flames. No matter what the under-servants did, Hembury would finish all his duties before he retired for the night.

"Good night, Hembury."

Richard picked up a branched candlestick to light their way upstairs.

"Good night, sir. Good night, madam."

Phyllida, following in her husband's footsteps as he mounted the stairs, happened to look down. The lined face of the butler, lit by his single dip, was gazing up at her, and there was no mistaking the mistrust and suspic-

ion in his expression. For a moment she was startled.
What could she have done to provoke such emotions? Just
then she lost her footing on the stairs. At once Richard
caught her arm to steady her.

"Are you all right?" he asked.

"Yes—er—yes." She recovered herself quickly. "I
wasn't looking where I was going, that's all." But as she
continued up to bed she was distinctly uneasy.

Ten

The first thing that Phyllida knew next morning was
Becky entering, one arm piled high with freshly laundered
linen, and precariously balancing a salver stacked with
the morning's correspondence in the other. Uncertain
which burden to relinquish first she succeeded in spilling
letters all over the coverlet.

"Bother the things!" she exclaimed angrily. "As if I
didn't have enough trouble getting them in the first place."

"Why, what do you mean?" asked Phyllida sleepily.

"It was that Mr. Hembury. He took so long sorting, it's
a wonder he didn't wear the ink off them all, just to be
awkward. Still, he's not the only one being difficult,
everyone's in a funny mood this morning. It must be the
late night."

Phyllida sat up and wrapped her arms round her knees.
She looked carefully at Becky who was looking over a
collection of muslin caps.

"How do you mean—funny?"

"M-m-m?" Becky was totally absorbed in her task.
"Just funny, Miss Phyll. A bit off hand, like, as though I'd
done something to offend, though for the life of me I
can't think what. Which cap will you wear, Miss Phyll?
The dormeuse or the Pultney? And will you have a ruff?"

"Oh, the dormeuse and a kerchief will do." Phyllida
dismissed her costume impatiently.

Becky's casual comments had disturbed her, particularly when she remembered Hembury's strange attitude the night before. But she had more to think about than overtired servants. In less than two hours she was to meet Gerard.

As she dressed she was torn between a desire to beg him to love her and forget Amelia, and an equally strong inclination to round on him severely for his behaviour at the dinner party. She was still debating the matter to herself while Becky put the finishing touches to her toilette when Richard arrived unexpectedly. At once she resented his intrusion because she was afraid he would delay her.

"You are dressed for riding!" she exclaimed. "You are going out already?" Then she noticed with a shock how tired he looked, and added in a rush of sympathy; "You were so late last night, surely the counting house can function without you for one morning at least?"

Richard gave a faint smile.

"I have already been there," he said. "I've spent two full hours going over the accounts while you were still abed. So now I am ready for some exercise. I must go to the Wool Exchange, just as soon as I've bidden farewell to Mr. Wilson and young Rogers. Shall I wish them a safe voyage on your behalf?"

"Please do. I had forgotten that they were going on the KITTIWAKE." She felt a pang of envy as she remembered the exhilaration of her own voyage. "I wish I could go with them."

"Yes, I agree. When these troubled days are over maybe we can go somewhere, a long trip to America, perhaps, or the West Indies." Richard was twisting his riding gloves in his hands. At the door he turned. "I don't think I told you how well you looked last night, your gown was most becoming. You quite easily overshadowed all the other ladies there without resorting to extremes of fashion. Such tricks are only for females with no beauty."

So saying, he left, leaving an astonished Phyllida sitting

at her dressing table. That was the first really personal compliment he had ever paid her, and his very awkwardness in uttering it proved his sincerity. At once all her eagerness to meet Gerard evaporated, leaving her consumed with guilt.

"I don't want to deceive Richard," she whispered. "But I do so want to see Gerard again. I almost wish I didn't love him so, then life would be so much easier."

Remorseful at her own weakness Phyllida left the house and headed for their rendezvous, a small clump of trees on a little-used lane. Usually her qualms about deceiving Richard melted away at the prospect of meeting Gerard, but today they remained over her like a dark cloud. Her uncomfortable conscience was not eased by having to wait nearly half an hour for Gerard to arrive.

"I'm surprised you bothered to come," she snapped, when he finally made the steep ascent up the rough track.

"What's this?" Gerard was taken aback. "I'm not late, am I?"

"You know full well you are. And not for the first time either," she retorted frostily, then added, because his behavior still rankled, "You are dallying with your colonel's daughter, no doubt."

A look of comprehension passed over Gerard's face, and he made to take her in his arms, but she dodged away.

"I see why you are angry, my darling," he smiled. "But it was very sensible, if you think about it."

"Was it?" Phyllida did not melt one inch. "I expected you to have a good explanation."

"In that case, at least listen to it."

Phyllida relented just a little.

"All right. I'll hear you. Why did you flirt with Amelia Wood?"

"Why did I flirt with her? Really, Phyllida, you ought to know the answer. Did you expect me to look at you adoringly? To exchange loving glances with you, while your husband stood at your elbow? Do you think I am so careless of your honour and reputation that I would let the world know what we are to each other? How could you have misjudged me so?"

He looked so downcast that she felt her heart melting, but she was unwilling to forgive him completely just yet.

"Why the flirtation, then?" she demanded.

"It seemed the best way to avert suspicion. No one who was at that dinner party could possibly suspect that it was you who held my heart, and not Amelia."

Phyllida had to admit that his reasoning was good.

"Very well," she agreed grudgingly. "But you appear on exceeding good terms with Miss Wood. Too good for my tastes."

"My love, she is the daughter of my commanding officer. You said so yourself. Of course I must be pleasant to her. I can ill afford to offend any member of his family; goodness knows I've few enough influential friends without that! Come alone now, say that I'm forgiven."

With the pleading tone of his voice every last vestige of Phyllida's anger was swept away, and she ran into his arms. As he kissed her passionately those dark shadows of doubt that had hung over her all morning lifted.

"I was so jealous of her," Phyllida admitted, half ashamed. "Your attentions seemed so real. I suffered agonies last night."

"How could you have imagined that I was attracted by Amelia?" smiled Gerard. "She is a pleasant enough young lady, true, but when compared with you she is nothing. And you need not fear that her heart is broken, either, because she is looking much higher than a penniless lieutenant, I can tell you." He broke into a chuckle. "Why, I was so absorbed by Amelia's beauty that I found time to keep my eyes open, in case I saw anything suspicious at Furze House."

"I doubt if you saw anything, not last night at any rate."

"No, true enough. But I don't think I'd trust that butler

too far. He looks a fly character to me. How eccentric to keep a butler who's a cripple."

"Hembury is most efficient, and he is devoted to the family." Phyllida did not know why she felt the need to defend him.

"I suppose he must be, or that husband of yours would not tolerate him. I can't imagine Compton putting up with anyone who didn't know his job."

"I'm not so sure. Half of the servants seem to have been collected from jails and poor houses, from what I can gather."

"You're not serious!"

"But I am. I know that one of the maids was transported for murder, she told me so herself. I've heard that the kitchen-maid was actually bought from cruel parents, and Joseph spent his childhood in a debtors' prison. Even Hembury has had one or two spells in jail. Goodness knows where the rest came from."

"And Compton actually took them into his service?" Gerard's tone was incredulous.

"Either him or his father."

"M-m-m." Gerard looked thoughtful. "That could account for a lot."

"In what way?"

"If he had some hold over his servants, then they would be afraid to betray him."

"No, that's not right, for they all adore him. I think they'd lay down their lives for him, and that's no exaggeration."

"Even better! Then they are grateful to him, and gratitude can be a much stronger force than fear. In such circumstances he need never worry about one of his servants informing against him, no matter what he did. That's a capital arrangement. I congratulate Mr. Compton. I had not thought him so astute."

The whole idea was so calculating, so completely out of character for Richard that Phyllida found it distasteful.

"No," she cried with such vehemence that Gerard

looked up in some surprise. "I'm sure it never occurred to him."

"What, defending Compton in his—smuggling?"

"No, of course not." She denied it hurriedly. "But why did you hesitate then? What were you going to say instead of smuggling? Surely you don't suspect him of something else?"

"Now it is my turn to say of course not." Gerard's answer came a little too hastily. "Why do you ask? Have you seen anything strange?"

"Not really, only . . ."

"Only what?"

"It may be silly, I know, but I feel that the servants are watching me again, just the way they did when I first came to the house. Becky has noticed it too."

"Has she? She's a sharp little wench that maid of yours. Has this been happening for long?"

"Only since last night, after the dinner party."

"And you can think of nothing that you've done or said that might have caused it?"

"Nothing at all."

Phyllida was getting weary of the way their conversations always turned to Furze House and its strange happenings. It was such a waste of their precious time. What did she care if Richard was a smuggler! He could drive a carload of contraband right through the house if he wished. All she was interested in was Gerard.

"I shall see you again?" she whispered, ready to plead, but Gerard nodded.

"Certainly we will. Where shall we meet? And when? If you are certain that your husband does not suspect."

"I am quite certain. But tell me at once, do you still love me? I want to hear you say it again and again."

"I love you. I love you. I love you. There, do you still doubt it, my adorable one?"

Gerard's arms slid round her waist, and she felt his lips on hers, but Phyllida had a disturbing impression that his mind was elsewhere.

After Phyllida returned to the house she realised how weary she was. Lunch was a quiet subdued meal, with Richard too tired or too pre-occupied to talk much, and with the servants still in their watchful mood she soon sought refuge in her bright little sitting-room. The autumn afternoon was short, though. The vivid sun glowed brightly on the horizon for a while, then sank out of sight, leaving a purple dusk to deepen into utter darkness. There was no longer enough light to see to sew or read, and being too indolent to ring for candles Phyllida soon fell asleep.

The penalty for her afternoon nap was a sleepless night. She closed her eyes in a token effort, but she remained obstinately wide awake. After tossing and turning for a while she gave up the struggle and tossed back her bedclothes, then she lit her candle.

"I may as well read," she decided. "Anything is better than lying in the darkness."

It was then that she found she had no book.

"I must fetch one from the library," she said aloud, but could she face the shadowy uncertainty of the hall? "What is there to fear?" she scolded herself. "Any activity down there will be flesh and blood, not spooks and spectres. Really, you are spineless."

Nevertheless, the fingers that tightened round the candle stick shook a little as she went down the inky well of the stairs. It was a relief to feel the cool tiles of the hall beneath her feet. It was only a momentary relief though, for when she turned towards the library she saw a thin sliver of light shining beneath the door.

The pounding of her heart shook her whole body, causing the candle to shake, and the warm wax to spill over her fingers. Two o'clock had struck long since so she knew that no servants were about. She knew she should rouse the household, but curiosity got the better of her. She felt that she had to know who was in the library. On silent toes she crept forward, a scream ever ready in her throat. Then she flung open the door.

"What the devil . . . "

Richard looked up in alarm at her intrusion. He was sitting at his desk in his shirt sleeves. Working candles burnt and a nearby table was strewn with papers. Phyllida stood there, unable to move.

"I thought you were a burglar," she said at last. "I couldn't sleep so I came down for a book, and I saw the light . . ."

"But you came just the same. One day there really may be an intruder, then what would happen if you barged in?" His tone was gentle. "Here, let me take that before you set light to the house."

He rose and took the candle from her, setting it on his desk. His action automatically brought her into the room.

"What are you doing, so late?" she wanted to know.

Richard glanced down at the papers strewn all over the desk top. He hurriedly collected them together and thrust them into a drawer.

"Just catching up on some work," he said, but Phyllida felt that she could not believe him.

"He's hiding something from me," she thought. "Now what was on that paper that he didn't want me to know about. Surely not simply a bill of lading for some calico?"

By now Richard had regained his composure.

"I'm sorry that you cannot sleep. Are you feeling well, or shall I call your maid?"

"No thank you. I'm not ill. I just fell asleep this afternoon—or do I mean yesterday afternoon? So now I'm not tired. I thought that to read a book would be more interesting than tossing and turning all night."

"Do you know what you want? Can I get it for you?" Richard turned towards the ranks of shelves that were packed with books.

"Something amusing perhaps. But I will get it. I don't want to disturb you."

"Here, have you read 'The Vicar of Wakefield'? It is very light and funny. It's by Mr. Goldsmith. I'm sure you'll enjoy it."

Richard reached up and picked out a volume bound in brown leather.

"But you are not disturbing me, I thing it's time I had a rest." He looked ruefully at a pile of ledgers on his desk. "I still have all these to deal with, and the prospect is not inviting."

Suddenly he noticed a tray, covered with a white cloth, on one of the side tables.

"Good heavens, I'd forgotten all about this! Hembury brought it in at about midnight." He lifted the cloth to reveal an array of food, cooked meats, pies and fruit. "Since you are wide awake won't you join me for a late supper? As you see, cook has provided more than enough." Phyllida hesitated, but he added, "Please, I should like your company very much."

"Very well. Thank you." She settled herself on the chair that he placed for her. "Shall I serve you with meat while you pour the wine?"

"If you please."

Richard brought some of the candles from his desk and set them on the table. In the brighter light Phyllida was shocked to see how tired and haggard he looked, even more than yesterday. His face had a pinched look about it, and beneath his eyes were shadows as dark as bruises.

"You look worn to the bone," said Phyllida frankly. "You really must stop working so hard or you'll be ill. Surely you can finish all this tomorrow?"

"Unfortunately I can't." Richard smiled wearily. "By tomorrow I shall have a pile of papers twice as high. I shall be better when I've had some food."

"Have a day off. Old Ned will just have to cope."

"Old Ned is first rate, but I keep telling you that the responsibility is all mine, and that involves a lot of head-aches these days."

"Then the war is still making a deal of difference to you?"

"Yes, indeed. For one thing the French privateers are at work, stopping merchant shipping, mine included. We

176

haven't got a cargo of coal through to Plymouth in weeks. There is no trade with the American Colonies, either, of course, and that used to make up a large part of our business."

"Then things are bad."

"Certainly not as good as I'd like."

Phyllida sat very still for a moment then she said,

"You must regret that no marriage portion came with me. Do you think it would be worth applying to my grandfather once more? I feel guilty that I've brought you nothing."

She might have added that she had other causes for her guilt, but she did not.

"You must not feel so. I know the circumstances when we married, and I knew your grandfather well enough never to expect a change of heart from him. You're still receiving regular letters from the Vicar of Barton, are you not? He has not written of any mellowing of character?"

"Not at all. Quite the reverse in fact. Grandfather refuses to have my name mentioned."

"Then I suggest that we forget about any expectations from that quarter, however much you feel you are entitled to them."

"I suppose it is hopeless," agreed Phyllida. "But what if I economise? I can do very well without so many gowns and jewels. I am used to having few, for my allowance from my grandfather was very small indeed."

Richard gave one of his rare smiles, and for a spell the deep lines of fatigue melted away.

"I am touched that you are ready to make such sacrifices, my dear, but I don't think that such extremes are necessary just yet, though I doubt if we can have any shopping trips to Plymouth for a while. I have made cuts in the business that should help. That's why I sit up so late, working out ways so that I won't have to lay off my men. Winter is coming, and if they don't work for me I doubt if they'll find employment elsewhere. Unless they fall foul of the Press gangs of course, poor devils. I've lost one or two that way already."

Phyllida remembered the day when Young Ned Prettyjohn had been chased by the Press gang, and she shuddered.

"You are cold!" exclaimed Richard. "How inconsiderate of me, not to have thought. Why, you haven't even a shawl. He rose swiftly and picked up his house gown that lay over the back of a chair. "Something else that Hembury brought, but I forgot about," he said, as he slipped the dull red silk robe about her shoulders.

Phyllida pulled it about her gratefully. It had a fresh tang about it, of Richard's shaving soap and pomade. She was quite warm enough, but she had just become conscious that she was only clad in a very flimsy cambric nightshift. At once she had felt embarrassed, stupidly so, since the man sitting opposite her was her husband. Similar thoughts must have occurred to Richard, for he glanced at his shirt sleeves, with their ink-smudged cuffs.

"If you'll excuse me, I'll go to get my jacket. I'm sorry to appear before you in such a way." He rose to go.

"There is no need," said Phyllida. "Neither of us is dressed to receive company, but does it matter at this time of night? Shall we eat? What can I help you to, the capon pie or the cold duck?" Richard sat down again.

"The duck, I think please."

He poured the wine. Neither of them spoke much while they ate, for they were both surprisingly hungry. Richard sipped the last of his wine, then looked at her over the top of his glass.

"This is very pleasant, having an informal supper together like this. We so seldom eat alone, just the two of us, and I find that I enjoy it."

Phyllida smiled. She was enjoying the unexpected intimacy of the supper too.

"It reminds me of the al fresco meal we had on the

KITTIWAKE. That was a day I shall remember all my life."

"I'm glad it gave you such pleasure." Unexpectedly Richard dropped his head to his hands.

"You are dead tired," said Phyllida with concern, and she stretched out a hand to him.

"I am tired, but that's not the trouble."

Richard looked up, then his fingers curled round hers. His grip was firm, and to her surprise Phyllida found that she had no inclination to pull away.

"What is wrong, then? she asked breathlessly.

"I am!" came the startling answer. "Phyllida . . . we have so few opportunities to talk together. I know that our marriage was not what you wanted, and sometimes you must be very unhappy . . . I don't find it easy to talk about my feelings . . . to you I must appear very dull and stern . . ." His words were disjointed as he struggled to express himself. "I do try to make you happy, though all too often I blunder and make a mess of things . . . What I'm trying to ask is . . . to say is . . . I hope your life with me is not too intolerable."

With all his worries that was the problem that troubled him most. Phyllida's fingers were still intertwined with his. She wanted to answer, to tell him how kind he'd been, how considerate, but the words would not come. All those times when he had infuriated her now seemed so trivial. Choked with tears she could not even look at him.

Foremost in her mind was the knowledge that she had betrayed him in so many ways. Because of her he was being hounded by the Preventive men. Behind his back she was meeting another man. She had brought him no inheritance, only disgrace. She had done all this to Richard.

Her sobs could be contained no longer. She pulled her hand away and ran from the room, leaving Richard gazing after her, a look of pain and bewilderment on his face.

In the seclusion of her room Phyllida sobbed until her whole body shook. Every particle of guilt and self-reproach that she had suppressed during these last weeks rose up within her. She knew that she could not go on deceiving Richard.

"If he was cruel or a drunkard, then it would not matter, but he's not. He has treated me well, far better than I deserve. What am I to do?"

She wept until no more tears would come, then she fell into a restless sleep. She woke at early light, and her first thoughts were that some great dread hung over her. Then she remembered it all, and she fell back on the pillows with a moan. Even when Becky came with her morning chocolate she did not stir.

"Lor, Miss Phyll, are you all right?" Becky peered at her with concern. "You look all done up."

Placing the tray on a table she put a cool hand on her mistress's forehead. Phyllida pushed it away.

"Don't fuss," she groaned. "I'm not ill, I just slept badly. There are things on my mind."

"Ah!" said Becky knowingly. "So that's it, is it?"

"What do you mean by that?"

"It's obvious, Miss Phyll. It had to come, didn't it?— Move over a little please, while I plump up your pillow. —Some day you were bound to have to make a choice between them. Things couldn't carry on as they were."

"I suppose you're right." Phyllida did not even have the spirit to scold her maid for impertinence. "I just don't know what to do."

"You have your chocolate while it's hot." Becky set the tray across her knees. "That'll revive you, help you think more clearly." She turned and began to bustle about, putting out Phyllida's clothes for the day. "Mind you, I know which I'd choose, if I were you, Miss Phyll."

"Well you're not me, so I'll thank you to keep a quiet tongue." The hot drink was already having its effect.

Becky shook out the folds of a stiff underskirt.

"What if he does indulge in a little free trading," she went on, ignoring her mistress's comment. "He's a real gentleman in every sense, and there's not many of those left on the tree, I can tell you. You wouldn't have much trouble either, not in the way of other women or drink or the like. True he does like his own way, but then he's generous with it, so what more do you want?"

"Becky, I'm warning you!"

"Then there is the small fact that you are already married to him. Had you thought a way out of that? Master'd no more countenance a divorce than fly."

"Becky!"

"Very well, Miss Phyll, I won't say another word." But as she reached the door she delivered one more parting shot. "There's one thing you might consider, Miss Phyll. Would the other one have you?"

Furiously Phyllida hurled a slipper at her maid, but Becky had nimbly slipped through the door and was gone. Just the same her words made Phyllida think more clearly, though she carefully ignored Becky's last comment.

"I have no choice," she decided at length. "I still love Gerard, but what if I went with him? He's bound for America any day now, and I could never follow him there. Who knows how long it would be before he came back or—or if he came back at all."

She tried to imagine Richard's reactions if she left him, and was surprised to find how painful the whole idea had become to her.

"I have to face the fact that I must part from Gerard." Tears fell at the thought. "I will have to tell him that everything between us is over, though I will always love him. I only hope he understands, and won't be too hurt. Goodness knows, I want to spare him that, poor darling. It will be so hard to say. But I must do it! I must!"

Phyllida wept for a little while, but she felt much more calm now that she had reached a decision. Soon she was composed enough to ring for Becky. She had to get dressed to meet Gerard for this final time.

A thick autumnal mist hung over the valley where they were to meet. It clung to the spikes of ripened blackberries in tiny drops, and Phyllida felt the minute beads of moisture brush against her cheeks.

"Like tears," she thought. "Everything is weeping for us this morning."

The poignancy of the occasion made everything seem more real, more vivid.

"I shall remember every detail of this," thought Phyllida. "I shall treasure it always. Keep it locked up in my heart."

She was quite glad that Gerard was late, for that gave her more time to drink in the subdued beauty of the morning. Gerard appeared, a scarlet blur among the mists. Phyllida watched him come with pain, eager to keep him in sight for as long as possible.

"I'm sorry I'm late." Gerard had run the last few yards towards her, and now he was slightly out of breath. "Can you forgive me? But just as I was . . . Why, what is it, my love? Is something wrong?"

Phyllida was unable to speak, but just clung to him, her face buried against the coarse wool of his jacket.

"Has something upset you? Surely you aren't still angry with me over this Amelia Wood business?"

Mutely Phyllida shook her head.

"No," she said at last. "Not that. I came to a decision last night. I know that I should have done it long since, it has been troubling me, but I've made up my mind at last. We are never to meet again."

She felt Gerard stiffen, then he held her at arms' length.

"What has happened?" he asked. "Does Compton suspect?"

Clearly he did not believe her.

"No. It's just that I can't go on deceiving him."

The look on Gerard's face was one of bewilderment.

"But we can't," he cried. "We can't stop seeing each other. After all, how many times will we have left? Let us enjoy them together, however few they may be."

"That was what I told myself last time, and the time before, and the time before that. We can't go on like this."

"Say you will meet me just once more." His voice was pleading. "Just once. That's all I ask."

He was so earnest that Phyllida almost weakened. She longed to give in, but she knew that to do so would only make her struggle harder.

"I've thought about it very carefully," she said in an even voice. "I love you very much, and because of that I've tried to hate my husband, but I can't. He's been so good to me. I won't do anything more to hurt him."

"Could it be that you've fallen in love with him?" There was a harshness in Gerard's voice that grated upon her ears.

"Of course not," she cried. "But he's a good man. I can't deceive him any more."

"So you'll be a dutiful little wife, eh?" The soft smile had faded from Gerard's face, leaving it hard and ugly. Phyllida stared at him, puzzled.

"I shall try to," she whispered, "though I shall never forget you."

"You most certainly will not forget me," sneered Gerard. "Nor will you reject me. You will go on meeting me, whether you like it or not."

Phyllida took a step back, unable to understand the change that had come over him. The handsome laughing Gerard had gone. Instead she faced a frightening stranger.

"I can't," she declared. Her voice sounded calm, masking the alarm she felt.

"And I say you will." His grip on her arms tightened. "Or how would you like your precious husband to learn all about us?"

"But why would you threaten such a thing? Gerard, darling, I know you must be distressed but . . ."

"Distressed? I most certainly am." His face came nearer and his dark eyes glistened. "But not for the reason you think."

"I don't understand."

"No? Well let me explain. I have taken note of all Compton's more—unusual, shall we say—activities,

183

thanks to information so kindly provided by you. And I am within an ace of seizing one of his illegal cargoes, and a big one at that."

"But what has that to do with you?"

A hundred confused thoughts whirled round in Phyllida's head. She must be dreaming all this. Nothing so terrible could really happen.

"You are such an innocent. Don't you see? When such a cargo of contraband is taken, on account of my information, that will be to my credit. I might even be in on the actual seizing. It must surely count towards my promotion."

His cold calculation made Phyllida gasp.

"And I thought . . ."

"Yes, you thought that I loved you for yourself alone." Gerard's smile was unpleasant. "True, you were amusement enough when I was in Barton, where diversions were few. But here you became much more important to me. Too important to let you leave my life so hurriedly."

"I won't see you again, and that's final."

"I'm sorry about that. Now I shall be forced to write a little note—anonymous, of course—telling your husband that his wife has been unfaithful. Do you think that he will like that? He is very liberal in his dealings with others, I wonder if he will be the same with his own family? Particularly when he finds that it was his faithless little wife who betrayed him to the Preventive men."

"But that's not true. I only told you. And I haven't been unfaithful, not really . . ."

"My dear, do you think he's going to believe you?"

"You wouldn't do such a thing." Phyllida was sobbing now, partly from fear and partly because his fingers dug into her arms like bands of steel.

"You know very well that I would. Now, before we part—to meet again tomorrow, I assure you—I want any news of the—er—smugglers. Have you noticed anything else of late?"

"Think harder." His fingers closed even tighter.

"No! I tell you, no!" But Phyllida remembered the paper that Richard had been so careful to hide from her. Her expression must have faltered, for Gerard cried triumphantly,

"So I was right. Come on, the truth. All of it, mind."

Phyllida tried to withstand him, but his fingers crushed her arms with such agony that she sank to her knees, half fainting with the pain.

"I won't have Richard harmed," she cried. "I won't do it."

"I'll send that letter," hissed Gerard. "He'll throw you out. You'll be on the streets where you belong. Never fear, it's only the cargo I'm after. I'm not fool enough to go after such a prominent man."

Pain and confusion whirled round in her brain, until, in a voice that sounded far away, she heard herself saying,

"There was a paper."

"That's much better." The pressure on her arms did not relax. "What was on it?"

"I don't know. Richard hid it so quickly."

"Then you've got to get it."

"Please no . . . it may not be there . . . it may not even be important."

"I'll take that chance, so you'll have to look, won't you? Now be a good lass. Go home and fetch it for me. I'll be waiting here."

"I can't."

"Then you must try."

"What if . . . if it's gone?"

"Then Compton will learn a few truths about his wife."

Abruptly he let her go, so that she fell in a heap on the damp grass.

"This can't be Gerard. This can't be Gerard." Her confused mind kept repeating the words.

"What are you waiting for?" She had so loved his voice, but now it sounded hard and cruel. "You'd best be off."

Weakly Phyllida got to her feet and stumbled away from him. She wanted to get away, far, far away.

"Be back within the hour," he called after her.
"Or . . . !"

Eleven

"Heavens, what happened?" Becky was too distressed at
her mistress's appearance to remember respect. Hastily
she put out an arm and steadied Phyllida as she all but
fell. "Did he turn nasty?"

"Nasty? Nasty? That's rich." Becky's masterly under-
statement brought a choking hysterical laugh from Phyllida. "Oh Becky, you must help me. I'm in such trouble.
I loved him, I really did, but he's so—so different now."

"Of course I'll help you. Just tell me all about it."

"We mustn't stop here. I have to be back within the
hour."

"What ever for?"

"Please, come along." Phyllida was running and stumbling
along the track, with her alarmed maid behind her. "He's
threatened to tell Mr. Compton about our meetings if
I don't get more information."

"What information? Miss Phyll, I don't know at all
what you're on about."

Becky sensed that here was something far more serious
than a lovers' quarrel.

"Against Mr. Compton and his smuggling, so that
fiend can take the cargo and gain promotion."

"But that's horrible. And you've to help him?"

"Yes, or he'll write letters about me, awful things."
They ran on a distance, Becky now nearly as distressed
as her mistress.

"What will you do, Miss?" she kept wailing.

Presently their aching limbs slowed them to a crawl.
Becky caught hold of her mistress and pulled her into the
shadow of a wall.

"Tell him, Miss Phyll," she insisted, her native sense

coming to the fore. "It's the only way. The master will know how to deal with that monster. He'll be angry, perhaps, but he won't throw you out, he's not that sort of a gentleman."

"But he might, and I can't take the risk. I've nowhere else to go."

Phyllida pulled away from Becky's grasp and hurried on her way. How could she explain the truth? That to have Richard regarding her with cold contempt for the rest of her life would be a far greater punishment than being turned out. To have to live with him while he thought of her with disgust and revulsion . . . To shut out the nightmarish picture from her mind she picked up her skirts and began running again. By the time Furze House came into view her breath was coming in great gasps. Becky caught her up at the edge of the common.

"You can't go into the front door like that, Miss Phyll. You'd have the whole servants' hall gossiping in no time. We must try through the garden."

There was a small door in the wall which fortunately was not bolted. Hand in hand they crept through the fruit trees, warily avoiding the gardener who was working at the far end. It was torture to have to move so slowly when every second was precious.

"Let the paper be there," Phyllida prayed. "Dear God, let the paper be there in the drawer."

They dared not use the doors into the house. Instead a low sash window into the morning room was open. Phyllida pushed it wider, almost screaming with tension as it protested, but no-one noticed the noise. It was no easy matter to climb over the sill, hampered as they were by voluminous petticoats, but at last they were in the room.

"The paper is in the library, I hope," whispered Phyllida."

"I'll make sure that all is clear." Becky crept to the door and peeped into the hall. "It's all clear now."

Phyllida sped across the empty hall, her hands fumbled with the door knob. For a heart-stopping moment it would not turn, then she was in the library at last.

The room had a tidy, empty air about it, and the smell of beeswax was fresh. No scattered books or papers littered its newly-polished interior. With a wave of nausea Phyllida realised that Hembury would never have allowed such untidy clutter to remain in one of the rooms under his charge. The only incongruous note was the copy of "The Vicar of Wakefield", still where she had left it, on the chart table, the only reminder of last night.

With shaking hands Phyllida opened the desk drawers. Neat piles of clean paper, spare tapers and wax, a personal account book, a pile of receipts clipped together, but nothing else. She had to fight her rising panic.

"I must find it. If I can't . . . No, don't think of that. Where else might it be? Think, you fool, think!"

Her foot struck the tall lacquered box that served as a waste paper basket. The paper might have been thrown away. It was a forlorn hope, but she knelt and feverishly turned it upside down. Its satin-smooth interior was quite empty. Hembury had been there before her.

By now she was shaking so much she had to cling to the table leg for support. The desk top was clear but for pens and ink well. All tables were clear. She staggered over to the chart table, lifting the maps one by one, but no paper fluttered out. Forcing herself to calmness she went over all the happenings of the previous night.

"It's little enough, but it might help. I opened the door —Richard looked up—he stood up and took my candle from me—then he put the papers in the top right-hand drawer of the desk."

The top right-hand drawer!

She dashed over to the desk and pulled open the drawer. Inside a neat pile of plain white note paper, all well cut, stared back at her. Only the top sheet was a little out of line. Phyllida picked it up and held it to the light. Faint marks and impressions showed up, and as she made out their shapes she almost wept. The original paper had gone, but here was the sheet that had been directly underneath it. Every word that Richard had written was impressed into the paper. If only this was the information that Gerard wanted then she was safe, at least for a little while. Becky's sudden appearance at the door startled her.

"Sorry if I gave you a fright, Miss Phyll, but time's getting on," the maid whispered. "How have you done? Have you got it?"

"No, but I've got something that I hope will do as well. Dare we chance the side door?"

"No. Joseph is clumping about, collecting the silver for cleaning. It's the window again, I'm afraid."

They were in luck. The garden was deserted this time as they made their way across, then it was a simple matter to slip through the garden door and out into the lane.

Gerard was still sitting where they had left him. Although the mist had lifted considerably he was very damp, and the uncomfortable wait had not improved his temper.

"I trust that you have succeeded, for your sake as well as my own."

"Here it is." Phyllida thrust the paper at him. "It's the best I could do."

He almost snatched if from her, and for a moment was about to protest at its lack of writing, then he saw the impressions. A slow, gloating smile spread over his face.

"I've got it!" he said in triumph.

Phyllida watched him as he attempted to decipher the scratches.

"I loved him," she thought with disgust, not noticing that she used the past tense. "I was prepared to give up everything for him, yet all the time he was a heartless, calculating brute. How could I have preferred him to Richard?"

"It's all a jumble." Gerard spoke harshly. "Now, did your husband use a code, I wonder."

"That's for you to find out," Phyllida retorted. "I've done my part."

Gerard looked up, a glint of approval in his eyes.

"Quite the spitfire," he said mockingly. "Bless me if I don't prefer you like this."

Her head in the air, Phyllida turned her back on him, but he spun her round.

"You will help," he said menacingly. "Look!"

The letters were clearly visible, but they did not make sense.

"Trans. frm K. to B.S.
Rend. 15m S. Pt. Bl.
4A.M. F."

"I've no idea what it means." Phyllida's lips were pinched tightly together. "And even if I had I wouldn't tell you."

"Yes you would!" Gerard spoke softly. "Otherwise you know what would happen. Now we will both concentrate." And he emphasized the word "both". "4 A.M. is obviously a time, so perhaps F. stands for Friday. Could that be tomorrow, I wonder? How does it go now. 'Rend,' that must be rendezvous. '15m.S.' M-m-m. 15 miles south of Pt. Bl. Where would you say Pt. Bl. is?"

"You seem to be doing very well on your own, so far," Phyllida said frostily, though inside she was terrified.

"Yes I am. Better than I'd hoped." Gerard was clearly enjoying himself. "Pt. Bl. is our worst problem. There is nowhere in this neighbourhood that fits. Perhaps if I looked a little further afield, Cornwall, say, or Dorset. Dorset! I have it!' Portland Bill! There is a rendevous at 4 A.M. tomorrow, 15 miles south of Portland Bill. That alone would be enough to take the cargo of contraband, I'm sure, but if I decipher the rest it may hasten matters. Would you like that, my sweet?"

"You are very confident," Phyllida spoke up. "But that could easily be an ordinary message to one of his captains. There is nothing about it to show that it is connected with smuggling."

"The only way to be sure is to be at the rendezvous at 4 A.M. and find out, isn't it? K. and B.S. could be ships. Now what was the name of the vessel mentioned at dinner the other evening? Ah, I have it—the KITTI-WAKE. Though she was bound for Plymouth, which is in the opposite direction. Something must have been transferred from the KITTIWAKE to another ship whose name begins with the letters B.S. All I have to do now is find a vessel beginning with those initials, and I'm certain that won't prove too difficult."

Phyllida had to admit that it all sounded reasonable. Too reasonable when she considered what was at stake. Already she had guessed the identity of that other ship, it was the BELLE SARAH, due to leave soon for Ports-mouth. Thanks to Mistress Edmund's tuition she also knew that its route would take it south of Portland Bill.

She surmised that some contraband must have been taken from the KITTIWAKE, which was well on her way to Plymouth by now, and put aboard the BELLE SARAH. The meeting was probably with a French vessel, but why? Phyllida always thought that contraband came from France, not went to it. Or was smuggling a two-way business? She did not know. Her only concern now was for Richard's safety. Thank goodness he had not signed that note, or put in anything that would incriminate him-self. He would lose the cargo, but that was a small matter.

"He's gone, thank goodness." Becky put her arms about her mistress. Phyllida had been too deep in thought to notice him leave. "I never liked that Mr. Lacey, a bit too smooth I thought, but I never dreamt that he was such a villain. Still, let's hope it's all over now, and he gets taken away to America in a hurry. There, you look exhausted. Something to eat is what you need and a little drop of brandy to revive you." From the folds of her skirt she produced some bread and cheese, and a silver flask. "That's the master's but he won't mind, I'm sure. I got the rest while you were looking for the paper. Here, take a sip of this."

Phyllida shook her head.

"I couldn't!" she exclaimed.

"Come on, just a little. It'll do you good."

More to please Becky than anything else Phyllida did indeed take a little of the brandy. She even managed a small portion of bread. It was small nourishment, but after she had finished Phyllida did feel stronger, and able to face the walk home. In her comforting chatter Becky had hit upon the best solution to Phyllida's problems.

"If only Gerard is sent to America soon. If only his sailing orders could come today." These were Phyllida's thoughts all the way back to Furze House.

A few hours ago those self-same orders were her greatest dread, now she never wanted to see Gerard ever again.

She was too overwrought to even think about entering the house secretly, and if Hembury was surprised by her dishevelled appearance he gave no sign.

"Madam," he said urgently, as he opened the door to her. "There is a mess . . ."

"Later, Hembury, later." Phyllida swept past him. She was in no state to talk to the servants.

Once in the safety of her own bedroom she collapsed on to the coverlet with utter exhaustion.

What had happened to the Gerard that she loved, the Gerard she had met so secretly in the woods at Barton?

"He didn't exist," she decided. "He was just part of a beautiful dream that I had built for myself. I wanted to fall in love, so I imagined him to be all that was beautiful and perfect, like the lovers I had dreamt about, but the real person was just the opposite—cruel, ruthless and vicious. Did he deceive me, or did I deceive myself?"

It came as a shock when she discovered that her heart was not broken. In the agitation of the moment all her worries had been for Richard's safety, and her fear in case he found out that she had been meeting Gerard. Now she had time to think she was surprised at how little remorse she felt for her lost love. Had Gerard killed all her feelings for him when he showed himself for what he was? Or had those feelings been gradually fading away, and she had not realized it?

"I know now that he is not half the man that Richard is," she thought. "Why, how could I even have considered Gerard to be his equal? I must have been blind, foolishly blind."

Suddenly she felt very much older than the naive girl who had dreamt such romantic dreams. She knew now that love was more than a handsome face and a smooth tongue. Phyllida only hoped that she had not learnt her lesson too late.

It was still afternoon when Becky came in.

"Mistress Rouse is below. Had you forgotten that you were taking tea with her?"

"Was that today?" Phyllida groaned and struggled into a sitting position. "Yes, I had forgotten. Chatting over tea is the last thing I feel like at the moment. What time is it? Surely it can't be just four? I feel as though today has gone on for ever." She fell back on to her pillows. "No, I can't face her. Tell Mistress Rouse that I am ill."

"Then she'll come up to see how you are," Becky warned.

"So she will." Phyllida groaned once more. "Very well. Tell her I'll be down directly, and give her my latest 'Lady's Magazine' to read. Then hurry back and make me presentable."

One glance in the mirror had been enough to convince her how hag-ridden she looked. Painfully she rose, stiff and aching. Cold water refreshed her, but all of Becky's skill with the hare's foot and the carmine pot could not prevent her from looking washed out.

"I'll put out your cherry gown with the grey ribbons,"

said Becky. "You need something to give you a bit more colour, Miss Phyll."

As she helped Phyllida out of her crumpled gown she gave a gasp.

"Your arms, Miss Phyll! Look what that devil's done to them."

Above Phyllida's elbows great livid weals stood out against the white skin, reminders of where Gerard's fingers had gripped her.

"Shall I bathe them for you, miss?"

"No time." Phyllida looked at her bruises with disinterest. "Later will do. I scarcely heed them now."

But she winced as the sleeves of her gown were drawn over her injured flesh.

Aunt Rouse was sitting in the Small Drawingroom, completely engrossed in the latest fashions from London. The old lady looked so comforting and so familiar sitting there that Phyllida could have wept. For a crazy moment she considered sending to Richard, telling him all that had happened, begging his forgiveness, but she dared not take the risk.

Aunt Rouse looked up at Phyllida, and at once her smile of greeting changed into an expression of concern.

"My dear, how peaky you look. Come and sit down for a moment." Then more brightly, "Perhaps you have some news for me?"

Phyllida flinched. Aunt Rouse was constantly hoping for what she termed "a blessed event."

"No, madam. I am fatigued, that's all."

"Then I shan't stay, my love. We can take tea some other time." Aunt Rouse rose to go, catching her shawl in the arm of her chair. "You must have a nice rest."

Phyllida stretched out a hand to help disentangle the flimsy silk. She found that she did not want to be left alone.

"Please stay," she said. "Some pleasant company and a dish of tea is just what I need."

"Nicely said, dear." Aunt Rouse looked so gratified that Phyllida's eyes grew misty.

"There, I haven't rung for tea yet." Phyllida was glad of an excuse to turn away for a second. "Though I'm certain that Hembury has had it ready this half hour or more."

She was right. Almost at once in came the silver service, the delicate china and an assortment of tempting confections. The entry of the servants and the hiss of the little silver tea kettle on its spirit stove made a welcome diversion for Phyllida. The diversion, however, became increasingly noisy.

"What can be happening in the hall?" Aunt Rouse paused, a sugary cake half way to her mouth. "There appears to be some commotion out there."

Phyllida listened too. From outside came the muffled sound of hurrying feet and subdued voices.

"A footman has broken something?" she suggested, though she had heard no crash.

Immediately, there was a tap on the door and Hembury entered. His face was quite expressionless as he announced;

"I beg your pardon, madam, but a party of dragoons is below. They wish to search the house."

The colour went from Phyllida's cheeks, leaving them even more pallid than before, then, almost in slow motion, the tea bowl and its saucer slipped from her grasp and shattered on the floor.

It was Aunt Rouse who took charge. With surprising briskness she tucked her trailing draperies out of harm's way and headed for the door.

"Come, Phyllida, dear." It was almost a command. "We must see what this nonsense is all about."

Obediently Phyllida followed, a sick empty feeling inside her. She did not even wonder when Aunt Rouse asked Hembury,

"I trust you have things under control?"

"Yes, indeed, madam. 'A servant of servants he shall be.' "

"Good. Thank you Hembury." This strange statement seemed to satisfy Aunt Rouse, though it completely defeated poor Phyllida's stunned brain.

The front door stood open, guarded by a very belligerent-looking Joseph, and beyond him the ladies could see a party of red-coated soldiers. As they approached, the officers moved forward to greet them.

"Your servant, ladies." The normally good-natured face of Lieutenant Parker was crimson with embarrassment. He bowed low. "You've no idea—I mean, this is most difficult—so sorry—"

"Mistress Compton, Mistress Rouse." A cool voice, ringing with arrogance, cut across poor Parker's apologies. "It is with regret that I must inform you that we are here to search this house."

Phyllida stared up at Gerard's face, and saw nothing but mockery in his eyes.

"Why, you . . . you . . ." She choked over the words.

There was nothing bad enough to describe him. He had betrayed her. She had done all that he had asked, but still he was not satisfied. There was no trusting him now, so what would he say? What could he do?

Aunt Rouse put out a restraining hand.

"There must be some mistake," she said coolly. "What reason can you have for searching here? I am sure that Colonel Wood . . ."

"Signed the order himself." Gerard completed the sentence for her. "So you see, there is no mistake at all. My orders are to search Furze House, its grounds, stables and all outbuildings, and this I shall do, with or without your permission. Of course," his voice softened to a sinister purr, "it would be more convenient if you gave it."

"And what if I refused?" Phyllida faced him squarely.

"Then I should have something to say." His meaning was quite clear.

With a sickening dread Phyllida saw that she was still in his power.

"Here, I say!" protested Parker. "Lacey, that's the outside of enough."

Gerard's eyes glinted like polished coal.

"Parker, I suggest that you see to the men," he rapped out. There was no denying who was in charge.

A new emotion swept over Phyllida—anger! Gerard had fooled her, deceived her, hurt her, betrayed her, and now her bewilderment was giving way to icy rage.

"You will not set one inch further into this house," she informed him. "I will not give way to your threats or your bullying. My husband will deal with you, no doubt a servant has already been dispatched to fetch him. And when he has finished with you, I should bid farewell to all your hopes of advancement. Indeed you will be lucky to remain even in the lowest ranks. You came here when you knew the master of the house was not at home, and you have tried to bully a houseful of women and servants. What a fine example of valour to send to fight the Americans."

"Well said, my dear," applauded Aunt Rouse. "I could not have bettered that."

"If you continue in that vein, madam, I shall be convinced that you have something to hide. While we wait for Mr. Compton my men shall surround the house. No one shall enter or leave. They will, I fear, be rather conspicuous. Think what a fine tale that will make for the gossips in the harbour-side taverns. That would dent the famous Compton reputation, would it not?" He eyed Phyllida in a cold calculating way. "And I hear your husband sets great store by his good name."

Icy fear went down her back. He was so sure of himself. What did he hope to find in the house, when surely the contraband was aboard the BELLE SARAH by now?

"You must wait for my husband," she insisted, with a confidence she was far from feeling.

"Very well, but if I wait, I would sooner be seated."

Gerard sat down on one of the straight-backed hall chairs, and stretched his legs in front of him. "But in the meantime I must insist that all your servants assemble here, under my eye. I want none of them tampering with the evidence."

"Evidence of what?" demanded Phyllida.

"That is what we are here to find out. Now call your servants, please. All of them, including those who work out of doors."

"Perhaps we'd better do that," suggested Aunt Rouse in a quiet voice. "He really is a most unpleasant young man. I was never more mistaken in anyone in my whole life. I think we'd better humour him until Richard gets here."

That was sound advice, so Phyllida nodded to Hembury, and the butler hobbled away to fetch the rest of the staff. A few minutes later he reappeared, followed by a procession of footmen, maids, and all the rest, who entered nervously.

"Have you brought them all?" demanded Gerard. "Groom, gardeners and the like?"

"They are all here. 'And they all went in, went in male and female of all flesh.' " Hembury even had a quotation for such a moment.

Gerard glanced at the line of self-conscious figures.

"Who, then, has gone to fetch your master?"

"No one, sir."

"Why not?"

The question was asked not only by Gerard, but by Phyllida and Aunt Rouse as well.

"He is from home, sir. He left unexpectedly this morning. I did try to tell you earlier, madam, but you were in a hurry."

Phyllida felt Aunt Rouse clutch her arm. What was she to do now?

"That changes matters." Gerard rose to his feet. "I'm not prepared to wait. The search begins now."

There was something about his attitude that frightened

Phyllida, as though he was mocking her. Did he have some information of which she was unaware? She sensed that there were things of which she was ignorant, but at least Richard was away from it all. He was out of danger.

"Parker, bring in the men," ordered Gerard. "You ladies can wait where you will, but the servants must remain here."

At once Joseph flung himself across the open door, to bar the way for the dragoons. With horror Phyllida saw a raised musket butt.

"No!" she screamed. "Let them through, Joseph. No one must get hurt."

Reluctantly Joseph fell back against the wall, and a tide of red coats came streaming through. Stiffly Aunt Rouse remained on the settee. Phyllida remained on her feet.

"Will you not sit beside Mistress Rouse?" Gerard did not sound at all concerned for her comfort.

"No. I shall accompany you while you search, since we appear to have little choice in the matter. I absolutely refuse to let you wander about this house on your own."

"And if I refuse to let you?"

She knew from bitter experience that tears and pleadings would get her nowhere with this man, he was without mercy or scruples. She was determined to stand up to him, no matter what the consequences.

"Nothing short of physical violence will prevent me, I think even you would balk at that." She stared back at him defiantly. "Gaining a reputation as a beater of women is not a good way to further your career."

"Suit yourself." Gerard turned away, and began issuing orders to his men.

It was a very small triumph, but it gave Phyllida confidence. The way to tackle him was clearly to stand and fight.

"With your permission, madam, I will accompany you." Hembury stood at her elbow. "I would not feel happy you being alone with that . . ." He did not trust himself to describe Gerard.

"Thank you. I will find it most reassuring to have you with me."

The butler's face was as impassive as ever, but he was certainly party to whatever secrets there were in this house. While he stayed calm, Phyllida felt confident that the danger could not be too great.

"You two men stand guard over the servants, with Lieutenant Parker." Gerard snapped out an order. "The rest, come with me."

The search began, and Phyllida and Hembury followed close behind as cupboards, chests and closets were emptied of their contents. Neither spoke.

"It's like some ghastly game of hide and seek," thought Phyllida. "With only me unable to tell whether they are hot or cold. I don't even know what they're looking for. It must be something large, for they haven't bothered with drawers or small cupboards."

It took a long time to go all over the house. Thoroughly, every place was scrutinised, from the cellars to the attic. The expression on Gerard's face began to darken as he found nothing.

"Outside!" he snarled at the luckless soldiers. "We'll go through the stables, the wash-house, everything." Turning to Phyllida he snapped, "There's no need for you to follow."

"Let me be the judge of that. And pray don't pretend to be concerned for my welfare at this late stage. I shall continue to accompany you until you leave this property, which time, I may say, can't come one moment too soon for me."

Out of doors the same wearying procedure was repeated in every outhouse, with Gerard's temper growing more and more foul.

"And this is the man I loved," thought Phyllida. "Just listen to him berating that poor soldier, as though it was his fault they've drawn a blank."

Dejectedly the dragoons trooped back into the house, inadvertently sweeping Hembury with them. Phyllida would have followed, but Gerard caught her arm, he was shaking with fury.

"You know what I'm looking for, and where it is. Now tell me, or I'll see that you are ruined. Do you hear?"

"I hear you very well." She was terrified. She knew he was capable of any treachery in this mood, but she stood firm. "I don't know, but if I did I wouldn't tell you. You've overplayed your hand. What's to say you won't spread scandal about me any way? What proof have I that you'd keep your part of the bargain? None! No, Mr. Lacey, you've threatened once too often. It would appear that this mission of yours is of great importance. Have you gambled everything on finding some incriminating evidence here? You've chanced everything at the outcome of this search, is that it? Well, what a pity you've been disappointed."

She'd struck close, she could tell that by the change in his expression. Then a deeper fear clutched at her as she realised something else. Gerard was after far more than just contraband cargo. He wanted to incriminate Richard. Why else come to the house?

"At least Richard is safe," she thought. "It doesn't matter what happens to me now."

Gerard had recovered some of his sneering bravado.

"I'm not defeated yet," he informed her. "Have you forgotten that little rendezvous off Portland Bill? I won't be there of course, but acting on my information a revenue cutter will be its way from Weymouth to intercept. It didn't take me long to discover that the ship with the initials B.S. was in fact the BELLE SARAH, a Compton vessel, mark you. What's more she sailed half an hour ago. Already she is heading into the trap."

"Your dragoons are waiting, sir." Hembury's voice interrupted him.

From his tone the butler could have been announcing the arrival of the morning letters. Phyllida let out a sigh of relief at his reappearance.

Without a word Gerard strode into the house and

through into the hall. It was a strange scene, with the dragoons ranged on one side and the house servants on the other.

"Parker, get the men out of here," Gerard ordered, as though at the end of his patience. Then as the orderly line of soldiers marched away he looked back at the collection of servants. "I shan't forget any of you. I'll be back with warrants for the lot of you, the whole traitorous pack."

Hembury permitted himself the luxury of a contemptuous sniff as he moved forward to usher out this most unwelcome guest. Gerard heard him and spun round, his arm raised. Phyllida stepped forward and caught hold of him.

"Thank you, Hembury, I shall deal with this." Facing Gerard she informed him, "Sir, have the goodness to go at once. We have suffered from you quite enough. And have no doubt that as soon as my husband returns I shall tell him everything that has happened." She paused for a moment, then repeated, "Everything."

He could not doubt her meaning.

Gerard Lacey stormed out of the house, and Phyllida slammed the door shut behind him. Then she leaned against the solid wood, her eyes closed, thankful for its support.

"I shall have to tell Richard everything, just as I threatened."

This thought was uppermost in her brain. If only she had taken Becky's advice and confessed earlier, then this whole terrifying experience would never have happened.

"I came close to putting him in real danger," she whispered. "Just through my own weakness and stupidity, but he is safe."

A dull thud behind her made her open her eyes. For a moment she thought one of the maids had fainted. When she turned she saw everyone frozen in their places, too stunned by the earlier events to move. Only the sprawled figure on the floor was different, the full skirts of the sprig dress spread wide. Joseph recovered first and bent down to support the inert figure. As he did so the full mob cap fell off to reveal a close cropped head and a man's face.

Phyllida's jaw dropped. The ashen face, so incongruous above the calico gown, was familiar. At first she could not place where she had seen it, then;

"Captain Merritt!" she cried.

It was the young American she had last seen at Mill Prison, in Plymouth.

Hembury had come up to help Joseph, and he forced some brandy between the unconscious man's lips. The American's eyelids fluttered, then opened. Phyllida sank on her knees beside him.

"Captain, are you all right?" she asked anxiously.

"My kind lady!" Merritt whispered weakly, and tried to sit up, but giddiness overcame him and he was forced to lie back on the cushion provided for him by Aunt Rouse. After a few seconds he opened his eyes again, and attempted a smile.

"Don't try to get up again," she pushed him gently back. "But will someone please explain. I don't understand what Captain Merritt is doing here. The last time I saw him he was in that dreadful place in Plymouth."

"The last time you saw him? Do you mean you've met before?" Aunt Rouse asked in astonishment.

"Yes, but that isn't important. I'll tell you about that later. Please explain about the captain."

"Well, madam," began Merritt, but Aunt Rouse cut in. "I'll explain. You just lie there and regain your strength. Hembury, help the captain to some more of that excellent brandy. Now my dear," she turned to Phyllida. "Captain Merritt was what those dreadful dragoons were looking for. You see, he has been a secret guest in this house for some time. Ever since his escape from Mill Prison, in fact."

"The soup bowl!" cried Phyllida. "Was that you, hiding in my sitting-room?"

Captain Merritt managed a pallid smile.

"Yes, madam, and a rare struggle Joseph had to get me out of your way in time. The bowl got forgotten in the rush. But I'd no idea who you were. You never told me your name."

"But I still don't understand. What is to happen to you now?"

"Your husband, God protect him, had arranged to ship me out into the Channel and rendezvous with a French boat. There are American ministers in Paris now, and I could have applied to them for aid. But unfortunately I went down with an inflammation of the lungs and was too weak to travel."

Phyllida's spirits soared until she could scarcely contain herself. So that was the true meaning of the message she had found. It had nothing to do with smuggling at all, and those Revenue men who were to search the BELLE SARAH would find nothing. She could have laughed out loud.

"And this dress is your disguise, I presume?"

Merritt looked down at his strange attire with wry amusement.

"It was Parsons who thought of it, clever girl. We had to do something quickly when we knew the dragoons were at the door, and this seemed the best thing. After all, who would look at a maidservant if they were looking for a rascally American sailor? Do you think I look fetching in this gown? To tell the truth, I was so weak I was afraid of swooning at the feet of that very nasty lieutenant."

"I think the colour suits you well," smiled Phyllida.

After the tension the relaxed atmosphere was beginning to spread. The servants stood about the hall in groups, and even Hembury was in no mood to send them back to their duties.

"But why did no one tell me about all this?" protested Phyllida. "I was the only one in the whole house who did not know what was going on."

There was an awkward pause.

"We didn't think you were sympathetic to Americans," Aunt Rouse said at last. "It was something you said."

Phyllida remembered that toast at the dinner party, "Death to all rebels," and blushed.

"I didn't mean it," she said hastily. "But Joseph could have said something. Surely he must have known that I had met the captain."

"Master said you were not to be told," said Joseph, then he looked sheepish. "Besides, I didn't fancy the task of telling him you'd been to a place like Mill Prison."

"A lot of things that have puzzled me are clear now. I must confess that I was sure I was in a house of smugglers." Phyllida waited until the laughter died down. "That was you, Aunt Rouse. You deliberately misled me. But wait! How can that be? There were strange happenings here when I first came, when I know for certain that Captain Merritt was still in prison."

"The good captain is not your first secret guest, my dear," Aunt Rouse informed her gently. "Quite a few poor American boys have passed this way, to be given help and shelter in this house."

"But isn't that against the law?"

"I suppose it is how you look at it, my dear. After all, why should these young men suffer because a lot of bunglers have caused a wicked and unnecessary war? Richard believes as I do, that this whole American business can still be sorted out with sense and reason on both sides, and without further bloodshed. It's all the fault of German George and his idiotic Government of fools. Why, I have as many friends and relatives in America as I have here in England! Many people think as we do and there are numerous homes where escaped prisoners can go for aid. Often these people bring the Americans to us. People like Mr. Wilson, for example."

"Mr. Wilson, the portly gentleman who came to dinner?"

"Yes, he has worked most courageously to help those unfortunate young men. Why, it was he who brought us both of our secret guests!"

"Both?"

"Yes, Mr. Rogers is also an American. Didn't you guess? That was a clever plan, wasn't it, to have him sitting at the same table as Colonel Wood? You see, getting from here to the ship is one of the most difficult parts of the enterprise, silly as it may seem, so what better way than to walk down openly? That's Richard's scheming for you. We hoped it would put the military off the scent, they've been so troublesome lately."

"But I thought he was going to Plymouth on the KITTIWAKE?" Phyllida asked the question, but already she knew with a sickening certainty what was to come next.

"That was what we wanted people to think. But once aboard the KITTIWAKE he was to cross over secretly to the BELLE SARAH, which was going to Portsmouth. On the way she will meet a French boat, and Mr. Rogers will go to France. Child, you've gone quite white. Hembury, some brandy for your mistress."

Phyllida waved aside the proffered glass.

"I must see Richard. I must get to him," she gasped. "Poor Mr. Rogers will be taken, and its all my fault. The Revenue cutter is lying in wait for the BELLE SARAH off Portland Bill. Oh, where is Richard? Take me to him. He will know what to do."

"You're too late, madam." Hembury's hand shook so much he had to put down the brandy glass. "He's already gone an hour since. He sent a message to say he's sailing on the BELLE SARAH."

Twelve

It took a moment for the full truth to sink in.

"He's what?" Phyllida asked stupidly.

"Mr. Compton has sailed on the BELLE SARAH. Seems there was some trouble about the Frenchies demanding double money before they took any more Americans. Master went along to sort things out."

All at once Phyllida began to shiver violently.

"Richard, oh, Richard!" She did not realise that she spoke aloud.

Gerard had got what he wanted. Richard would be arrested by the Revenue men. A heavy silence hung over the hall, no one spoke, the servants had stopped their chatter. Only Aunt Rouse murmured,

"Dear Heaven, what are we to do?"

"She's still there." Becky's voice made them all jump. No one had seen her leave, but now she was dashing down the stairs. "I went to your sitting-room, Miss Phyll, and looked through your spyglass, just to make sure. The BELLE SARAH is still there, though by the look of her she'll be gone any minute."

"Then we can warn Richard!" Phyllida sprang to her feet, clutching desperately at this one hope. Then she clasped her hands in despair. "The dragoons will see her as they go by the harbour."

She had a vivid picture of Gerard's gloating expression as he confronted Richard.

"They've gone by the road." Joseph was already on his way to the door. "If I go by the back ways I can beat them, maybe."

"I must come too," said Phyllida. All at once her brain was crystal clear, and she took command of the situation. There would be questions and explanations, she knew, and she was certain that Richard would despise her for ever, but that did not matter. To save him was the only important thing.

"Hembury," she called to the butler, as she made to follow Joseph. "Captain Merritt must be found a new hiding place, he is no longer safe here in the house. And can you arrange for the dragoons to be delayed, even for a few minutes?"

"This way, missus." Joseph took her wrist and fairly dragged her towards the servants' door. Neither of them noticed his familiar way of addressing her. "Here, take this." In passing he snatched a cloak from the back of a door. "It'll make you less noticeable."

After that there was no time for talk. Joseph took her out of the side gate and down through a series of winding alleys and steps that she did not even know existed. The backs of the cottages opened onto these narrow lanes, and many heads poked out to see what was happening, but none tried to hinder them. Instead, many a small child or basket of washing was whisked away from their path. Phyllida's feet slithered and slipped beneath her, but she dared not slacken her pace. To get to Richard was her only thought.

She knew with a sickening clarity that all hope of happiness with him was gone, destroyed by her own stupidity. The least she could do was to spare him as much pain as possible.

Pictures of Richard came into her mind. She saw him entering the inn room at Exeter, saving her from humiliation, she saw him on the KITTIWAKE, bound for Plymouth, carefree and happy, and with deep pain, she saw him during their late night supper together, worried for fear he had made her unhappy. Now, unless she reached him in time, his whole future would be ruined, there would be disgrace for him, maybe even prison.

They were on the level now, and ahead of them, hard against the harbour wall, lay the BELLE SARAH. Phyllida swallowed hard as she saw that the ship had already weighed anchor, the foremast hands were already aloft. The ship was within minutes of setting sail.

Joseph almost pushed Phyllida across the gangplank and down towards the captain's cabin. Three puzzled faces turned towards them as they tumbled in. Phyllida had slid to her knees after her swift descent from the companionway, but she did not bother to rise.

"You must go," she panted, her sides heaving and hurting with each breath.

"What's amiss?" demanded Richard. "For heavens sake tell me."

"Go—and Mr. Rogers—and Mr. Wilson. The dragoons will be—here—soon."

"How do you . . ." began Richard, then decided that this was no time for questions. "Rogers, Wilson, you go to the counting house, quickly. Old Ned will get you away. I will divert the attention of the dragoons as much as possible."

"That is too much danger for you, Compton." Mr. Wilson's face was grave. "I'm in no danger, but young Rogers, here, must be got away at all costs."

"They're bound to look in the counting house, sir," put in Joseph.

"True, but where else?"

"I'll make a run for it," said Rogers. "I'm the one they're after." He looked desperately through the stern light to see if the dragoons were coming. "I might make it going across the harbour from boat to boat."

"No you wouldn't. They'd soon see you and may be open fire." It was Phyllida who spoke. "You must go back to Furze House. Hembury will soon find you a hiding place. You can go dressed as me. It's a trick that has worked once today, there's no reason why it can't work twice."

"You are not serious." Mr. Wilson stared at her.

"I am. Mr. Rogers is not very tall, there's scarce an inch separating us, and with the cloak to cover him . . . oh, don't stand there arguing. It's the only way."

"Missus is right," agreed Joseph. "I'll take the gentleman back to the house."

"I can't let you take such a risk," protested the American.

"Yes you can, for much of this is my fault. Now for modesty's sake go. Oh, my laces. I can't undo them myself. Richard, you must stay and be lady's maid."

Too bemused by her insistence, and unable to think of a better plan, the men did as they were bid.

Phyllida and Richard were alone. In silence he struggled with his unaccustomed task, but Phyllida knew the question that was to come.

"It was your fault?" he said at last.

"Yes." There was no way of softening the blow. "I found the message about the BELLE SARAH, and gave it to Lieutenant Lacey. He made me do it. Otherwise he would send you a letter. I have been meeting him, you see. I—I . . ." Despite her good intentions her voice faltered. "I thought I loved him."

The silence that followed seemed to press on Phyllida's ears, as she waited for Richard's reaction.

"We had best discuss this later," was all he said.

Unable to face him, Phyllida stepped out of her gown. Richard picked it up, and together with the cloak he took them to Mr. Rogers. At the door he said,

"There are some things of mine in that valise. You'd best put them on." But he did not look at her.

Outside the cabin door, in the confined space at the foot of the companion way, Mr. Rogers struggled into the folds of the silk gown.

"It won't do up at the back, but no matter. The cloak will hide it." Whatever Richard's emotions were he was not allowing them to interfere with the business in hand, and the light was too bad for his companions to notice the changed look on his face. Richard examined the American's disguise critically.

"No, that's not good enough. The hood doesn't cover all of your face. You'll have to be weeping. Here!" He thrust a handkerchief at Rogers. "Keep your face buried in that. Yes, that's much better."

"They're coming, sir," hissed Joseph, who had been standing look out. "We'd best go if I'm to get the gentleman back to the house."

Rogers shook hands with the others. "I can never thank you enough," he said. To Richard he added, "And please offer my gratitude to your wife. Perhaps in happier times . . ."

There came an urgent interjection from Joseph.

"Hurry sir, please hurry."

On the quay, Young Ned Prettyjohn, the ship's manifest in his hand, was checking that all of the consignment of hemp was safely aboard. It had arrived late, and had had to be loaded in a hurry because the tide was slackening fast, and the BELLE SARAH was already an hour late in sailing. He had just signed off the last items when Mistress Compton appeared on deck, supported by Joseph.

Gallantly, Young Ned offered his arm to help her ashore over the precarious gangplank, but the hand that took his was firm, muscular, and decidedly masculine. For a moment he stared open-mouthed, then he recovered himself. Out of the corner of his eye he caught sight of an advancing line of scarlet heading towards the harbour. Deciding that there must be a connection between the two he acted promptly.

"You are overwrought, madam," he said loudly, for the benefit of a group of idlers who were lounging on the quay. "Shall I get you a chair to take you home?"

He did not wait for an answer, but ran off to return in two minutes with Tormouth's one very elderly and motheaten sedan chair. With Joseph's help he assisted "Mistress Compton" into it, no easy matter since "she" refused to remove the handkerchief from her eyes.

As the chairmen departed on their rickety way, with Joseph trotting at their side, Young Ned realised that the incident had created some interest.

"Don't you wish your wife was in tears every time you

left home, Will?" He addressed an old man who was mending nets near by.

"In tears? 'Er'd split 'er sides more like."

The reply brought a ripple of laughter from the onlookers, then they immediately forgot the tearful Mistress Compton. The advancing dragoons who clearly meant business promised them a greater diversion.

As for the small group of perspiring soldiers, they hardly noticed the sedan chair that passed them. Their descent down Hill Road had been marred by more obstacles than had seemed possible. An upset barrow of mackerel, a string of obstinate donkeys, a hoard of urchins involved in an energetic mud-slinging fight, and last of all, an even longer delay as four men attempted to get a very large bed through a very small doorway. Hembury had worked quickly, and since his requests for assistance had been liberally accompanied by shillings, the inhabitants of Hill Road had come to his aid with enthusiasm.

Gerard Lacey knew that it was all deliberate, but could do nothing about it. Nor could he understand the reason for all the obstacles until he neared the harbour, and caught sight of the BELLE SARAH still at her moorings. To compensate for the delays he moved his men at such a rate that the perspiration was soon trickling down their backs. The speed of their marching meant that all their attention was devoted to keeping their footing among the slimy cobbles of the harbour area. They had no time to notice passing sedan chairs.

When they arrived at the BELLE SARAH only the gang plank and one mooring rope gave her a tenuous hold on the shore.

"Leave that!" roared Gerard to the bosun, who was about to have the gang plank removed. "I'm coming aboard to search this ship."

"That you're not!" came back the reply. "Not till I've informed Mr. Compton."

Gerard ignored this, and made to set foot on board, but the bosun was too quick for him.

"You do that and I'll tip you and the plank overboard."

There was no mistaking it, the bosun meant every word. Gerard looked down at the narrow strip of water between the hull and the wall. It was dark, dirty and most unpleasant-looking. Hastily he retreated, perfectly aware of the sniggers from the crowd that was rapidly collecting.

"That's more like it." The bosun gave a nod of approval, then without taking his eyes off the lieutenant he bawled, "Boy! Take my compliments to Mr. Compton, and tell him I'd be grateful for his company here on deck."

Gerard was forced to cool his heels and fume. Behind him his own men were as delighted at his discomfiture as the local people. They had had more than enough of Lieutenant Lacey for one day.

Down below in the cabin, Phyllida changed into the only clothes she could find, a pair of breeches and a shirt belonging to Richard. Normally she would have felt most awkward being in men's attire, but today it was just one more unimportant detail.

When Richard returned from saying goodbye to the American, he sat down at the table and faced her squarely.

"I think I'd better hear all about this matter," he said.

In his absence Phyllida had been practising a dozen ways of beginning her explanation, but now none of them were adequate.

"He was the man I was waiting for at Exeter," she blurted out.

"Who, Lacey?"

"Yes, but he never got my letter. I had no idea that he was in Tormouth until the day he helped Aunt Rouse, then we began to meet. Each time was going to be the last, but some how we went on and on. I thought I was in love with him, and I also thought he loved me in return."

She paused, but Richard did not interrupt her.

"I happened to mention some of the strange things I'd seen at Furze House."

"What things?"

"That man who left in the middle of the night, for example, and that letter in the lobsters, and much more. He—Gerard—questioned me a lot about them, but I thought nothing of it at the time. I was sure that you were connected with the smugglers, but I see now that Gerard suspected the truth all along."

"You knew more than I thought. I had hoped to keep you out of the whole matter."

"What, when I was living under the same roof?"

"Perhaps that was expecting too much. But how did he find out about the BELLE SARAH?"

"I told him that I was not going to see him any more. He got angry and threatened—threatened to tell you about us if I didn't get him more information. He was going to tell you lies, to make the whole affair look much worse than it really was. That's why I took him the information—the letter that you hid in the drawer that—that night. You'd sent the message of course, but the sheet you had rested on was there, and the letters had come through." So far Phyllida had almost recited her confession, only by keeping to a dull monotone could she prevent herself from breaking down, but now she could stand it no longer. Bursting into sobs she cried,

"But I still thought it was just contraband. I didn't want you hurt—he promised that nothing would happen to you. Please believe that, Richard."

For a moment she sobbed uncontrollably, and she made no effort to staunch the tears, not even when Richard handed her a handkerchief. She waited for him to say something, but his reactions were far worse. He buried his head in his hands, and in a voice of sheer pain, whispered,

"What a mess I've made of the whole business."

Phyllida, her face still wet with tears, sank on her knees beside him.

"A mess?"

"Of our marriage. I wanted it to be so splendid, but I've tried to explain, I have a talent for blundering. Why, I couldn't even keep my activities secret from you, though, goodness knows, I tried hard enough."

Phyllida was bewildered by his attitude, but she knew that she had hurt him deeply.

"But you did succeed," she cried. "Be angry with me, but don't blame yourself. I don't understand why you think of yourself as a failure. I had no notion of the Americans at all. I was convinced that you were smuggling, right up to the time that the dragoons searched the house . . ."

"What!" exclaimed Richard, startled out of his distress.

"It's all right, Captain Merritt is safe. Parsons disguised him as a house maid, but it was only after the search that I knew the truth. I knew, too, that Gerard had lied. He told me that you would be safe, but in fact it was you he was after. He thought that if he helped to arrest you then he would get promotion. He had arranged for a Revenue cutter to intercept you. If you hadn't been late sailing you would have gone into a trap."

A sharp knock at the door interrupted her.

"Bosun's compliments, and he'd be grateful for your company on deck, Mr. Compton, sir." The boy faithfully chanted out the message he'd been given.

"It seems that every important conversation we have together must end abruptly. What is the matter, Jacky? Do you know what it's about?"

"There's dragoons, sir, as want to search the ship." Jacky's tone was much more conversational now. "Bosun won't let 'em aboard without your say-so. He's threatened to throw the officer overboard."

Richard turned to Phyllida. "I think it best if we conduct the interview down here in private."

Miserably Phyllida nodded her head.

"Are you still there, Jacky? Will you give the bosun my compliments and ask him to send the officer down here. No other soldiers are to come aboard. Do you understand?"

"Yes, Mr. Compton, sir."

There was a patter of bare feet and Jacky was gone.

There was a long silence, while they listened to the activity above.

"You said that you thought you loved Lacey." Richard spoke at last.

"Yes."

"Do you still love him?"

"No."

"Are you sure?"

"Quite."

"And—and you have told me everything?" For the first time Richard's voice was not quite steady.

"I have—all the important things anyway."

"First I must deal with Lacey. Afterwards there are—things we must discuss."

Phyllida's heart felt heavy at this but it was no more than she expected. Footsteps began to descend the companion way, boots this time, not bare feet. Phyllida drew in her breath and automatically backed away from the door. She sank down into a dark corner of the bunk.

There was a hurried knock at the door. Before anyone could answer, it burst open, and Lacey confronted them. By his arrogant expression and his self-assurance he meant to sweep in upon them, but his intentions were thwarted by the low doorway. He had to check his stride and stoop to enter. Richard took full advantage of this.

"Lacey," he rapped out. "A word with you."

If Gerard expected to see guilt and fear he got no satisfaction from Richard. He opened his mouth to speak, but Richard went into the attack right away.

"I understand that you want to search this ship, as you have already searched my home. Well, Lacey, as the very sight of you offends me I will give you fifteen minutes exactly. That is all the time we can spare before we lose the tide. You may go."

Gerard had clearly intended to carry out the interview on his own terms. This swift shift of tactics threw him off balance.

"Compton," he began.

"That's thirty seconds you have wasted." Richard consulted his gold hunter. "We sail in fourteen and a half minutes, with or without you. However, if you wish to accompany us to Portsmouth I must warn you that there is a deal I want to say to you, and little of it is to your comfort. Do I make myself clear?"

"I warn you . . ." blustered Lacey, but Richard looked at his timepiece again.

"Thirteen minutes," he said calmly.

With a snort of rage Gerard turned on his heel and left.

"He didn't even notice me," Phyllida exclaimed. Seated in her dark corner, she had been completely overlooked. It was almost laughable.

"There's a man who is easily flustered by the tone of authority," Richard observed. "Let's hope we can continue to keep him in confusion, for no doubt he'll be back."

Richard was right. Above them, feet thudded across the planks, hatch covers crashed, and above it all sounded the belligerent voices of the crew, who having just finished stowing away the last of the cargo, objected to having it all disturbed again. There was a cry of triumph, followed by more protesting, then footsteps came towards the cabin again. This time Gerard did not even bother to knock. He burst open the door.

"Well, Compton, we've got one of your precious American rebels. Where's your high and mighty attitude now? Bring the prisoner forward."

A rather dishevelled Mr. Wilson was thrust into the cabin.

"That's not an American, that is Mr. Wilson, as you should know full well, since you sat at dinner with him."

"So you say." Lacey's tone was full of insolence. "Why then was he skulking in the forward hold?"

"I was not," protested Mr. Wilson hotly. "I packed my spectacles in my large box, by mistake. The mate kindly suggested that I should get them before we sailed. He would have been there helping me, but for this invasion of red-coats."

"You said you were going to Plymouth, not Portsmouth," objected Lacey.

"So I was," agreed Wilson reasonably, "but then Mr. Compton told me that there was room for me on the BELLE SARAH, if I wished to go to Portsmouth. I happened to mention to him that I have a sister in that town who is in poor health, you see, and my chances of visiting her are few. This was an opportunity I couldn't miss, so I had my things moved from the KITTIWAKE to this ship. My son in law will tell my wife where I am."

"Rubbish, that's what you are talking," insisted Gerard. "If you aren't an escaped American then you are something to do with them. What is it, man?" He asked of one of Mr. Wilson's guards, who had been trying to attract his attention for some time.

"Beg pardon, sir, but that gentleman is definitely Mr. Adam Wilson, as he says," the dragoon informed him. "I've seen him often enough. He's the Free Church minister at Plymouth Dock."

"You are from Plymouth, too, then?"

"No, sir." The dragoon looked affronted. "I'm a Saltash man, myself, but we sometimes cross the river of a Sunday, especially if there is a good preacher to be heard."

"That will do!" Gerard's brows lowered in anger. "You, sir, may go," he said abruptly to the elderly gentleman. "Though I'm still not satisfied about you."

"Thank you." Mr. Wilson looked relieved. "I wonder if I still have time to find my spectacles?"

When he and the dragoons had gone Lacey turned round.

"I smell a rat on board this ship," he began, then for the first time in that ill-lit cabin he noticed Phyllida, who was still sitting in her corner.

"What are you doing here?" he gasped. "I left you at Furze House just a few minutes since."

"Is they any reason why I should not accompany my

218

husband? We are both particularly fond of sea voyages."

"But you are dressed in men's clothes." Then he added, more suspiciously, "There's something wrong on this vessel, and I'm sure it is to do with escaped prisoners."

"I assure you that there are no prisoners, escaped or otherwise, on the BELLE SARAH." Phyllida looked him straight in the eye, challenging him to prove her wrong. "And as for my attire, which, by the way, is no concern of yours, I find petticoats cumbersome on board ship, not to mention indecorous upon occasions."

"So it's no concern of mine, eh? We'll see about that." Gerard was mocking her again, but she stood her ground. "There is a small matter I wish to discuss with your husband, one that he'll be glad to hear."

"No time, sir." Richard's voice cut in. "I have no wish to discuss anything with you, even if we had the time." Going over to the door he shouted, "Bosun, we'll get under way at once, if you please."

"Aye, aye, sir," came the reply.

"Now, Lacey, we'll be at sea in a matter of minutes, and there will be no turning back. I suggest that you leave."

"You're up to something, the pair of you, aye, and Wilson too," snarled Gerard. "Watch out when you return, that's all I say. I shall have you marked."

"If I catch so much as a glimpse of your shadow when I return you will have cause to regret it." For the first time Richard lost his temper. "I know just what treatment to mete out to a blackguard who ransacked my home and terrorised my family and servants."

"Call me out, will you?" jeered Lacey.

"No, duelling is for gentlemen," Richard spat out. "For you a horse whip will suffice."

Gerard went white, but before he could reply the ship gave a shudder.

"We're moving," Richard warned him. "Make up your mind. Do you sail with us or not? Bear in mind, though, that Portsmouth is a fair distance off, and I can use a rope's end as well as a whip. There's none on board this ship who'd come to your aid. Tackling me might prove more difficult than a house full of ladies."

Lacey began to back away.

"And one more thing." Richard stood close to him. "You are destined for America, I believe. Well, if you so much as breathe one word about certain matters concerning my family—I hope I make myself clear—it would be as well if you remember one thing, I have as many friends in America as I have in England. Many who would not hesitate to act swiftly if they heard the name of Compton abused. That should be plain enough for you."

Lacey was now pinned against the cabin door, a thin dew of perspiration on his brow. Fearfully he licked his lips, still wondering if Richard was bluffing, but then the ship gave a lurch and began to rock gently. Without another word he scrambled out of the cabin, and they heard his feet as they scrambled up the companion ladder.

"He'll have to jump for it," Richard remarked. "We are a fair way off the quay."

Sure enough, a few seconds later, there came a derisive cheer from the crew as Lacey just made the harbour wall. Richard began to gather up some charts, preparing to leave, but Phyllida could not bear it any longer.

"Don't go just yet," she begged. "If you are going to shout at me, do so now. Shout, yell, swear, anything, but don't be so calm."

He put the charts down again, but did not look at her.

"I don't feel like shouting," he said quietly.

"You were angry enough just now. Were you in earnest about those things? About your friends in America?"

"Certainly. I've always held my family name very highly, you know that."

"Yet you are not angry with me because I nearly ruined that reputation?"

"I'm angry with myself."

"To say that I'm sorry is very inadequate, Richard, but I am. I would give anything to put it all right, but I suppose it's too late for that. All I can do is to leave you."

"What will you do, go to your grandfather?"

Phyllida shook her head, afraid that her tears would betray her. She wanted so much to run into his arms, but he looked so forbidding, standing there white-faced.

"Signor Giorgio once said I could make a career singing if—if I was not married to you. I will go to him. I'm sure he will help me."

"I will make some financial arrangement for you. There is no need for you to be in want."

"No, I won't take any money from you. That would be the final straw, I've failed you in so many ways."

"Good heavens, Phyllida," he cried. "Let me do something, since money seems to be the only thing I have to offer. I handled our whole marriage exceeding ill. I should have learnt my lesson after my first experience, but clearly I didn't. My parents were so happy together that it didn't occur to me that others were not the same. I soon found out, though. Maria made it very clear that her affection was purely for the Compton money. I thought that with you it would be different."

"I don't care about your money. I won't have any of it. You have given me so much already, I can't take any more." Phyllida was half weeping now. "I have taken so much and given nothing. But how could you expect our marriage to be so different when you only offered for me because of the Barton inheritance?"

"I never cared a fig for the inheritance." Richard's voice was tight and strained. "I was heartily glad when your grandfather disinherited you. It meant that you were free of him."

Phyllida could not believe it.

"But I always thought . . ." she began. "Then why did you . . . ?"

"Why did I offer for you?" A wry smile twisted his lips. "For a very good reason. I had fallen in love with you. Did you really think that I had to visit your grandfather quite so regularly? No, I went to see you. Is that so hard

221

to believe? How often did I dine at Barton Hall during the last year or two? A score of times? More like two score. And it hurt me to see you bullied by that old tyrant. Yet you never let him break your spirit. You were so young and lovely that I could not help loving you. I wanted to protect you, to take you away from your grandfather, to give you all the things that he had neglected to provide for you. Oh, I knew you thought of me as dull Mr. Compton, your grandfather's associate, but I hoped that may be in time . . . you might . . ." Again he smiled that bitter smile. "I never could say anything to you, the words wouldn't come, especially when I realised that you had run away sooner than marry me. The last thing I wanted was your gratitude for giving you a home. I didn't want to trap you into marrying me, but there was no alternative, was there?" He still would not look at her, but scratched a pattern on the table with his finger. "So there it is." He sighed.

"You loved me?"

Phyllida felt as though her heart was breaking. Richard had loved her, and she had thrown her chance for happiness away for the sake of a scoundrel like Gerard Lacey.

"It's hardly surprising you didn't know, is it?" Richard managed a laugh. "After all, I treated you like a child, made you take lessons, wouldn't take you into my confidence, I meant to make up for all the things your grandfather denied you, and I just made myself a dictator in your eyes. I should have seen that your grandfather denied you love as well. No wonder you turned to someone like Lacey to find it. I'm not blaming you," he added hurriedly as she started. "From what I've seen of him he'd deceive a far more worldly heart than yours. It must have been a cruel blow when you found out what he was really like."

"I was more concerned about losing your . . ." she wondered if she could go on, "losing your regard."

"You were?"

He looked at her for the first time. Gently he reached out and brushed away the tears that lay on her cheeks.

"You told him that you would not see him again?"

She nodded.

"Why?"

"Because I couldn't deceive you any more. I-I was afraid of hurting you."

"You were?" There was surprise as well as hope in his voice.

Again she nodded. "You were so good to me. I'll admit that you made me cross at times, but it was all over little things. I think then I was already . . ."

"Yes?"

"I was already in love with you, but I didn't know it."

There was a silence, broken only by the lapping of the waves against the hull.

"Will you say that again?" Richard spoke in a whisper.

"I was already in love with you. I've grown up a lot in the last few days. I see that it wasn't really Gerard that I loved, it was some romantic image that I'd dreamt up. I thought I was deceiving you, but the truth is that I was deceiving my own heart too. But it's all hopeless now, I know that. I've spoilt it all, and the only thing I can do now is to get out of your life."

She pressed her face against his hand and wept. Then at once she felt his arms about her, and he was holding her very close.

"You aren't going out of my life now," he cried. "I don't care about Lacey, your grandfather or anyone else. All that matters is that you love me and I love you. The only place you are going is Portsmouth and you are going there with me. Now, please say it again."

Phyllida looked up, unable to believe that this was happening, but she saw him smiling down at her, and she knew for certainty that this wonderful miracle was true.

"I love you, Richard Compton," she said deliberately. "I love you, I love you, I love . . ."

But she never finished, because Richard was kissing her with greater passion than she could have believed possible.

Above them the white sails of the BELLE SARAH took the breeze, and carried them further and further out to sea.